CONTROLLED CONVERSATIONS

KAROL LAGODZKI

MILFORD
HOUSE
an imprint of Sunbury Press, Inc.
Mechanicsburg, PA USA

MILFORD HOUSE

an imprint of Sunbury Press, Inc.
Mechanicsburg, PA USA

NOTE: This is a work of fiction. Names, characters, places, and incidents either are the product of the author's imagination or are used fictitiously. While, as in all fiction, the literary perceptions and insights are shaped by experiences, any resemblance to actual persons, living or dead, events, or locales is entirely coincidental.

Copyright © 2024 by Karol Lagodzki.
Cover Copyright © 2024 by Sunbury Press, Inc.

Sunbury Press supports copyright. Copyright fuels creativity, encourages diverse voices, promotes free speech, and creates a vibrant culture. Thank you for buying an authorized edition of this book and for complying with copyright laws. Except for the quotation of short passages for the purpose of criticism and review, no part of this publication may be reproduced, scanned, or distributed in any form without permission. You are supporting writers and allowing Sunbury Press to continue to publish books for every reader. For information contact Sunbury Press, Inc., Subsidiary Rights Dept., PO Box 548, Boiling Springs, PA 17007 USA or legal@sunburypress.com.

For information about special discounts for bulk purchases, please contact Sunbury Press Orders Dept. at (855) 338-8359 or orders@sunburypress.com.

To request one of our authors for speaking engagements or book signings, please contact Sunbury Press Publicity Dept. at publicity@sunburypress.com.

FIRST MILFORD HOUSE PRESS EDITION: April 2024

Set in Adobe Garamond Pro | Interior design by Crystal Devine | Cover by Igor Andrić | Edited by Gabrielle Kirk.

Publisher's Cataloging-in-Publication Data
Names: Lagodzki, Karol, author.
Title: Controlled conversations / Karol Lagodzki.
Description: First trade paperback edition. | Mechanicsburg, PA : Milford House Press, 2024.
Summary: In 1982 Soviet-controlled Poland—a place and time of suspicion and mistrust—when geopolitical forces and violent men descend upon her little town of Zygmuntowo, Emilia must decide if she's willing to risk prison or worse for self-respect and for her unexpected lover.
Identifiers: ISBN : 979-8-88819-206-1 (softcover).
Subjects: FICTION / Literary | FICTION / Historical / 20th Century / Post-World War II | FICTION / Thrillers / Political.

Designed in the USA
0 1 1 2 3 5 8 13 21 34 55

For the Love of Books!

For Meg

CHAPTER ONE

SOKOŁOWSKA

Wednesday, June 30, 1982. Zygmuntowo.

Emilia Sokołowska jammed the plug into a worn hole and drawled into her headpiece, "This conversation is being controlled." She listened with half an ear. At first, back in December, little would have been exchanged. A tentative hello, how are you, did you sleep well, oh that's nice. But now, six months into martial law, she and her ear had grown into the circuitry like just another resistor.

"I miss you," the doctor said, "I wish you'd never had to leave." He blew the ether a kiss.

"Oh, Danusia," Mrs. Brozio giggled in response, "sure I'll stop by for tea at five." Then she whispered, "You call too often! He's still at home."

Emilia turned off the remaining half ear. Dr. Szukała wasn't even Emilia's gynecologist, and she had heard this conversation a dozen times. When she began to learn who was sleeping with whom, she found goosebumps on her arms at the strangest of times. When she met Maria Brozio in a store queue after the first time she'd listened, the other woman twenty years older and with a homemade perm the size of a small poodle, Emilia smiled. Brozio screwed up her forehead and sniffed. Emilia wondered if she had given anything away in her eyes.

Now, few surprises remained. She would snag a plug and stab a hole next to a blinking light. "This conversation is being controlled," she would say and pay it little mind. If Mr. Brozio—or any of the other men—ever learned who'd conspired to make him a cuckold, it wouldn't be from her.

Emilia had started at the telephone station as soon as she'd failed university entrance exams after high school. *I'll try again next year*, she'd told herself. Maybe she still would one day. Now, five years later, she continued to read and memorize Baczyński, Miłosz and Hłasko, others, for love rather than credit toward a literature degree.

Back in the fourth year of high school, the old Polish literature teacher, Prusak, told her she'd never amount to anything right after giving her a final marginally passing grade. She knew the low mark wasn't for her writing or literary critique. He'd been doling out punishment for most of the preceding two years.

You'll never become anyone. Had she begun to believe him? She grimaced thinking of Prusak's nicotine-stained hands on her shoulder and his breath on her cheek. He seemed to be with her in the exam hall at the University of Gdańsk when she bombed the analysis of Szymborska's "Notes from a Nonexistent Himalayan Expedition." Her mind betrayed her by filling up with Prusak's lewd little backward steps, his ass-cheeks clenched as if in charge of holding a live grenade. That smirk.

Somehow, everything had gone wrong.

Now, it was June 1982, and Emilia sat and monitored sin, love, and banality.

***

The night shift on December 13th, 1981, ended hours past the 6 A.M. quitting time. A few minutes after midnight, two uniformed Milicja Obywatelska policemen, accompanied by a few armed soldiers in fatigues, walked into the telephone station and ordered Emilia and Frania Nowak, the only two women on the shift, off their headpieces and to their feet.

Emilia held Frania's shoulder, as her shiftmate seemed to have trouble breathing. Pani Frania could have been no more than fifteen years her senior, but as soon as Emilia met the woman for the first time, she sensed in her a frailty that couldn't be explained by age. Now, they hobbled to the opposite wall and stood under the searching eyes of the men, and the sharp, naked neon light that for the first time made Emilia shiver.

One of the Milicja uniforms silently prodded a young, skinny soldier, the only one with a bar of rank on his chicken chest. "Nothing to worry about," the boy said, stumbling forward. He fixed the AK-47 on his shoulder, then fingered his gigantic knob of a nose and exhaled. Emilia wondered if the gun's strap had left a bruise against the bone. Her urge to stare oscillated between the rifle and the nose. She could think of nothing to say.

The boy swallowed, glanced back, and remained silent. The man who seemed to be in charge bobbed his head down and back up in a clear mix of irritation and resignation, took off his hat, and scratched the flaking skin on top of his bald pate. He walked up to the console wall and stared at the row of plugs, lights, and sockets. With a sigh, he dropped into a swivel chair and spun to face the room.

"All telephone communication has been suspended. No phone, no telegram, telex, whatnot. As of," he glanced at his watch, "fifteen minutes ago, we're under martial law."

"Martial law?" Emilia didn't know if she asked about what that meant or what exactly happened, but she was glad to get some words past her throat. How was it that she'd never met the sweaty, bald man before? Zygmuntowo was a small enough town that she should have known all the local Milicja: the patrolmen, the six men on traffic detail, and all the other uniforms. The other man looked familiar, his shifting feet told her he'd much rather be anywhere else, but his name escaped her.

"All telephone stations are getting little visits right about now," the bald man said, then gave a wry smirk. "Lucky me, I got to come all the way to this dump. Let's go."

In short order, the Milicja and the soldiers herded Emilia and Frania upstairs and into the administrative office. The janitor and the boilerman were already sitting on the floor in the middle of the room under the guard of two uniformed boys with guns. The main Milicja man pointed to the floor, and Emilia complied. His gaze fixed her down and moved on to the others. With a nod to the soldiers, he turned and left the room, followed by the local man in a steel blue uniform.

The soldier who had tried to comfort them slouched, then sunk to a crouch with his back against the wall, his gun held between the knees. He gestured around, and the other boys followed his example. "Let us know if you want any water," he addressed Emilia and Frania. "We have no food, but if you want some tea, we could make it in the kitchenette."

"Tea would be nice." Emilia smiled at the boy. He smiled back. She decided he wasn't as young as she had thought now that most of the fear had fled him. Perhaps even approaching her age. He sent four of the other men to the kitchenette, and when they returned, they carried enough tea cups to go around.

Emilia sipped her tea, back-to-back with Frania, next to the janitor and the boilerman, and surrounded by six soldiers with automatic rifles, each resting against the wall. All she could hear for a time was sipping. A faint mechanical scent, like freshly oiled door hinges, rose in the room. Probably the guns.

"What's happening?" Emilia heard Frania say. "I've got children at home." The woman's first words since the soldiers barged in barely shook. Emilia sought Frania's hand, squeezed, and held.

"Martial law," the soldier in charge said. "Służba Bezpieczeństwa and the military have taken over. They've put lots of people in prison. I don't know how many. Thousands. That's what the bald Bezpieka major said. Wałęsa and all the Solidarity brass. And Gierek, Jaroszewicz, and a bunch of the old apparatchiks, too, for good measure. We're under curfew now, until the morning. The major came from Gdańsk, with orders."

"But he's wearing a Milicja uniform," Emilia said.

"Ubeks wear what they want. I saw his ID. Definitely from the Security Service, but I don't know if the name was real. Stelmach, or some such."

"What is *your* name?" Emilia asked.

"Marek."

"Emilia," she said. "Behind me, that's Pani Frania." She smiled and worked on deciding how much that nose bothered her.

***

Within days, the telephone station got back to business, now militarized. Local and national operator-assisted connections resumed under strict monitoring. Being part of the military made Emilia feel no different than she had before. Having to tell people she would eavesdrop on them made her feel sticky at first. But the days turned into weeks, months and rubbed the muck off until the smooth surface of duty and routine shone unobstructed.

Now, at the end of June, snow had long melted, the birds had come back, and the water in the lakes was warm enough for swimming. The morning shift ended at three, and Emilia had plans. She filled another socket with a plug, and a light stopped blinking.

"This conversation is being controlled," she muttered the script.

"I have a kilo of smoked eel for sale," a woman's voice on one end of a long-distance call said, having waited for no hello. Emilia's ear perked up. Few things made her drool as much as smoked eel.

"I'll take two kilos, but only if they're fresh," a man answered. A Pomorze Region number. Somewhere on the Baltic Sea. Gdańsk? Elbląg? Emilia didn't know off the bat—she didn't have Frania's spooky savant memory for phone numbers.

"As fresh as December," the woman said. A pay phone, somewhere in town. "The holy mass is scheduled for six in the morning on July 6th. In the intention of Antoni's spirit."

The connection clicked as both hung up. Emilia returned the plug to its resting spot with a shake of her head and caught the sight of the wall clock. A minute to three. A report would take a good hour to file. The door opened, and her successor walked in. Emilia disconnected her headset. She had a place to be.

Marek waited by the door to the bar and put out his cigarette with the heel of his left boot as soon as he lifted his head and spotted her preparing to cross the street. A few seconds later, Emilia grunted in his skinny but solid hug and gave him a kiss. She screwed up her nose.

"I'll stop smoking when I get out of the army," Marek said, as he had so many times before. He inhaled and cleared his throat. "Ready?" He smiled.

The smile was what had gotten her to start with. And the eyes. She was willing to overlook the nose and much more for the kindness in these eyes.

The nose, the shape of a ski jump ramp, if somewhat smaller, was difficult to overlook.

Marek led her to a table and walked off to get their drinks. Sitting by the open window, Emilia looked out at the trees lining the avenue and at the occasional passersby, most in short sleeves. Cars came across every so often, most of them Fiats, sometimes a Trabant, a Škoda, a Syrena.

Trucks smoked worse than Marek, and a majority were civilian. Birds sang with the happiness of the uneducated, drowning out the smaller engines.

Marek placed the beers on the table and hefted his.

"Na zdrowie," he said.

"Na zdrowie."

Emilia drew deeply and licked her lips. Beers at a bar. How much of his soldier's pay was he spending?

Marek's fingers worried over the mug's handle. "How was your day?"

"Something wrong?"

"I love you."

"I love you, too," Emilia said and smiled.

"I'm getting transferred to Białystok."

Emilia's smile slipped.

"I'll come visit," she said. "It's just two hours on the bus."

Marek took a drink and stared at his hands. "I know," he said. He pushed his chair back, and before Emilia could react, Marek was kneeling in front of her with his hand out. A ring rested on the open palm.

"Will you marry me?"

Emilia focused on placing her mug on the table without spilling. She closed her left hand around his extended wrist. Then she folded his fingers around the silver band with her right. A few breaths later Marek looked up, and tears welled up in his eyes. He knew. But it would be too easy, cowardly to leave it at this, unspoken. She liked this man. She might not even have lied much when she'd said she loved him, but he would never understand, and neither would anyone else, why she had to shake her head and say, "I cannot."

That night, Emilia cried a little. Then, as she waited for sleep to cover her, instead of the hurt in Marek's eyes, she thought about the mysterious voice asking to buy two kilos of eel.

CHAPTER TWO

THE MAN CALLED ADAMCZYK

Thursday, July 1, 1982. Frombork.

Antoni Adamczyk stole two sideways glances before he dumped the fish entrails off the pier. He took enough risks, and even though he had never seen a Milicja patrol on this proletarian stretch of the coast at six-thirty in the morning, shortly after curfew, it didn't pay to be stupid. As he put the carcasses in a cooler filled with ice, a fish's eye caught his before he closed the lid. He grimaced. He killed them but didn't like the necessity.

Adamczyk. He answered to this name as his own now. Every so often, he'd stand in front of the mirror. Sometimes he addressed himself out loud to try it on. *Adamczyk.* It fit. One day he'd get his own name back, but not today. At least his given name was common enough to keep. He was still an Antoni. Antek, for short.

He carried the bicycle along with the cooler to the top floor of the four-story apartment building on the outskirts of Frombork. Wiped the sweat off his forehead and unlocked the door. Once in, Antek locked both deadbolts.

Having done most of the butchering by Wisła Bay, he now made the scales rain, coated the fish pieces in egg and flour, and floated them onto melted butter in the frying pan. He soon sat down with a plate of fried fish and a few slices of dense, dark bread he picked up on the way home. Breakfast.

He couldn't get his hands on ration cards, not legally, and money grew scarce quickly when one had to pay double for a loaf of bread. He could think of no other easy source of cheap protein. But the dead fish stare had a way of sticking in his head. The cold vacuum where the life he had taken used to be. Having long ago taken the measure of his courage and conscience, he understood that no matter the consequences, he could never kill a human being. He found comfort in knowing it.

Antek licked off his lips and stood over the sink long enough to wash the frying pan, the plate, and the fork, and to hum all of The Clash's "Should I Stay or Should I Go." Then he brushed his teeth, put on dirty clothes, and headed out to walk twenty minutes to the car garage.

The sign read *Naprawa Samochodów*. The squat cinder-block building crouched over two garage bays sealed at night by wooden gates reinforced by steel bars. During business hours, open, it yawned with two deep trenches covered with a patina the color of tooth decay.

Antek checked to make sure the young fool working yesterday's afternoon shift had left the tools where they belonged. He chased a couple of the wrenches down by the office and retrieved them to reunite the set. Idiot boy. All zits and a sad attempt at a mustache. But a necessary idiot. Bolek was the one of the two of them on whose meager income Pan Stefan, the owner and Bolek's father, paid taxes and insurance. Antek's role, played under the table, was to be the mechanic.

"A smoke?" Stefan said, getting off the office phone. He presented a butt of a filterless tube out of a white pack. "And good morning."

"Morning." Antek lit the cigarette off Stefan's.

The men walked out in front of the garage and stood in silence. Stefan must have had considerable connections to have been able to build in the middle of the housing co-op's designated green space and to appropriate half of the parking lot for his own. Gray, prefabricated concrete apartment buildings rose across the full one hundred and eighty degrees of his field of view. Young trees came up to a few feet above Antek's head throughout the landscape. Crows perched on the branches when they weren't chasing seagulls away from roadkill.

Crows knew what they were about. When a part of a flock skittered out of a bush, cackling, Antek suspected they were having great fun at his expense. Telling dirty jokes about the size of his junk. Perhaps a thing or two about his mother. Or his sister. Probably both.

You always knew where you stood with a crow.

"Son of a whore," Stefan muttered and stomped on the cigarette butt while sucking on his fingers. He rubbed them. "Do the Łada and the Zaporozhets today. That'll do. Got to respect the work."

"Didn't Bolek do the Zaporozhets?"

Stefan squinted. "Second opinion," he said and stalked back to the office. Antek got the keys and brought the twenty-year-old miracle of Soviet engineering over to rest above a trench. His ears and nose told him most of what he needed to know. Bolek had changed the sparkplugs. Meanwhile, it was the gasket that threatened to split in half like Nadia Comăneci. That, and the brakes.

Antek was not a tall man but broad in the shoulders and strong from working with his hands. If he were willing to risk a hernia, he could have lifted the engine block out of the Zaporozhets. He sighed. One of the freighter engines he used to build in the Gdynia shipyards would have made him crane his neck and smile. You knew where you stood with a ship. If you loved her, she took that love and gave it to the men and women who trusted her with their lives.

No one fell in love with a shitty, twenty-seven-horsepower Zaporozhets.

**

Antek had always pursued two things: machines and love, the latter broadly defined. He delighted in the ships he built. Adored his wife. Yearned for the freedom to say what one thinks, to travel, to drink French wine, that others, further west, enjoyed and took for granted.

He loved his first and, thus far, only job. After graduating from Gdańsk Polytechnic, he joined the Gdynia Shipyards in late 1976, around the time the new three-hundred-meter dry dock came on-line. The Gdańsk plant wasn't going to hoard all the most exciting orders anymore. About forty minutes on a bus and a tram separated the two shipyards, but it would take more than a new dock and a few prestigious builds to change the perception of Gdynia's shipbuilding as second-best.

Antek, who always rooted for the underdog, loved that fact, too.

His first real assignment—after a few months' training because "there is book learning and there is real learning," according to his boss—was on a tanker that was to become the Marshal Zhukov: a 105,000-tonnage, 245-meter-long beauty, that even Gdańsk would have been proud of. Antek joined the team a few weeks before the job was done, and since he couldn't have screwed anything up too much at that stage, he suspected this had still been part of his "real learning."

On a summer morning in 1978, a month after his wedding, Antek arrived at work and proceeded to his station only to be met there by old Matusiak, the boss. What he had lacked in formal education, Łukasz Matusiak gained through thirty years of hands-on practice.

"Antek," Matusiak said, "you're almost late."

Antek knew there would be no profit in pointing out he was on time. "Good morning," he said and waited for the older man to make his next move.

Matusiak motioned for Antek to follow, and a few minutes later they were both sitting in the boss's office, with Matusiak leaning over the desk and offering the other man a cigarette. Antek accepted; it would have been rude not to.

After the boss leaned back with the cigarette stuck in the corner of his mouth and a minute later still said nothing, the hard silence finally broke Antek's resolve to wait the man out.

"Panie Matusiak," Antek said, "how can I help?"

"Not me you'd be helping." The man took another few moments, grimacing, his eyes wandering as if trying on and discarding several options for what to say next. Then he continued, "Paying your Solidarity dues?"

Antek nodded, coughed—Matusiak's favorite smokes were the filterless *Sport*—but said nothing, now completely at a loss about the purpose of this meeting.

"I've always said the best cigarettes came from Zygmuntowo," Matusiak said. "Must be something in the soil. Isn't that where you went off last month after the wedding?"

"Camping."

"Went into town, though?"

"Boss, what's this about?

Matusiak leaned back, flicked off the ash from his cigarette in the vicinity of the ashtray, and stared at the younger man, his face expressionless as if deciding what size coffin would fit Antek.

Antek was about to get up and excuse himself when Matusiak said, "Had to go into town to deliver all that print paper to the girl running that silly underground rag."

Antek did spring up now, would have sprung up, had he not tripped over his chair trying to back off and stand at the same time. Motion stopped after his head bounced off and then settled on the floor, and his jarred elbow rang a peal of pain heard loudly by his fingertips.

"Jezus Maria, son, what in the world are you doing!?"

Matusiak's voice came from the front of the room. Antek turned his head and was glad to find his neck obeyed. Not broken. His boss had closed the door and likely locked it since he was putting a set of keys in his pocket. Matusiak then knelt by his side.

"You think you can get up?"

"Possibly. But what's the point? Are you from Bezpieka or just working for them?"

"What? My God, no. Get up." Matusiak clasped Antek's arm, the aching one, and hoisted him up. The old man was strong. Once Antek was on his feet, his boss picked up and placed the chair in front of his desk, then gently guided the younger man to it.

"Sit."

Antek did. He slouched, staring yet not seeing the papers on the desk's surface, while his right hand rubbed his sore left elbow.

"Have you met the third shift foreman? Blond hair. Not tall, but wide. Has got these wispy, curled up Pan Wołodyjowski mustaches?" When Antek didn't respond, Matusiak went on, "Lucky skurwysyn got the papers to go to France and left yesterday. He said his brother-in-law had set him up with a construction gig. Never mind the names now, but he was the treasurer for the union chapter here, for Solidarity."

Antek raised his head and stretched his neck both ways. It didn't hurt much at all.

"You've been active in Solidarity, even taking risks," Matusiak said. "Trustworthy, I'm hearing. And in your personnel file, it says you've done some accounting."

"That was a two-year certificate in retail management," Antek said, relaxing, finally sensing the purpose of this meeting. "I had to do something when I didn't get into the polytechnic the first time. And the second time. Mostly to get a military deferral until I could get a diploma. Six months of that useless torture beats the two years you have to do without a master's degree."

"Sounds like we got ourselves a new chapter treasurer."

Antek nodded. But there was something else. He filled up his lungs. "They're doing good work. Taking risks, too. A small-town free press doesn't seem like much. I know. But the least they deserve is some respect."

Matusiak threw his hand up and nodded a bow of contrition.

"How did you know, though? About the paper?" Antek said.

"I helped teach them how to set it up. Maybe I should have started with that."

Later, as he attempted to work, Antek re-lived the guilt he had felt when, in his wife's company, he stammered like an idiot handing over the paper and ink to the press operators. One specific operator. Antek had always thought that only machines—made for a purpose, perfected through as many iterations as needed—could achieve what some might call perfection. Organic life was messy. Always blemished. Often simply disgusting.

That's when Kalina—who had met them and their heavy backpacks in the town square and led them to the newsletter's unadvertised location—had proved him wrong. He did his best to fight slack-jawed awe as if he had stood in the presence of a Batillus-Class tanker and its 64,800-horsepower engines, while she revised his idea of what's possible by doing nothing more than being. Base physical attraction never entered into it. That would have felt wrong, somehow. Still, his wife—as perfect in every way as soft, breakable, inconstant humans could get—though she hadn't said anything at the time, that night picked up a separate blanket, turned around, and went straight to sleep.

***

In a Frombork repair shop, about four years after Antek and his wife went to sleep angry and hurt for the first time, the Łada just needed the new sparkplugs Bolek put in all the cars by default. Antek double-checked to make sure. He felt like a fraud when he was done with both the Zaporozhets and the Łada ten minutes past noon.

He lit one of his own cigarettes and leaned against the side of the garage with his right sole resting against the wall. If he had a wide-brimmed hat, he could have been a cowboy out of *The Magnificent Seven*. Steve McQueen, preferably. Maybe he'd rent a videotape and a VHS player and see a movie tonight. He drew hard enough to make his head swim. Exhaled.

Antek pinched the cigarette, took a deep drag and, as he did most days, allowed himself to worry just a bit about Stefan. The man knew where Antek had come from and who he was. Stefan's garage served as a safe house, a safe identity, and yet Antek could never draw him out on politics, on Poland, on Solidarity. Stefan kept his mouth shut and paid the going wage.

Antek rounded the corner to where the bushes behind the garage provided a refuge in which to piss in peace. He ground the cigarette into the clay soil and sighed when the shiver of a long, satisfying leak shot through him. The trick rested in getting far enough into the bushes to secure a cover, but far enough away from the wall to prevent the backsplash from wetting your shoes. "Fuck," Antek said, forced to shake off both his cock and his boots. As soon as he zipped up, he heard the growl of four-cylinder engines on compressed gravel.

He came around and peeked in from behind the corner. His ear hadn't lied. Two Milicja Ładas had stopped in front of the garage. But the men who got out wore the military green instead of the steel blue of Milicja footmen.

Antek had seen enough. He backed off and began to walk away toward the apartment buildings across the street while making sure to keep the garage between him and the cars. He hoped they wouldn't think to check around the building until he could disappear among the concrete obelisks.

Going back to his apartment was stupid. But not going back meant failure and betrayal. He walked steadily while surveying the street. The effort of pretending not to hurry and not to look around made his calves and neck hurt. He'd seen nothing unusual as he approached and entered the building.

Two locks. He scanned the apartment. No one. Two bolts.

Having grabbed his sharpest knife from the kitchen, Antek huffed into his bedroom and dissected the mattress in one stroke. He completed the butchery so that the mattress lay dead and splayed open to reveal a notebook and a thin stack of green American cash. He prayed that the rest—all twenty thousand dollars—was still resting safely at its destination. Most people would never see that much cash at once, but Antek had been trusted to count it and keep it safe. Then, expecting arrest late last fall, he'd had to say a prayer and let it go, trusting others with so much more than just a fortune.

He stuffed the rainy day money in his pockets and paged through the notebook. He considered holding the pages over a stove burner. No, he and others needed the information. He put it in his breast pocket instead.

Carrying his bicycle, he measured his steps down the stairs.

"Citizen Adamczyk," the mostly bald man loitering on the bottom landing said. "Come with us?"

Despite the tone, Antek knew the words were no suggestion.

Us? Aside from a pile of trash swept into a corner, there was no one else.

He couldn't tell how long he stood staring into the man's eyes. Some say there is no such thing as time, that it's personal. Take a look at the long hand of your watch. It always seems to take more than a second to take that first tick. All embarrassed because you caught it dawdling. Then it keeps on ticking, as if nothing notable happened, hoping you'll take it at face value.

By the time he blinked, Antek had had all the time he needed. He let the bike go and, knocking the man aside with his larger body, he bolted. The building's door thundered like a rifle.

"Halt!" someone yelled. Antek ran. Another rifle-like shot of the door rang out. He kept his head forward and his eyes on the space between two apartment buildings. Somebody slammed the door again, and something bit Antek's calf. He stumbled for a step but kept his legs churning.

When something pierced his right side and took his breath, Antek tripped again but ran on.

* * *

He hadn't been shot before. And now he'd been shot twice, and all within seconds. It didn't seem so bad at first. When he fled, he had taken off toward the pier, a kilometer away, though he hadn't realized that until he saw the water.

He stopped in the shade of an oak, struggling for breath and seeing spots.

A summer afternoon. The sea. The pier. People. Suddenly adrenaline swept away the haze. He glanced up and down the street. People, but not too many. Whoever saw him run, unless they worked for Bezpieka, would have been likely to turn around and convince themselves they had witnessed nothing. His right side pulsated, but the bullet had gone clean through and there was less pain than he would have expected from getting shot. True, his right love handle might have absorbed the bulk of the damage. The mostly sedentary existence of the last couple of months—home, work, sleep, fishing, and back to the start—might have left him a bit wider than he had ever been.

He glanced up. A young tree still, the oak would one day command this street corner and probably get cut down for its impertinence. His wife's affection, engineering, liberty, and definitely water and trees—if he could have these things, he'd never ask for anything else. But for now, a sight of water from afar and this tree behind his back were all he had and staying here so long had been dumb.

Antek stepped out from under the shade, and, God, did his side sting all of the sudden. With each jarring step, he felt as if something with teeth clamped down hard on his side. His shirt seemed to stick more damply to his skin. But he couldn't stop, not until he got to his destination.

Where to go? Zygmuntowo, eventually, to find and move the money somewhere safer. But first to see to the wound. Antek took a course for Stefan's repair shop. It was another stupid thing to do, but he couldn't think of another place with disinfectant, tape, and the privacy in which to wrap up his side.

Stefan's first. But then Zygmuntowo. The presbytery of the Most Sacred Heart of Christ Cathedral where he'd delivered twenty thousand American dollars of Solidarity's money. In the first week of last December, when the so-called Polish Unified Workers' Party's grip began to fray, Antek boarded a train to Zygmuntowo—alone this time—with stacks of bills taped to his body. On the way back, he'd hoped he had done the right thing, that the priest would follow directions and pass it through a couple more hands until neither he nor Antek could spill its location under questioning. The fortune could buy hardware for printing presses, transportation, food, and bribes. God have mercy, weapons. He prayed it never came to that.

Antek's mind still worked well enough to take a roundabout route to the repair shop. Whether that helped or only bought him more pain, he would never know, but when Stefan's building came into view, only a couple of stray mutts were hanging around.

CHAPTER THREE

STELMACH

Thursday, July 1, 1982. Frombork.

Major Roman Stelmach sweated his ass off by the time he rounded the corner of the building. He bent over with his hands on his knees. The man had fled like a rabbit. Heavy steps announced Roman's junior partner before the idiot came into view in uniform and still holding his pistol.

"Put that thing away and start checking the houses," Roman said between breaths. He pulled out his radio and called in the other two units. Then, he clenched his teeth and kicked a rock in frustration. He kept his teeth clenched determined not to bend down and rub the achy foot.

Roman sighed and looked around. He couldn't help but smile at the crows perching on a tree, unfazed by all the ratatat. You always knew where you stood with crows.

"Drobina! Zenon!" Roman called out to his junior partner who'd just run out of another staircase and seemed as if he might have twisted an ankle but persisted. "Stop! Stop."

The big man's momentum broke, and he ground to a rest. "Stop?"

Roman walked toward his mentee. "Three buildings, five staircases each, each staircase's got four floors, with three apartments on each floor. Do the math."

"One hundred and eighty apartments."

The moron was showing off. "Regardless. A shitload of places to hide. And you forgot the basements. Keep an eye on the exits. We need help." Roman ran his hand over the mostly barren scalp, wiping off what was left of his sweat. The back of his pants and his shirt had stuck to his skin, and, despite the late June heat, he shivered. It would figure if he got laid out with sciatica. He crimped his lips. His wife was the only person ever entitled to pain. Whenever something ailed Roman, Bernadeta said nothing, but her eyes made him feel like a fraud and malingerer. One with an achy back.

Roman kept scanning the open space between the three buildings. The time of the day could explain the lack of foot traffic around them. And Zenon Drobina's pistol with two fewer bullets might have played a role. The three new radio cars had now arrived, the men throwing open the doors to get out, and still no one had exited the buildings. Roman waved everyone over to him. He beheld the team under his command, snorted—*was this a cold coming on?*—and issued the orders.

* * *

At age ten, Roman Stelmach told his mother he wanted to be an architect. At nineteen, he cleared the waiting list and got into the Gdańsk Polytechnic. The next nine months comprised the best years of his life.

In August 1966, before he was to start his studies, Roman went to mass for four consecutive Sundays to say thanks. The Oliwa Archcathedral got all the press because of its famous organ, but he preferred St. Mary's in the city. As one of the largest brick churches in the world, it rose as a monument to God and its builders. Roman would stand, or sit in the pews on slow days, and admire the work with self-taught professional insight.

The builders had broken ground to lay the foundation stone in 1343. Different hands placed the last brick and pronounced the work complete in 1502. Roman often thought about the men who drew these first plans, who dug the trenches for the foundation, and who fired the first bricks. About the architect who sent his creation into the future, into the hands of those who came after him. What did he think? Did he care that the cathedral remained faithful to his vision?

Roman was fairly certain that if he had been the St. Mary's architect, anxiety would have chased his thoughts and propped his eyelids open every night.

He met Bernadeta in October. Poetry readings and art shows in the Old Town always brought in a few eggheads from the Polytechnic to pockmark with gray the more colorful crowd from the Arts Academy and the University of Gdańsk. Most of the Politechnika men came for the girls, but Roman considered himself part of this more subjective, mystical world as fully as the one filled with math and physics. Architects were hybrids, and in his mind, he already was one. Three years older, Bernadeta was well into her work at the Faculty of Painting at the Academy, and Roman discussed the relative advantages of social realism over modernism with her and her friends as an equal.

She told him she was pregnant in April. In May, instead of sitting for exams, he stopped by the Milicja headquarters and asked about work.

* * *

At the beginning, after he'd gotten out of training, Roman Stelmach surprised himself by how much he had taken to the work. But now the luster of excitement, of control, had worn off, had with time lost its new-leather smell. As he watched the men, including Drobina, fan out into and between the buildings, the sensation foremost in his mind was ache. In his back. In his throat. But an inseparable fusion of anxiety and excitement came as a close second.

After he could be sure that none of the men had turned around to clarify his orders, Roman set off toward his own goal. He'd never really lost track of the treasurer. Not for long. Once he'd realized who was sitting in a cell in the basement of the Gdańsk headquarters, he knew precisely what he was going to do.

Formerly storage, the HQ basement had been converted into cage-sized enclosures hosting a droplet of the penitentiary overflow after the nationwide pacification of December 13. The guests were fed two or three times a day and had cots—nothing fancy but better than concrete. A radio piped in a mass every Sunday. Very humane.

It was simple. Drobina, believing it a step in an undercover operation, had followed Roman's orders and arranged for the treasurer to be left unguarded in front of an open gate to the grounds. It took a minute for the man to bolt, and when he did, they followed. *He'll lead us to their nest*, Roman had told Drobina.

The man might, at that. But Roman wasn't interested in making arrests. He was now after a different, inanimate target.

So when the man seemed to have settled in this little town—with a job and a place to live—going on three months now, Roman knew something had to be done. He had to make the treasurer run.

Roman Stelmach stopped a good fifty meters short of the repair shop and from under the awning of an apartment block's entrance watched a somewhat hunched figure test the shop's door and enter. The man was on the move now and wasn't likely to stop until Roman stopped him.

A scraping of concrete. Roman jerked his head to the left, then relaxed. A small charcoal-furred mutt, judging by the slight waddle not yet fully grown, hopped up the stairs toward him wagging its frayed tail. Roman crouched and extended a hand. A sniffing nose, then a lick greeted him. He scratched the pup behind the ears, and the tail blurred from speed.

"Good boy. Or whatever you are," Roman whispered.

The brown eyes stared up with a mix of hope, fear, and admiration. This here was one of the last truly honest things left on this Earth. Roman petted the dog a few more minutes until he saw the boy, Bolek, whom he had called on his way here, enter the garage. It was time to go.

CHAPTER FOUR

YOU'LL PROBABLY LIVE

Thursday, July 1, 1982. Frombork.

Antek tested the doorknob. It surrendered and the door opened. He had no backup plan. He stumbled then straightened and bolted the garage door. He prayed that the Bezpieka police wouldn't think to return. Not right away.

He dragged himself over to one of the shelves and squinted until he spotted a roll of tape. He took off his shirt and shuffled up to a tall, sheet-metal tool cabinet. A bottle of purple denatured alcohol stood on top, the skull and crossbones on the label advertising the effects of ingestion.

Antek unscrewed the cap and, with gritted teeth, sloshed fire at his flank. Once the gasps and the shaking subsided, he tore small bits of tape and secured strips of clean shop rags over both the entry and the exit wounds above his right hip. He finished applying the battle dressing by unspooling the tape around his torso until only the cardboard center remained.

Then, Antoni Adamczyk attempted to lean over to see to his leg. He passed out as soon as a bend in the tape armor dug into the hole in his flesh.

* * *

He woke up to the sensation of soft plastic under his back. A cushion. Someone had built a hot, steel spike right into the middle of this resting spot and decided it would be a good idea to throw Antek's body on top.

He slowed down his breathing to avoid moving his middle and wished he could stop altogether. For a while. If only he could make himself faint.

Antek cracked open his left eye. A fake crystal chandelier dominated his field of view. The white of the ceiling, marred to one side of the light fixture by a greenish stain, reminded him of his wife's nursing uniform. Did she think he was dead? Bezpieka wasn't in the habit of confirming political arrests. Or escapes. Did she care?

The burn beneath his ribs hadn't subsided, and he decided against further movement. A clock kept the beat somewhere on the periphery, each tick robbing Antek of a second, not to be outdone by the tock which hurried to follow. His ears registered soft cawing—the windows must have been shut. The light in his eyes didn't come from above. A shadow fell. A step. A splash.

The footfalls moved away. When they returned, a wet coolness trickled over him. A hand stuck a searing blade where his flesh ought to be and chased away all other sensations.

Antek's mind shut down again.

* * *

Antek decided that the splotch over his head must have come from someone uncorking a bottle of bubbly without the necessary expertise. Now that the pain no longer commanded most of his attention, he did his best to focus. Mold. Definitely. He liked the idea of Soviet-made "champagne" turning to rot.

When Antek woke up for good, he smelled chicken soup, sunlight streamed through the window, and Bolek sat on the stool by the cot. The aroma of chicken broth came from his direction and dulled the body odor. The boy's pimples converged as his lips attempted a smile. They managed a quiver.

"Hungry?"

Antek shook his head and winced. "No," he whispered. "Water?"

When Bolek returned it was to prop Antek's head up with one arm and bring a glass to his lips with the other. After a few sips, Antek waved his fingers to dismiss the drink. The boy let the head he held descend.

Antek wanted to gulp air as if he'd just played a full soccer match, but that hurt too much. He settled for shallow breathing. A bead of sweat tickled his temple. He lifted his forearm to wipe it off, then let the limb fall back down. Nothing for it—a tickle never killed anybody.

"How did that feel? Just wow. I never met anyone who's been shot before." Bolek cleared his throat and added, "Sorry."

"It's alright."

"Do you need anything else?"

"It hurts if you really want to know. It did then, and it still does. You end up surprised. Disappointed. How a little thing like that takes your strength. Someone stitched it up?"

Bolek nodded. Then, he attended to the blanket, making sure Antek was properly covered.

"I hope it was a doctor. Did they say anything?"

"A pathologist. He said it wasn't much deeper than superfacial, or some such. The doc said it's fine to move, just don't bust your gut at the seam."

The next morning, Antoni Adamczyk, body and mind, left Frombork.

CHAPTER FIVE

DUE EAST

Friday, July 2, 1982. Leaving Frombork.

Antek recognized the Zaporozhets and congratulated himself on never cutting corners. The car sounded like a bouquet of aluminum cans as it dragged itself across the cobblestones, but it made steady progress at sixty kilometers per hour. Slumped in the back seat, Antek had spent the last hour shifting and twisting, but all his efforts failed to dull the discomfort.

Bolek drove and every so often touched his forehead where his father had made a sign of the cross. The skin on his neck had broken out in a horizontal pattern corresponding to the folds in the fat. Sweat stood out like dew.

The young man wiped his forehead again. "Comfortable?" he asked.

"No."

"Beautiful day, isn't it?"

Antek shifted. Some of the pain seemed to waft away as he exhaled. He froze in the position.

"Almost there," Bolek said over his shoulder. "Just a few kilometers."

They turned into a side dirt road. It shook the car less than the 1930s Prussian cobblestone, and Antek allowed himself to sit up and take note of the landscape. The destination turned out to be an old tobacco shed—empty until the harvest—a kilometer or two away from the thoroughfare. Bolek took his foot off the gas and let the Zaporozhets die. It came to a stop in front of the shed's crooked entrance. There was no door, and the mesh screens, where they weren't missing, offered no protection from anything.

"Now we wait," Bolek said.

They did.

The sun had reddened by the time a horse-drawn cart pulled up next to the car.

"Woa!" said a man sporting a handlebar mustache and a wisp of gray hair. He let the horse clap to a stop, threw the reins aside, and lowered himself from the bench with a grunt.

Bolek got out and the two shook hands. Antek heard the murmurs but couldn't make out the words. The old man nodded and produced a pipe from the inside of his jacket. He tamped it as he continued to nod. Bolek stepped closer, opened the car, and pulled the front passenger seat up.

Antek scrabbled out while struggling to keep his torso straight. He stood up, leaning back against the Zaporozhets, and extended his hand.

"Antoni Adamczyk."

"Wacław Hurynowicz," the man answered and squeezed back. "Call me Wacek."

Bolek cleared his throat. "Good luck. Pan Wacek has some clothes for you to change into . . . May God be with you." Then he gave Antek his own handshake, turned around, revived the car, and soon disappeared around a bend in the road.

"Get in," Wacek said.

Antek made an honest effort. He ended up getting hoisted up by Wacek, who then got back on the bench, grabbed the reins, and whistled the animal to attention. The clapping, muffled by the dirt, punctuated the jabs in Antek's side.

He decided not to complain. Strewn with last year's hay, the bed of the cart offered more comfort than the automobile had. The sides of the cart, made of wooden stakes connected by a couple of rails, did enough to contain the cargo but allowed Antek to watch the passing fields. He'd spent little time in the country and was finding the landscape interesting. Antek could imagine resting for a few days among these fields dotted here and there by clumps of pines and other trees he couldn't name. But this was no vacation.

Having gone close to an hour in silence, Antek said, "Panie Wacku, why are they keeping half the fields fallow? Some sort of agricultural science?"

Wacek took his pipe out and spat. The mustache wiggled sideways and up-and-down as the man thought.

"Party answer or God's truth?" he asked.

"Truth?"

"No seeds or fertilizer."

Antek nodded and asked no more questions.

Wacek stayed silent, too, until he turned and soon pulled up to a wooden house the size of a couple of garage bays. An outhouse stood a few meters to the side. The old man held onto the pipe with his teeth while he helped Antek disembark. He shuffled into the house. The younger man followed at his own, slower shuffle.

The room they entered took up most of the building and combined a kitchen, a dining space and a bedroom. An open door revealed a smaller area and another bed. There was no rug on the floor to cover the square, wooden lid of the root cellar.

"Rest." Wacek pointed to a narrow bed by the wall.

Antek complied. He reclined and closed his eyes.

When he woke up the next morning, it took the ache in his side and the smell of burning tobacco to help him remember where he was. He felt for his wound. He could touch it without wincing and decided to consider that good news. Antek smelled Wacek's pipe, but the whistling came from outside.

He propped himself up to a sitting position and twisted to lower his legs to the floor. He was still wearing his regular clothes, but Wacek must have removed his shoes. Right, there they were. Antek bent to put them on with a surprising lack of aggravation in his flank and walked out.

"Up? Good," Wacek said and threw another handful of something to a couple of chickens following him around the yard. "But don't overdo it. My brother-in-law came back from the war shot. Didn't go well for him."

"Thank you. But I thought we were going to try to cross the regional security line?"

"We will. Today. Don't be in such a hurry to get shot again."

"Anything I can help with?"

"Don't get an infection. I left bandages and iodine on the table." Antek went back inside.

* * *

Two men rode a horse-drawn cart down a cobblestone road. The animal kept snorting, and it might have been because of the smell of manure both he and Wacek carried. The old man had insisted on dragging both his and the frayed pants he'd lent to Antek across the floor of the pig shed. Antek's own clothes rested under the load of straw covering the cart up to the railings.

He put his hand on the breast of the work jacket Wacek had also lent him and felt for the identification booklet. When Antek had signed up to run the union treasury at the shipyard, he hadn't planned on this. Now he felt like a fake. He was no James Bond or Hans Kloss.

In fact, the papers in his pocket made him Wacek's son.

Was he getting used to it, or had the stench and the anxiety blunted the pain? Perhaps he was healing? He decided to hope for the latter.

The horse rounded a corner, and there it was: a bar painted white and red with a stop sign nailed to its middle reached across the width of the road. Three soldiers smoked while loitering, boredom wafting out of their bodies with the smoke. Wacek kept the unhurried pace unchanged until a few meters away from the checkpoint. Then he called out, "Woa!" and the animal clapped to a stop.

"Papers!" One of the soldiers dragged himself over, the cigarette hanging from a corner of his mouth.

After both men produced the green identification booklets, he walked off and bent over a few sheets of paper he had pulled out of a bag suspended from one side of the gate.

Antek focused on breathing. When he glanced over at Wacek, the man might as well have been daydreaming about a beer and some kiełbasa.

One of the other soldiers lifted the bar. The first man threw the documents onto the cart's bench, making sure not to linger. At his gesture and Wacek's "woa!" the horse resumed its plodding.

"Why are you doing this?" Antek said, once they had gone a safe distance.

Wacek rested the reins on his lap and took out his pipe. He filled it. Tamped it. He lit it and took a puff.

"Boring, being alone."

"This isn't safe."

"Ever had to convince the Germans you weren't with the partisans? Or the Soviets you had nothing to do with the Germans? *Safe*." He scoffed, then coughed and took another puff. "My wife died ten years ago. The kids all went abroad before that. What else am I going to do?"

Antek nodded. He hadn't thought of it that way.

"Why are *you* doing this?" Wacek asked.

"I want freedom. If I live to have children, I want them to have freedom, too."

"So, what is that, then? Your *freedom*?"

"Just like America. You can do or say anything."

"My brother went to America. He started in construction. Then went to school, worked at a bank. Some asshole shot and killed him for a few dollars."

"But see? He had freedom!"

"He's dead."

Wacek turned down a dirt road. He gathered the reins and stopped the animal next to another tobacco shed. A different Zaporozhets waited next to it. The key would be inside, under a floor mat, where Antek would return it having left the car at the Braniewo train station's parking lot. A horse drawn cart filled up with hay would draw attention in a city.

"May St. Christopher bless your travels," Wacek said. "Go find that freedom."

"Right. As soon as I change my pants."

CHAPTER SIX

OLSZTYN MAIN

Friday, July 2, 1982. Olsztyn.

After exchanging a couple of green bills for złotych at an illegal but tolerated kantor, Antek bought a ticket and soon boarded the train from Braniewo to Olsztyn without any trouble. In less than three hours he'd be at Olsztyn Main. Three hours to figure out what to say. He chose to dispense with looking for a seat in a compartment and opted for standing by an open window in the corridor. Standing hurt less. As the train pulled out of the station, the breeze cooled down the summer heat and dried the sweat Antek had forgotten about. He rested his elbows on the top of the open frame and leaned out.

When Bolek had told him who'd meet him at the Olsztyn train station, Antek blinked but forced his face into stillness. He hoped Bolek couldn't hear his heartbeat. The memory of the saxophone solo steaming from the speaker he'd rigged up came flooding in.

Nineteen seventy-four. On the floor of his barren, student's room, on a mattress, Grażyna lay near-naked in front of him, her rear nestled against his belly. The bodies' heat under the blanket matched the sax. He reached around and pushed aside the elastic of Grażyna's panties. She parted her thighs, inviting his hand. It took him a second to find the point, erect. Antek reached into her for moisture and began to stroke across. Grażyna moaned, opened wider.

Antek stood by the train window, cooling off his suddenly flushed face. Grażyna Duńczyk. They'd gone on to make a home in that room for more than a year. They had not spoken since.

And now only three hours to figure out what to say.

* * *

An hour out of Olsztyn, Antek was still standing by the open window. The air had chilled his nose. He sniffed. The clouds reflected the sun in cotton-candy pink. The hour or two before sunset had always been his favorite time of the day.

Not this time. Too soon, the train crawled into the station, shuddered to a stop, and Antek still hadn't come up with anything profound to tell Grażyna. He had been the one who insisted on making the break clean. No calls or letters. He'd convinced himself he'd felt more lust than love for her. And yet.

Antek patted the legs of his pants to ensure the money and the notebook were still where they belonged, taped to his thighs, waited for his turn, and stepped off the car's steps onto the platform. He hadn't seen her from the window. Now, when he looked around, he realized he'd been looking for Grażyna from eight years ago. He was still wearing the same haircut, but had she changed? Could she have changed enough that he'd failed to recognize the face and the body he had known so well?

Antek walked down the platform, up the stairs, and over to the station's ticketing hall. Still, none of the women looked right. He found a bench and sat down. *You'll meet Grażyna Duńczyk*, he had been told. Antek let his face fall into his open palms and closed his eyes. Funny how he hadn't felt tired a few minutes earlier. Now, lifting his head up seemed almost impossible.

"Antek," a familiar voice said.

He looked up and saw a belly. Above it, there was Grażyna's face.

She looked down, and then back at him. She smiled. "Yes, I am expecting."

Antek rose and Grażyna came in for a friendly hug. Then she sat and patted the spot he had just warmed up. Antek joined Grażyna on the bench and studied her face. The smile.

"I didn't know you married," he said.

"I heard you had."

Antek nodded.

"We have a room for you," Grażyna said. "The committee head got a call a couple of days ago. I volunteered."

"Funny to think, there was a time we both imagined this for us," Antek said without a trace of humor.

"You're the one who dumped me."

"I . . ." He shook his head. No use.

"I know."

"How far along?"

"Seven months." She took his wrist and guided his hand to her belly. He imagined her skin, the freckles and the appendectomy scar, under the thin cotton. He felt her inverted belly button. Antek let his hand fall and return to his knee.

"Any kids?" Grażyna asked.

"No, and there won't be. Not anytime soon, at least. My wife asked for a divorce last November. There just hasn't been time to tie everything off."

"Antek, what are you going to do with your freedom when we win it?" Grażyna rose, pushing a fist against the small of her back. "We've sat here long enough. If anyone had followed, Józef and his brother would have seen them by now."

Antek remained on the bench.

"What?" Grażyna asked.

"Go home."

"Why are you being an idiot?"

"I have a reputation to live up to." Antek smiled. "But, really, I have a plan." He kept the smile on his face even if it felt like a scab. What had he been thinking? From now on, no handlers, especially ones he'd once cared about. He'd zig before he zagged.

Antek hoped Grażyna wouldn't argue but expected her to. When instead she nodded and gave him a smile of her own, the irrational disappointment gripped his chest with a heartburn made of ground glass and vinegar. He kept his face straight.

"Where will you go?"

"Best you don't know," he answered.

Grażyna touched her fingertips to her lips and pressed them against Antek's forehead. He closed his eyes as he received the blessing. When

Antek opened his eyes, he watched the tall figure of the first woman he ever loved walk away.

He could not stay here during curfew, but he hadn't lied to Grażyna. He did have a plan. Antek dragged himself over to the train station's toilets and stopped in front of an ancient attendant. The skin of the woman's face had shriveled, shrunk, and darkened as if it had been left hanging in a smoker. She rested, hunched, macerating bits of sausage with toothless gums.

"Droga Pani," Antek said, "I have nowhere to go during curfew. Could I sleep inside until the morning trains?"

The woman's lower jaw stopped its work but still trembled like a poorly tuned engine on idle. She looked up and squinted. "What is this? A hotel? I lock up at nine, anyway."

"Perfect. Lock me in, then let me out in the morning."

"No. Impossible."

Antek pulled out his wallet. He placed a one-dollar bill on a low table next to the rest of the woman's sausage.

That evening, too tired to care about the smell, Antek curled up on ceramic tiles and fought to find sleep. When it failed to come despite exhaustion, he sat and felt the bitterness in his gut return, then rise. Once it reached his throat, he wept.

Antek still hadn't slept when, liberated from the toilets, he spent most of his remaining złotych on a ticket and boarded the 6:36 headed south.

CHAPTER SEVEN

WHAT KIND OF MAN DO YOU THINK I AM?

Friday, July 2–Saturday, July 3, 1982. Gdańsk and Olsztyn.

Roman watched the kid blink. Then the boy blinked again when the pistol rang out hot metal through the prototype P-64 suppressor the brass had asked Roman to test. This should count. Roman fired three more times, three more hammer blows on a blanket-covered anvil, before the body had a good sense to crumple to the garage floor. Louder than he would have preferred, but Roman didn't expect to write and turn in his review. He shrugged his backpack off and pulled out a sheet of plastic he had left over from building a greenhouse last fall. Funny how he would never have guessed then how he'd end up using it.

He backed his car up and opened the trunk. Roman was sweating and the sun had mostly set by the time he pulled away from the repair shop—closed for business early on Fridays—and headed out, then northwest. The moon had already come up when Roman stopped the car by the gate to his garden plot on the edge of Gdańsk. Once he had dragged the boy in and closed the gate, now shielded by the two-meter fence, he allowed himself to relax. Roman stretched, pushing his hips out. He was going to be sore in the morning. All this lifting was murder on a man's lower back.

Roman crouched and frisked the boy. His name had been Bolek. Roman had made sure to use the name and smile when they first spoke. Bolek had agreed to inform before Roman could tell the youth the running rate. Having sifted through all the pockets, on the inside and out, Roman hiked the body's pant legs. The twenty American he'd paid the boy had been stuck inside a sock, wrapped in plastic foil. Bolek couldn't have been more than twenty, likely younger. Briefly, Roman had considered letting him live, but then he thought about the risks and squashed the weakness. As he stood back up while fighting the sudden vertigo, the necessity and rightness of what he'd done settled over him.

He had flushed the treasurer out. Now all he had to do was not give the man enough time to think. Keep him running. Straight to where he'd stashed the cash. Roman brought the foil-wrapped banknote up to his face. The green was gray in the moonlight and no detail showed, but in his mind, Roman could see every line and signature on a thousand more identical pieces of paper.

He pulled the body into the greenhouse. The hole he'd dug earlier gaped. Between the digging and the dragging, it was an even bet which one was going to lay him out. Roman pushed the body over the edge with the treads of his shoe and threw the plastic, which had come loose, on top of it. Sweat dripped off his temples when he'd finished shoveling the dirt back. Then he spread out a bit of compost and mixed the top layer with it. He dragged over a crate of containers.

When it was time to straighten up, Roman stood and beheld a couple of rows of tomato plants, each stalk accompanied by a stake driven into the ground. Well past midnight, he unfastened the plastic cover and dragged it back off the greenhouse's skeleton. He stashed it in the shed for October. Then he paused. A life in which he would still need this piece of plastic in October wasn't worth contemplating.

A half-hour later, Roman Stelmach pulled up and parked the Łada in front of his house. He opened, then gently pushed the steel gate in the fence closed, locked it, and double-checked the handle. He walked up the concrete stairs on his toes and winced when the key grated in the lock. Without turning on the light, he closed and bolted the door. Then he headed straight for the shower and used the lowest pressure that would do the job.

Naked, Roman sneaked across the hallway and into the bedroom. He lowered himself onto the mattress and pulled the blanket. Caught somewhere under Bernadeta, it stopped short of covering his groin. Roman didn't care about his uncovered legs and torso, but he had never been able to sleep with his junk hanging out. Too vulnerable. He pulled again, exerting a gentle but inexorable force.

"Romek?" Bernadeta muttered. Not even what he had left of friends called him Romek anymore.

Roman stopped pulling.

"If they make you work nights, they should pay you more," she said.

"Can I have a little bit of this blanket?"

Bernadeta shifted, releasing a few centimeters of slack. With the cover over his groin, Roman felt a measure of calm. Safety.

"Do you even remember your children's names?"

Roman closed his eyes. "Good night," he said. Soon, he heard Bernadeta's soft puffing. It still had a way of lulling him to sleep.

By the time his wife woke up in the morning, Roman Stelmach had already left for Olsztyn.

***

A couple of blocks down from his house, Roman pulled over and double-checked his briefcase. Identification papers. A service booklet. A thin money clip with a few green bills. A larger one with the Polish pulp—worth a few percent less today than yesterday. Two passports. A Stanisław Lem novel.

A duffel with a pair of shoes, toiletries, and a few changes of clothes sat in the trunk.

Roman stopped by an apartment building twenty minutes later. Young Zenon Drobina ground down a cigarette and got in.

"Good morning," he said.

Roman rolled down a window.

Many people carried a few extra kilos. Many sweated. Roman himself broke a sweat when he sneezed. But Drobina's body managed to take that fertile ground and cultivate a stench strong enough to challenge a happy hog. The cigarettes didn't help.

Roman wished Drobina hadn't been necessary. But leaving the city without his partner would have raised eyebrows and brought questions altogether too soon. Besides, the man might yet have a role to play.

Drobina wiped his forehead. "Hot."

Roman nodded. The sign marking the end of Gdańsk's city limits allowed him to accelerate. The breeze picked up and he risked a deeper breath.

He thanked the Łada for its speed. In stretches, it hit a hundred kilometers per hour. In the two hours to Olsztyn, neither of the men offered any further conversation. Roman pulled up to the Milicja headquarters. He produced his papers and the gate swung open. Before they left the car, Roman rolled the window back up, making sure to leave a five-centimeter slit on top.

As a major, he outranked all the local yokels. In less than thirty minutes, Roman sat behind a desk in what was now his office. Having sent Drobina out with his orders, he closed the door. He checked his watch. Then he made a call to reserve rooms in an Interior Ministry hotel in Zygmuntowo. He could always cancel them if Olsztyn proved more fruitful than he expected. The last thing he wanted, though, was to sleep in some drafty, flea-infested shithole.

Drobina returned at fifteen hundred hours. He drew his stomach in—the flesh disappeared in the now closed gap between the bottom of his civilian polo and the top of his pants like a frightened mollusk—and saluted. Despite himself, Roman sighed; this sudden attention to forms didn't bode well.

"Spit it out."

Drobina let his gut back out and stuck the hand, with which he'd just delivered a passable salute, into a pocket of his slacks. So much for forms.

"No sign of Piekarski or Adamczyk or whatever name he's going by now. No one home, in fact."

"How do you know?"

"I knocked," the fat man answered.

Roman ground his jaw and reminded himself of the possible use he had in his mind for Drobina. "Go back out and keep an eye on the place until the evening. Pretend you're checking meters or something."

Once Zenon Drobina left, Roman opened the window to let some air in. Then he pulled out his notebook, sat at the desk, and began to check every step of the plan for the hundredth time. On occasion, he jotted a note. Then he doodled another rendition of Mount Corcovado and Sao Paulo's Christ the Redeemer.

If he had ever become a working architect, Roman would not have taken the job of building the giant Jesus statue. He suspected it must have been fun. Some would consider it beautiful. But for what? What shelter did it offer anybody? Rain still fell on the faithful as they beheld the Christ, the sun still burned them. He'd never seen anyone with skin darker than a mild tan in real life, but something stirred in Roman at the thought of dark-skinned girls in bikinis.

He'd learn Portuguese. Perhaps it wasn't too late to go back and get his degree.

When Drobina returned at eighteen hundred hours to announce that all he'd seen were the pregnant bitch and her husband, Roman worked hard to keep his temper. He put everything back in his briefcase, rose, and led the idiot to the Łada.

* * *

Roman had left the car two blocks away and walked to Grażyna Duńczyk's building, listening to Drobina huff. The dead boy had written the address down before pocketing the twenty American dollars. The crisp bill had seemed to give Bolek joy. It was good that the boy could experience some of that before what had to happen, but now Roman wished he could shoot the zit-ridden oaf again. Assuming Drobina's report held up.

They walked up to the second-floor apartment. "Close and lock the door behind us," Roman said. Then he knocked.

A man—not Piekarski—answered and held the door as open as the chain would allow.

"Our technician reported a problem with your electric meter," Roman said. "Mind if we take another look at it? Sorry about the time. Hard to keep up with this crap breaking all the time."

The man lowered the chain.

Roman gave him a smile. Then he swung his right arm and ruined the fellow's nose with one punch fortified by the butt of his pistol. He drove the wound deeper into the head with three more jabs before the man fell. Then he trained the pistol's sights on the woman standing three or four steps away.

"Shut up," he said, just in case, and stepped forward until the barrel hung less than a meter from her throat. His arm was steady even if he felt a bit winded.

The woman—lanky, her belly sticking out like a volcano out of a flat—began to hyperventilate, instead.

"Breathe," Roman said. "Where is Antoni Piekarski?"

She fell to her knees, her eyes trained on the bleeding man on the floor. Roman looked down at the body. He couldn't tell if its chest still moved.

Roman lowered the weapon and said, "We'll call an ambulance as soon as you answer my questions. Grażyna? Grażyna Duńczyk?"

The woman nodded.

"Grażyna, be smart. Where is Piekarski? I know he was coming to meet you."

"I don't know."

Roman's arm started to come up.

"I don't know, I swear to Jesus. I saw him at the train station last night. That's all."

"If he's hiding in this apartment, I *will* find him and I *will* kill you."

As if uncorked, the woman's eyes flooded. Soon, the tears and the snot mixed and began to drip on the linoleum. Somehow, she was still straining to muffle every sound.

Roman gestured at Drobina, and the fat man stepped around the woman and into the living room, holding his own P-64. Next, Drobina checked the bedroom—the last of the rooms in the two-room apartment. Finally, he investigated the bathroom.

"Nothing," he reported.

Roman squeezed his eyes shut and took a moment to think. This turn of events had been unexpected—his least favorite kind. Nothing for it now.

"Take your best guess," he told the woman.

She took a break from weeping and shook her head.

"Try again," Roman said.

"He was just going to stay the night. Maybe two."

"Consider this. If I don't find him, I'll come back to ask more questions."

"Maybe he went back home?"

Roman pursed his lips and wiped an imagined smudge off the barrel with his thumb.

"He has no other family," Grażyna said. She had started to drool again.

Roman pitched the pistol's barrel up like a director's baton.

"Mazury? He knew people in the Lakeland." Grażyna tried again.

"Anything more specific?"

"Zygmuntowo. He's mentioned friends . . . in Zygmuntowo."

"Names?"

Instead of answering, Grażyna pushed her forehead against the floor and wept, blind to whatever the pistol did next.

Roman lifted his arm and felt his finger on the trigger. He watched the woman's body over the sights. If she still kept her eyes open, all she could be seeing was the brown flooring. She'd drawn her knees up and wrapped the one arm he could see well across her abdomen. As if an arm could stop a nine-millimeter Makarov round.

He aimed at the head and flexed his finger a bit more. Some people complained about how much effort it took to fire a P-64. Some preferred a hair trigger. Roman liked the heavy trigger pull. It meant intention. You had to earn the right to fire it.

The woman had compressed into a ball not much larger than her stomach. She no longer cried. Roman couldn't tell if she still drew breath. He gritted his teeth.

Roman Stelmach lowered his arm and waved at Drobina to follow him. They got back to the Łada three or four minutes later. Neither had still said a word when Roman started the car and pulled away.

"Major, I almost thought you were going to off the bitch," Drobina said a few kilometers down the road. He giggled. "You almost gave me a scare."

"What kind of man do you think I am?"

Drobina made a noise in response.

Roman wasn't going to turn back north to Gdańsk. He expected he'd never see the city again. Instead, he headed east.

CHAPTER EIGHT

CONTROL

Friday, July 2–Saturday, July 3, 1982. Zygmuntowo.

Emilia watched as Frania Nowak connected a call and clicked off in silence.

"This call is being controlled," said Emilia, having connected her own call.

She looked forward to putting on the swimming suit she'd bought at the market. She got it back in September. As she saw it, the benefits were twofold: September swimming suits were cheaper and getting one in the autumn committed her to walks and staying off cookies. Or maybe not completely off. If she could only come up with a way to move the rolls from her hips to her chest. Looking in the mirror each morning, she felt content, if not entirely happy.

Emilia preferred her face straight on—a profile revealed a slight hook in the tip of her nose. The eyes blinking back would flash a blue the hue of Virgin Mary's flag. Emilia used a touch of shadow to bring the color out. Her skin, under a brown bob, shone clean, unblemished, unpowdered. Her cheeks hadn't needed to camouflage bruises since she stood up to her father, who left soon after she turned seventeen and had no address she knew.

The swimming suit was an athletic two-piece, with a hip-hugging bottom and a stuffable top. Red polka dots contrasted well with the powder-blue of the fabric. She couldn't believe her luck when the fat Russian woman at the market gave it away for two American dollars. Emilia pretended to haggle—one had to keep up appearances—even though she'd saved up for months and had been ready to spend twice as much.

Three o'clock couldn't come soon enough.

"They arrested old Marelski." Pani Frania's voice failed to register at first. Frania used it so rarely when she didn't have to—and never to talk about herself—that Emilia needed a moment to realize the woman was speaking to her.

Emilia glanced sideways. Frania Nowak stared at the blinking lights in front of her as though she hadn't said a word.

"From Baraki?" Emilia asked. As if there were another Marelski in town.

"Someone reported him for listening to Radio Free Europe."

Emilia's jaw clenched.

With a nod to the shift manager dozing at her desk, she tore off her headset and rushed out of the room and up the stairs. Emilia stopped in front of the door labeled DYREKTOR, then took a step one way and the other. She stretched her fingers and took a couple of deep breaths.

"Come in." The voice rang out before she could make herself knock. Emilia pushed the doorknob and stepped in, leaving the door ajar.

"Good afternoon," she said.

"Sokołowska? What is all that racket and the sighing about?" Director Czarniecki always sounded irritated, whether he used his bass to fire someone or announce a promotion.

Emilia grasped for what she had planned to say and missed.

"Sokołowska, I don't have all day. Spit it out."

"Pan Marelski. They arrested him."

Czarniecki picked up his pen and tapped the papers scattered in front of him with the side of his palm. "Do I know him?"

"I made a report. A call report. On him. Now he's in jail."

"Good. Keep up the good work."

Emilia lost the rest of her words. An image of a freckled face hovered in her mind. Beata Marelska was a close friend once, before she got into university and Emilia didn't. God, had Beata failed like she had, would she have reported on her father?

Czarniecki looked up and rubbed his right eye under the rim of eyeglasses thick enough to be bulletproof. "What?"

"Thank you," Emilia said. Then she slipped out and closed the door. She stopped by the women's lavatory. When she was ready, she washed and dried her eyes and went back to work.

A light flickered. She grasped a plug, measured out a slow breath, and made the connection. "This conversation is being controlled," she said.

Three o'clock couldn't come soon enough.

***

"Emilka!" Agata squealed and bombed the water's surface holding her nose with one hand and her top with the other. Her ponytail disappeared.

Kalina rolled over, jumped off the beach towel covering a couple of square meters of the pier, and hugged Emilia hard enough for two or three ribs to crack. Not for the first time, Emilia decided to try windsurfing. It gave her best friend superhuman strength and made her butt cheeks scamper up and down like the bars of one of those railroad handcars Emilia had seen in silent movies. The bruise on Kalina's thigh must have come from falling on a board, but Emilia would have been happy to pay that price.

"Sexy!" Kalina said.

"What? This old thing?"

That's when both Kalina and Emilia swore and jumped.

"Agata! Quit it!"

Agata giggled from the water, having just sprayed the other two women. She slapped the surface to spray them again and set off toward the other side of the lake, a kilometer away, at a practiced backstroke and with a grin on her face.

Of the three old high-school friends, Kalina was the athlete, excelling at windsurfing during the short summer seasons and speed skating in the winter. Agata was the clown and, built like a seal, a rather strong swimmer. Emilia was . . . She wasn't sure. She struggled to come up with a succinct definition of her role in their triangle. She read books, as many as she could get her hands on, wrote badly, and she listened. That didn't seem like a lot to her, but the three had become known as The Trinity among their classmates early. Now, five years on from graduation, The Trinity persisted.

Kalina sat her butt back down on the now damp towel. "It'll dry," she said.

"What a whore," Emilia said. "One day she'll drown. I may or may not go to the funeral." She sat cross-legged, knee-to-knee with Kalina.

It had been fifteen years, and her friends no longer noticed, but Emilia couldn't miss the stunted middle toe on her left foot, standing out like the starving youngest pup in a litter. She had started with a full-length toe. A broken beer bottle at the bottom of a lake and an infection had claimed it down to the first joint. She now forced herself to go barefoot or wear open-toe sandals whenever possible. Let them gawk.

Emilia nodded toward a point a kilometer or so to the north, along the shore of the lake, where an inlet partly shielded a complex maze of piers, assorted sheds, and a single-story brick building. "Ready?" she asked.

Kalina stretched her neck and grunted.

"You'll do fine. This is the year. I can feel it," Emilia said.

Kalina grunted again and spread out face-down on the towel.

Emilia knew that anything she said would be as helpful as an aspirin for a beheading. Kalina had failed to qualify for the national team at three world championship trials in the past two months. This was the last chance for Japan, and none came as gilded as racing in her own backyard, where she knew how the winds changed and how the depth affected the currents.

Agata splatted over, water dripping from her dark hair onto her Sasquatch feet. Emilia put a finger to her lips.

"Nice suit," Agata stuttered, having changed what she had been going to say. "What's up with her?" she whispered.

Before Emilia could decide how best to punch or slap the idiot, Kalina sat up and fixed them both with a stare.

"Sure, it'll be fine," Kalina said, rose, and walked away down the pier toward the small snack stand and the row of toilets on the shore. As she got further, Kalina picked up speed, until she zoomed into a stall and slammed the door.

"That bad?" Agata said.

"Try not to make it worse," Emilia said and hoped for the best. Kalina always exorcised her pre-race anxiety as diarrhea. Given the stakes, Emilia expected puking to follow. "Thanks again for the canned pork," Emilia continued. "Mother has said a few Hail Marys in your intention."

Agata waved it off with a *don't mention it* twitch to her lip but came up and gave Emilia another hug. There was little, if anything, that Kalina and Emilia could do to repay her for the canned meat she stole from work a couple of times a month, and all of them knew it. Emilia loved her friend for not being an ass about the matter.

***

Emilia and Agata met Kalina at her apartment and walked her to the club's pier early the next morning. A chipped sign reading *Zygmuntowo Water Sports Club* guarded the broken gate and seemed to stare at them saying, *I tried*. The gate had been broken as long as Emilia could remember so she couldn't say either way if it had.

"Good luck," Emilia said, once they stopped at the gate.

"We'll be back for the race," Agata added.

Kalina nodded with a face the color of a skid mark on dry grass, hugged each of them, and walked off without a word toward the club's buildings to meet her coaches and teammates. To prepare and warm up.

With two hours to kill, Agata and Emilia shuffled back to town and, like two pigeons, homed in on a coffee shop about a kilometer away from the beach. They dropped into their seats with matching sighs. After a couple of minutes of a stationary, silent game of chicken, Agata rose and ordered two coffees at the counter.

Agata's sigh after the first sip reminded Emilia of her grandfather's last breath, except in reverse. Emilia's grunt expressed the same relief that coffee had been served at last, mixed with the certainty of a hell soon to come.

It was going to be just like the other times. Kalina would come in third or fourth, not high enough to qualify but too close to avoid asking *what if*. Would she have won had she taken tighter turns? Would more upper body work have made a difference? What if she had picked a different board?

Once they finished their coffees, Emilia got up to get a couple more at the counter. The clerk waived off her five twenty-złoty coins. "She paid for unlimited refills," he said.

Emilia placed the cups on the table. "Thanks," she said.

"Did Kalina ever show you how to windsurf?"

Emilia shook her head.

"She tried to teach me," Agata said, and slapped her left bicep. "Thought I'd be a natural. Big arms, fins for feet, a low center of gravity. But every time I got the sail up, the breeze pulled it out of my hands. I finally told her I didn't think I was strong enough."

Emilia smiled. She could imagine what Kalina might have said to that.

"She said I was an idiot, and it was more about technique, not muscles." Agata proved her correct. "I think she was disappointed when I didn't ask for another lesson."

"I hope she gets over this one sooner than the last," Emilia said.

By the time Agata and Emilia left, they'd had four cups of coffee each and had formulated no plausible plan for how to help their friend overcome the impending heartbreak.

* * *

The bleachers faced the lake and ran about thirty meters long. The four rows could have seated a good three hundred, maybe more, but Emilia thought they stood about a tenth full. Kalina came out of the boathouse and turned her face toward the bleachers, shielding her eyes. She waved.

Emilia and Agata waved back. Emilia's gut tightened, and she wondered if it was the coffee or if she'd finally caught Kalina's weak stomach. She hated the powerlessness. Especially over Kalina's fear. Her anguish.

Kalina had dressed for the sun and the heat. She wore her favorite white one-piece she'd bought two years before. Her blond braid fell halfway to her behind. Emilia allowed herself to admire her figure.

The race followed the damnable pattern. This time, only the winner qualified. Kalina came in second.

"Let's go over to my place," Agata said to Emilia, as they walked toward the club house, steeling themselves for whatever came next. "I've got some beers in the fridge."

They greeted Kalina with hugs. Emilia embraced her friend and let her bury a wet face in her neck. "Shhh," she said, as nothing else seemed right. She stroked Kalina's shoulder, making sure to avoid the constellation of bruises. One would think the girl played rugby, rather than sail. Agata carried Kalina's bag, while Emilia led her, silent, a couple kilometers to Agata's apartment.

Agata's one-bedroom made for their usual haunt. She was the one with her own place. That it was thanks to Agata's father's connections and probably a few cases of vodka, did not bother Emilia. One used what tools she had. She and Kalina would likely have to wait for their own bit of space until their parents died or until the economy started hitting the five-year plans, whichever came first. Somewhere between thirty years and never.

Emilia deposited Kalina on the sofa, and Agata disappeared into the kitchen from which the mini explosions of beer caps soon sounded. Tip-toeing back in, Agata held the overfull glasses like baby birds until she alighted them on the table.

"Tyskie." She announced the drink. "Only the best for the best." Then she dipped back into the kitchen to fetch the half-full bottles.

Emilia leaned forward to sip the crowning head before she lifted her glass. Kalina made no motion.

"It was the closest of the four." Agata sat on a corner of the coffee table. "You'll make it next year."

"Next year?" Kalina's voice came through a stuffed-up nose. "You said that last year."

"Look, you're just twenty-four, you've got years to make it to the top," Emilia said. "And you will. We all know it." She looked around as if inviting an audience to nod and took a long draw out of the glass. Tyskie was a good brew. Emilia never kept beer at home. It cost too much money, and her mother had never approved of alcohol, anyway. No, *never* wasn't quite right. She'd seen Zofia Sokołowska unsteady with some regularity since December. Emilia drained the glass in seconds and swapped it for a partly full bottle.

"Japan." Kalina's whimper came amplified like a sneeze one tries to stifle in church. "Japan," she keened, and the tears began to flow in earnest. Kalina bent over, hiding her face and covering her head.

Emilia caressed her shoulder but stopped when it stiffened. "Hey, what's so special about Japan? Next year's Italy, right? Easier to defect."

When Kalina straightened back up, her face had changed. "What do you know?" she said. "All you want is to eavesdrop on people and feel like you know things. Like nothing is happening. Like all this. . . ." She raised her hands up, then splayed them out. ". . . like this is a normal way for a person to live."

Emilia's breath caught.

"And you." Kalina turned to Agata who was now perching on the corner of the table, looking as if she were trying to avoid crossfire. "You just want to eat and fuck, and you're happy." A direct hit.

"Kalina, stop—"

She wouldn't let Emilia stop her.

"I could have been out of this shithole, cooped up with. . . . I can't stay and pretend this is real life like you."

"Kalina, don't—"

"You just gave up! Want to report me for the social order criminal I am? Here, I've been working with the underground for months!" Kalina spat out. "I thought you had a soul, once, but you're a fraud. You're walking around dead inside!"

Emilia had clenched her jaw. Now she felt something break. It wasn't her mandible. It hurt worse than snapping a bone.

She rose and left Agata's apartment with a dry face and a beer bottle in her hand. She bought three more on the way home and drank all of it alone, ignoring her mother's stares and tsking, to put herself to sleep.

CHAPTER NINE

ZIG ZAG

Saturday, July 3, 1982. Warszawa.

Antek got off at Warszawa Wschodnia well before eleven in the morning. He counted the change in his pocket and decided to walk instead of springing for a tram ticket. If there was anything he possessed today it was time. His destination—a hospital in a southern part of right-bank Warsaw—lay, by his estimate, three or so kilometers away. Antek set out, initially focused on putting one foot in front of the other.

He had been walking, too, when he first met Dorota. Except, instead of sunshine, it had rained and the wind from the sea had forced him to hold his coat together because the zipper was broken. The solid umbrella he carried that day had been one of the last gifts from his father before he died the week prior. All his life, whether his choices were met with approval, Antek knew he could count on his father's hug and, once he'd been found to have crossed the boundary from boyhood to manhood, a beer and a meal. Antek's eyes stung as if seawater had mixed up with the moisture in the air.

He bumped into the girl when she'd stopped in the middle of the sidewalk, working to unfurl her collapsed umbrella. She would have fallen had he not reached an arm and steadied her. The useless mass of wire and red fabric she'd held sailed off in the wind. Before she could vent the anger he saw in her eyes, he apologized and gave her his father's gift.

That's when her face changed. Instead of grabbing his umbrella and huffing away, she suggested he walk her to work. A hospital. And that he meet her after work, of course. *Who knows, it might continue to rain.*

Today the sun shone and had already made it at least thirty degrees despite the relatively early hour. Five minutes in, Antek felt a drop of sweat meander down his back. Then another. Soon, a waterfall. The wound in his side had started to smart again, too. Passing through a park, he spied a bench under a tree and sat down to cool off in the shade.

He sniffed and realized he could smell himself. Not much he could do about that. It's not like Dorota could sue him for divorce any harder because he stank. Still, he decided to slow down the pace. When he saw a street seltzer water vendor, he bought and downed a couple of glasses mixed with cherry juice.

Antek shuffled up to the hospital entrance in the early afternoon. He walked in—blessed shade—located the information desk and asked about the nursing station in the Neonatal Intensive Care Unit.

The woman behind the desk squinted. "What's your business?"

"My wife is a nurse there. Dorota Piekarska. I need to speak with her. It'll only be a few minutes."

The woman was as large around as one of the thick lobby pillars and seemed at least as solid. The reinforced concrete might have carried more fat than she did. Antek's mind conjured a picture of her throwing shot put in the Olympics.

She huffed and muttered something under her breath.

"Really," Antek begged. "Just two minutes."

"Name?"

Antek obliged.

The strongwoman picked up her phone. She asked to be patched through to the NICU. "Can you give me Piekarska?" she said. "There is a man here," she continued. "He says he's your husband. A bum, if you ask me. But polite. He says his name is Antoni Piekarski. Never seen him before."

She hung up. "She'll come," she said. "When she can." The woman pointed to the rows of benches in the lobby.

Antek found a spot by a wall, sat and leaned back, cooling off against the stone. He let his eyes close. Just a year earlier, on a sunny summer day like this, Dorota and he would be planning a picnic dinner on a pier in Sopot. They'd watch the seagulls. The men with their fishing poles, casting and failing. They'd laugh and plan a future. It all went wrong, somewhere.

He felt a body sit next to him and opened his eyes.

"Good God, Antek, you look terrible," Dorota said. She took her glasses off and buffed the lenses with a corner of her white nurse's jacket. Then she blinked. "What?"

"It's good to see you," Antek said. He found himself grinning stupidly at her green eyes. "That's all."

"You smell terrible, too."

"Nothing a bath couldn't fix," he lied. His side burned now. He thanked the heavens the graze in his calf had closed without an argument. Given the look he got in exchange, he didn't think Dorota believed him.

"Here's my key." She put it in his palm. Then she walked back up to the information desk and returned with a piece of paper and a pen. "Here's the address. Do you have money for a bus?"

Antek nodded.

"Go take a bath. A long one. Then sleep. Feel free to lock the door. I have a spare key. I'll see you in the evening."

The strongwoman behind the desk escorted Dorota with a disapproving stare. Antek suspected he got the same or worse as he walked out of the lobby but chose not to look over his shoulder.

* * *

The bus let Antek off less than a block away from Dorota's apartment in the Gocław district. Inside the building, someone had painted *ZEPSUTA* on the elevator door in capital but cursive black letters. Antek pressed the button anyway. Nothing happened. Broken, indeed. He turned up the staircase and began a twelve-story climb to the top. Apartment 12d. Two landings up, he stopped for a breath.

When Antek arrived on the twelfth floor, he took a moment to rest with his hands on his knees. Then he pulled out the key and unlocked an apartment he'd never seen. His wife's apartment. The burning in his thighs and middle floated to his chest as he opened the door and closed and bolted it behind him. Then he stood, uncertain what to do next.

The kitchen lay across the hallway, in front of him. To the right of the kitchen was the only room, spacious enough to show a good bit of uncluttered floor among Dorota's usual books, magazines, and knick-knacks.

An open door at the end of the two-step hallway revealed a sink, a toilet, and a bathtub.

Antek headed straight for it. He stripped naked. Then he plugged the sink, put his underwear and shirt in it, and filled it with hot water mixed with shampoo. He decided to let them soak as long as possible. He drew a lukewarm bath and lowered himself into the water.

Antek's breath caught, and he would have tsked if he'd had any air. His side had submerged and with it the scab in the process of becoming a scar. He ran his fingers over it and was forced to decrease the pressure. The thing looked redder than the last time he had taken a good look at it. A soak and soap were probably exactly what the wound needed.

Once washed and rinsed, Antek stood up and pulled a towel off a wire shelf. Dry, he wrapped the towel around his hips and scrubbed his undergarments in the sink. Rinsed them. Wrung. Then he hung them on a line above the bathtub.

Antek kept the movements of his torso to the minimum—his side was beginning to sting. Naked, except for a towel around his hips, he shuffled into the main room of the studio apartment and surveyed the surfaces.

Dorota had never been much for photographs. She insisted she did just fine focusing on the experience and keeping it in her head. But she was also the kind of person who'd take time to think through her relationship to images. One who'd as soon read about Paris as go there. Well, maybe not that last part. Not that either of them was ever likely to make it to Paris.

A set of shelves built upon a base of low cabinets running the length of one wall supported at least two hundred books. A black-and-white photograph of a couple stood in a clear space in the middle. Acting out spontaneity, the man gazed down at the woman's face. The woman, supported by one of his arms, gazed back up. Their smiles appeared genuine. Dorota's parents had been married for two years before their little girl came. Antek wondered what they would have thought of him had they lived long enough.

A television set, its screen lifeless, rested in a square receptacle built into the shelves for this specific purpose like a sarcophagus. Antek usually found he had too little time to waste on television. An L-shaped sleeper sofa—Antek remembered it well—took up the opposite wall's length.

Antek wriggled his nose and moved closer to the off-white, sheer window curtain. It gave off a stale tobacco stench, one he wouldn't have noticed a few years ago when he smoked at least a pack a day. When had Dorota started smoking again? They had celebrated their engagement by quitting together. For the children. Well, he had relapsed recently, too.

Two armchairs surrounded a table set against the wall opposite the balcony. Antek sat in one, but the sting in his side soon became too much. He scrambled out of it and decided to lie down. In search of a blanket, he began to open the cabinets, starting from the left. Dorota's clothes, some folded, some thrown in. Aside from a few professional pieces, most of the garments appeared her preferred airy style.

To one side, a couple of pairs of lace thong panties stood out from the professional and hippie masses. Antek had tried to talk her into wearing something like it a few times. Dorota would tell him to get himself a pair if he liked to walk around with a wad of rope stuck between his ass cheeks. He had no idea she'd gone and bought some.

No blanket.

Antek opened the middle set of cabinet doors. Having stared for a moment, he finally understood he was looking at neatly folded stacks of men's shirts and pants. Some underwear. A sleeve of Eros condoms stuck out from under a pile of socks. Antek closed that cabinet. He found a blanket behind the next and last set of doors.

With the blanket cocooned around him, Antek crawled onto the sofa and put his head on a quilted pillow. The image of the condoms constricted his throat. He rubbed his palm across his forehead, and it came off dripping like a windshield wiper. He shivered and wished he'd grabbed another blanket. No way was he getting back up. Antek pushed against his thoughts, hoping to force them to disperse. The pain, with its own mind, lingered. Antek's last thought before falling asleep was the resignation to never sleeping again.

* * *

A film dripping with hues played on the wall above the table and chairs as if someone had set up a projector in the darkness. The images on the wall alternated between popping out in three dimensions and losing sharpness altogether. In one corner, beachgoers romped around chasing a rainbow-colored ball. All attractive, two—both women—wearing not a stitch and intimately familiar. Antek smiled and decided to embrace the hallucination.

In the opposite quadrant, Boniek had just scored to put Poland in the lead over East Germany.

Above the soccer game, Kojak was sucking on a lollipop and solving Bezpieka crimes.

In the last corner Dorota and Grażyna, wearing white lacy dresses, sat hip to hip and smiled at him with their entire faces.

Antek squeezed his eyes shut. When he opened them, the movie his mind projected was still playing.

A shade on the floor caught his eye. A form, feminine and petite, rested on it under a blanket, her chest rising in the rhythm of sleep. Dorota.

This wasn't right. He should be the one sleeping on the floor. Antek moved to get up but passed out before he could fall off the sofa.

CHAPTER TEN

REASONS FOR JAPAN

Sunday, July 4, 1982. Zygmuntowo.

Mother answered the telephone. Yes, she would attend the committee meeting tomorrow. No, she had no questions. Yes, the arrests had been unfortunate but necessary. For public safety. For the Party and the Country.

Emilia had tried to convince Kalina and Agata a thousand times that her job had nothing to do with her having a telephone at home. She might have worked at the telephone station but had no such pull. Seeing as both of their families had waited a decade or longer for a line, and neither had one yet, she couldn't say she blamed them for disbelieving. She wondered why she couldn't tell them the real reason why the company had installed a telephone for her mother in mere months.

Mother carried the Party ID booklet in her purse like anyone else who wanted a job or a decent place to live. Everyone did it.

But few were true believers. Most spoke little or espoused the party line in public. In private, some relaxed, and others spoke even less, afraid of their children ratting them out. Emilia couldn't imagine Mother afraid of her.

"With you being so important and everything, how come we can't get a couple extra ration cards?" Emilia said, walking into the room. The space functioned as a living room and—with a sleeper sofa—Mother's bedroom. She had hung up and been staring at the brown squiggles on the wallpaper.

Mother's head turned. "Shut up," she whispered.

"I went to school with Beata Marelska."

Mother blinked. "I remember. Nice girl," she said.

"Her father's been arrested."

Mother shrugged.

"I'm done making reports. No matter what you say," Emilia said.

Mother shrugged again. "If you want to put your ass on the line."

"Can you speak to someone? Help? He's an old man."

"No more than ten years older than me."

"Please."

Mother blinked and nodded.

Emilia did her best to get a thank you past her lips. In a different, better world, none of this would have needed to happen. She'd get a passport. A visa. She'd take Kalina to Japan to see the cherry blossoms.

* * *

In a different, better world, Emilia would have preferred to be able to call ahead. She could never hold on to anger at Kalina for long, even if the impossible woman knew all her buttons and seemed to push them often but usually with no more malice than that of a rain cloud on a picnic day. Instead, to see Kalina and speak with her, Emilia walked two blocks over to a gray apartment building, a clone of her own. She stopped on the third-floor landing to catch a breath. Then climbed on to the fourth and highest.

She raised a fist to knock when a murmur stopped her.

No, a choked breath struggling to escape. When a half-sob sailed through the door, Emilia forgot about knocking, pushed the doorknob—unlocked—and charged.

A man's naked ass the width of half the hallway shocked Emilia into halting. He threw a glance over his shoulder. Pan Zalewski. He bent to grab his shorts, and only then did Emilia spot the figure crouched before him. His daughter.

Kalina scampered on all fours, squeezing around the legs the size of pine stumps, scrambled to her feet, and bulleted into Emilia still stuck frozen in the doorway.

The impetus carried both women out. Emilia had no questions about what had happened—that had been clear enough. The other questions could wait. She raced down the stairs, skipping a few at a time, covering Kalina's retreat.

Emilia rushed out of the building a few steps behind Kalina.

"Jesus Christ, Kalina!" she called out.

Kalina ran. Emilia stumbled to a stop and rested her hands on her knees. She knew of few people who could keep up with Kalina. When she could breathe again, Emilia mapped out all the most likely spots in her mind and set out in search of her faster friend. She could see well enough through her tears.

***

Emilia walked across the five-meter-long swing bridge across the inlet canal to the Zygmuntowo Watersports Club marina. She was beginning to feel the burn in her thighs. ZWC was her third bet. She struck out at Agata's—no one home. Robert, Kalina's on-and-off-again—mostly off—boyfriend, had no idea where the "crazy woman" was.

The marina had been built at a corner of a triangle formed by the river Netta and two canals. Emilia had already traversed two of its shorter lengths—a good three kilometers—and was beginning to promise herself a more regular workout regimen. The blob around her hips bugged her more than she admitted to anyone, but getting winded after a walk was worse.

At least the trek had given her enough time for the tears to dry. Kalina would need to see calm and strength.

A fastened lock hung off the club's gate and the main door had been bolted. Right. Sunday. That explained Agata's absence—she made sure to get to mass every week. Mother went regularly, too, but didn't seem to care if Emilia did.

Emilia circled the building until the pier spread out in front of her. On the far end sat Kalina, her feet dangling above the water.

The boards creaked as Emilia picked the drier ones in an effort to alert Kalina. She'd read that one had to approach a flighty animal with care. She had little energy left for more walking or, God forbid, running.

Kalina kept her face trained on the waves, her back set in a hunch. Her hair fell in strands as thick as the twigs of a weeping willow but reflected the sun more brightly than a birch's bark. Emilia's breath caught in her throat, and she paused, convinced that her friend's hair had gone snow-white. A cloud cut across the light—the white rippled and became the familiar gold again.

Emilia approached and lowered herself to the boards, her shoulder touching Kalina's and their legs dangling together just as they had so many times since they'd met. Had they been five or six? Preschool or kindergarten.

Kalina's feet froze, and Emilia made her body still, too. She tried to will her love to flow through her shoulder and into Kalina. Stupid. That's not how things worked.

How *does* love work? She tried anyway.

"I could just slip off. One deep breath. Why shouldn't I?" Kalina whispered.

Emilia's relief at not having to speak first fled when she really heard the words.

"Things usually get better," she said. "Also, you swim too well."

"Haven't you ever . . . ?"

Emilia nodded. "I puked the pills out."

"So, did things get better?"

"Yes," Emilia said. "You broke Prusak's arm."

Kalina finally lifted her face to the sun, her eyelids shut and wrinkled. She offered the sky a sob. Emilia held her until the writhing stopped and Kalina began to draw deliberate, measured breaths. She stroked Kalina's head. "You won't go back there," she said. "I'll take care of you."

CHAPTER ELEVEN

WHOSE CLOTHES AM I WEARING?

Sunday, July 4, 1982. Warszawa.

Antoni Adamczyk—no, Piekarski now—woke up in a swamp of sheets, under a comforter. Lovemaking could turn a bed into a bog, and he and Dorota often had, but not this time. This time he was sick as a run-over dog with a nail through its throat. Whenever he tried to swallow, the nail jerked and jabbed and jabbed.

He was pretty sure he hadn't hallucinated the body and the blanket on the floor, but they were gone, and the expanse of green carpet, like a forest clearing, lay unobstructed between him and the wall cabinets. And the men's clothes in them, and . . . the other things. The nail in his throat and another one in his side jabbed again. Need water.

A shadow fell on him, and a woman perched on the edge of the sofa. Freckles, hair the color of henna but without henna—Dorota. Antek imagined smelling her herbal shampoo, but all his olfactory faculties could make out was the stink inside his head.

"I'm going to find out everything about that hole in your side. For now, I cleaned it out. Take this." Dorota opened her palm and presented a white pill the size of an average submarine. "I know, but you need to be on antibiotics." She held a glass in her other hand.

Antek forced the pill down his throat without trying to get up, and his eyebrows curled up in pain.

"These, too." Dorota produced two smaller pills from her pocket. "Aspirin."

Stab. But he got them down.

"There. That's a good boy. I'll make you some tea with honey and lemon."

Dorota had found the right profession. When they'd first met, Antek would sometimes delight himself in being pampered as she played the nurse—using her nursing school uniform and little else—opposite his role of the convalescent. The game died soon after she had started working. When he asked, she told him to engineer her an orgasm instead, if he was so stuck on bringing work home. And then she kissed his pout and fucked him to within a hair of a stroke. The love he carried for this woman back then paralyzed most other emotions.

Now, about four years later, Antek Piekarski lay sweating through several days of grime on her couch in a life they no longer shared. He hadn't thought he could taste anything, and yet he tasted bitter. Jab, went the nail in his throat again. Tears tickled Antek's cheeks.

Dorota sat down on the sofa's edge, holding a steaming glass of yellow liquid with a lemon slice in it. Her eyes met his. She grimaced.

"Try to raise your head," she said, as she reached to the back of his neck to help. "Just a little sip. Let's not waste honey and lemon."

The honey-sweetened tea dulled the blade cutting through his throat. Dorota held up his head, the bulge of her bicep showing little strain, and fed him one sip at a time. Tears continued to drip from his eyes as if something solid the tea melted inside him needed a place to go.

Dorota seemed satisfied once he'd consumed most of the tea and lowered his head back down onto the clammy pillow.

"We need to find a way to clean you. And these sheets. I might just throw you and them in the tub together." Her face remained blank and serious as a funeral. At that, she left the room, and Antek soon heard water running from the direction of the bathroom. How long had it been since Dorota had drawn him a bath?

Most likely sometime last November. Before he had to tell her that he was leaving, before internment, and before the strangest day in his life, in January, when a guard made Antek follow him outside, and then left him in front of an open gate. Dorota and he had shared a home and a cause back then—Poland, democracy, Solidarity. But they hadn't shared a bed in months; the passion they'd once had for each other had been consumed by these higher needs. Within three years of marriage, lovers became comrades like steam becomes water.

Dorota crouched by his side.

"This is going to hurt," she said. "Keep your torso and stomach straight. I'll help."

It did hurt, but not as much as Antek had expected. The aspirin might have started working. Or he might have begun to get used to this. Dorota used her body for leverage, anchored her feet against the sofa, heaved, and Antek rose, a stick-figure Frankenstein's Monster.

They shuffled to the bathroom together. There, she helped him strip naked with professional efficiency. Then she lowered him onto the toilet, his body bent in exactly three spots—hips, knees, and ankles—and turned around to give him privacy. He gave thanks for being able to empty himself. Once he was done, Dorota hoisted Antek back to his feet.

"Now the hard part." She first had him rest his buttocks on the edge of the white, enameled tub. Then she helped him swing one leg in. The fact that he noticed the discomfort of the tub's wall digging between his ass cheeks cheered him up—the pain in his side had receded to background throbbing. The other leg. Dorota then gripped him by his underarms and helped him lower himself into the two centimeters of hot water. It was little more than a puddle. He squinted up at Dorota.

"Don't want to submerge the wound," she said. "A sponge bath will have to do."

Antek wiped the sudden sweat off his forehead. "Thank you," he said.

Dorota had prepared a sponge and began to dab at his face. She slid it across his skin and alternated it with the tips of her fingers.

She took her time. Dorota caressed Antek's face, caressed his neck, her touch gentle as a moth, all the while staring him straight in the eyes, her lips still set as if in mourning for a life. She broke eye contact when she began washing Antek's shoulders.

He sat and made no attempt to take the sponge, to protest that he could wash himself. Instead, Antek let his hands fall down and rest, focusing on the searing cramp in his chest, as if he'd swallowed a boiling pieróg whole. The scalding became a tremor, and it shook him from the inside: no harder than a passing train would; hard enough to turn him inside out. His throat had shut. He couldn't have opened it for holy communion, or for a denial of guilt, but tears no longer beaded in his eyes.

Dorota washed his chest and his back. She circumnavigated the swollen redness in his side. When her hands dove down across the surface of Antek's stomach, his breath caught again. She worked over his penis, his testes, as she had over his hands, at the speed of meditation and with the force of gravity, as if no body part were more or less important, and Antek dared not move. Fully erect now, he saved her the need to pull back his foreskin. Dorota had aimed her eyes at her work, and all Antek could see of them was the blinking of her eyelashes. He begged her in silence to look up, look into his face, but then his middle contracted in pleasure and his side contracted in pain, and he ejaculated into the shallow bath water.

While Antek's breathing worked down the gears, his wife drained the tub, turned the faucet back on, and went on to clean his thighs and calves. Rubbed his feet. Then she washed his hair using a hand-held shower head.

Only then did she meet his eyes again.

"Turn sideways, and I'll help you up," she said.

* * *

Dorota dressed Antek's wound in bandages, dressed his body in men's clothes he hadn't seen before—a brown sweatshirt and matching loose warm-up pants—and made him a nest on the sofa. Once he had pillows behind his back, propping him up, and a blanket over him, she looked him in the eye, raised her index finger, and left the room without another word.

A cap popped off a bottle, followed by a prolonged splash. Another cap pop. A door of some sort made a sound of breaking suction like a wet kiss—the refrigerator. Utensils jingled, toneless cracking announced the breaking of shells, and Antek was soon drooling over the aroma of what could only be scrambled eggs with fried onions. Maybe he wasn't as sick as he felt if he could have so much desire. He thought of Dorota's hand finding him in the tub.

She brought out a plate and set it down on his lap atop a tray improvised by a wooden cutting board. The steam enveloped his nose, and Antek realized he couldn't remember his last meal. He picked up the fork Dorota had stuck right into the yellow scramble and licked the tines. Saliva flooded his mouth.

"Just the way you like it," she said, her voice thin. A shade of a smile dimpled her cheeks, but her lips remained pressed into straight lines. "I made some mulled beer. It's cooling off."

Antek brought a clump of egg up to his mouth and chewed. He grimaced as he swallowed, but nothing was going to be easier to eat than eggs. "Thank you. It's delicious." He took another bite. He lifted morsels small enough to make an etiquette teacher happy, put them in his mouth, chewed as if it were a job, and swallowed through barbed wire. Bite after bite.

Dorota rose and left the room. She returned with a steaming mug in one hand and a bottle of beer in the other. After she placed the mug on the cutting board, she crossed the room and took a chair, resting the bottle on the table after taking a long pull.

"Who shot you?"

"Bezpieka," Antek said. Then he cocked his head. "You didn't seem surprised to see me," he added, having just realized how true that was. "Why? As far as you know, I'm supposed to be in prison."

"Someone sent me a note you got out."

Antek swallowed and put the fork down. "Something like that. I had to go underground."

Dorota studied him. Took a sip of her beer.

"What time is it?" Antek said.

She glanced at her watch. "Breakfast beer."

When all she would do was keep staring into his face, Antek couldn't work up the irritation he thought would have been the proper response. Instead, he put another bite in his mouth and chewed. He ate the eggs, sipped his spiced brew, and stared back into Dorota's hops-colored eyes. She didn't flinch from his gaze and took breaks only for her own beer.

Soon, Antek felt a giggle start to work its way up his throat. This was juvenile, ridiculous. It made his chest feel warm.

He smiled instead. "One morning," he said, "a guard came to my cell, took me out, had me change into civilian rags, and left me in front of the gate—"

"Was he someone you recognized?"

"No, but I didn't have to. I saw a chance and took it."

"And not a single message."

"Wasn't safe," Antek said. "Besides, you wanted a divorce anyway."

Dorota let her shoulders drop. "For someone so smart, you're an accomplished idiot."

Antek lost interest in the rest of his eggs. His irritation, no longer playing hard to get, made his heart race, but he found his voice, when it finally returned, flat and thick like a boiler door.

"What did I miss?" he said. "Share the wisdom, please."

"When was the last time we went for a walk together? Or cuddled, before falling asleep?"

"Are you being serious?" Antek didn't roll his eyes only because the whiplash made him forget to. What the hell was she getting at? Walks tend not to be a great idea when you're a Solidarity treasurer and have a tail every time you leave your apartment. Besides, there isn't a lot of time for walks when a man is busy fighting a dictatorial regime animated like a marionette by the Big Bear to the east. As for the cuddling, by sleeping on the sofa, Antek and his roaring epiglottis had been doing Dorota a favor; she'd made a sport of complaining about his snoring.

Dorota's face did appear serious.

"Wanted a divorce," she repeated Antek's words at him. "No, I asked for a divorce. I didn't want it. To keep a marriage, you need to act like it matters."

"It did matter." He blinked to clear his eyes. "It still matters," he said, because it was true.

"Why did—"

"But you're better off, safer, without me. I should leave as soon as I can."

She said nothing. The beer sat on the table, ignored now.

"I left twenty thousand dollars of Solidarity cash in Zygmuntowo," Antek said, "with someone you don't know. It was supposed to be temporary, just until things relaxed. I must go. Secure it. It can't wait."

"It's waited all this time."

"Whose clothes am I wearing?"

"Antek, I'm too young to be some strange thing, one part nun, one part widow. I'm not going to spend the rest of my life with him, but when he's here, I know, in that moment, I matter. That little moment, it matters." She seemed to remember her beer and took a long drink. Then she rose, said, "Are you done?" and grabbed the tray with Antek's food without waiting for an answer.

As she walked away to the kitchen, Antek let his head fall back. His thoughts numbered in thousands and none of them offered a good solution or made him feel better. But at least Dorota was going to come back to this room. They would speak again.

CHAPTER TWELVE

TRACKS

Saturday, July 3–Friday, July 9, 1982. Zygmuntowo.

Roman made Drobina carry their bags up the steps to the lobby of the Armed Forces Resort perched on Zygmuntowo's Lake Białe.

"We have reservations," he said to the receptionist. "Two rooms."

"Papers," the woman behind the counter said.

Roman waved to Drobina and then pulled out his identification. "SB. Security Services. Make sure his room has an attached shower." He tried to clear the grit from his throat and fought the weakness that had spread throughout his body in the last few hours. An early night was in order. He'd wake tomorrow feeling all better.

Roman slept and dreamed about a beach. The unobstructed sun made the air shimmer and painted the black sand with different shades of green, blue, and gray. The heat beat down on him and radiated up from the ground as if it were a seasoned iron skillet.

Water rolled up the beach in pulses like heartbeats and left no slick. Steam rose over the dry black sand, it thickened into fog and hovered, making the air between Roman and the sea look scratched-up and greasy. The water kept up the violence, like a piston, like a mounting bull, and made more fog, and soon Stelmach saw no sea, no water, no aqueous heartbeat.

Any hint of black had disappeared. He stood amid white blindness. It had risen around him or maybe just turbaned up his head, either way, Roman's mind floated. That didn't last. The heat returned, but now he couldn't see where it was coming from. The furnace blew into his face. Roman knew a step forward would ignite his body, and he remembered the moths that had died under the magnifying glass his father had given him for his birthday in third grade. He'd hold them by the wings until they began to smoke and stopped struggling. The power such a simple thing conferred had made the back of his neck tingle harder than sneaking into a movie with a naked lady in it had.

Maybe he wouldn't need to move to die. The heat grew all on its own. He felt his eyebrows curl and melt. His eyes sizzled, but the white blindness held him. Roman's body shrunk away from the blast into itself like a stick of butter on a frying pan, but all he could feel was discomfort no greater than having a drop of candle wax alight on his palm. This was not death. Too strange for that.

A dream. He needed to wake.

A face broke through the screen of white. Roman had no eyes, and yet he saw skin cratered with zits under a cover of dark brown hair seeming more worn out than a theater wig. The young punk—not much older than his children—he had put in the ground. The heat Roman felt radiated from this face, from the eyes fixed in permanent surprise.

Roman woke up. The room illuminated only by a dim streetlight half a block away tumbled around him like a runaway spare tire and made his stomach rear up. He had kicked the blankets off in his sleep, but the sheets had still soaked up enough sweat to wring. The heat he had endured had evaporated, and now Roman shivered, but he couldn't find enough balance to lurch and yank the blankets back over him. He felt pressure in his lower belly.

Darkness rose and covered him like a black hole.

When Roman woke up to the sun in his eyes, he discovered he'd wet the bed.

***

Five days later, Roman Stelmach still hadn't left his sick bed and felt no better. Zenon Drobina came every few hours and brought water, broth, and hot, spiced lager beer. Roman's fever continued to return on its own schedule, every few hours, but he kept fighting it with the mulled brew.

Drobina never let any cloves fall into Roman's mug from the saucepan he used to mull the beer in the hotel kitchenette. *Thoughtful.* It surprised Roman. He hadn't seen that side of the fat man. And to think the sweaty pile of shit might have been dead now if not for the flu. Well, when it was Drobina's time to go, it was going to have to be peaceful. Painless. Happy, really. The least Roman could do in return. Brazil was his no-extradition destiny. An easier death was now Drobina's.

If Bernadeta were here, she'd likely tell him to quit acting and get his ass out of bed. Then, she'd slam the door and go . . . somewhere. *Tea*, she'd say. At Elwira's, Bożena's, Renata's; she knew he could never keep track of her girlfriends. But she had no proper appreciation for Roman's decision not to keep track of her boyfriends, either.

He had just started as a beat Milicja private when their baby girl was born in the autumn of 1969. Eyes of the bluest steel in all of Gdańsk. Deeper than the Baltic. The nurses said they'd never seen as beautiful a baby. He chose to believe them. The smile in Bernadeta's own tired eyes told him he'd made the right choice. Why build a cathedral if he could make this?

Like a large celestial body, his daughter pulled his disappointed parents back into his orbit. Mother cooed over the heavy bundle of heat and sometimes forgot to stop smiling when she turned her wrinkled eyes over to him. His father bought him a cigar—a top-notch Soviet Золотой Олень—and when the man stiffened in Roman's hug, the son chose to appreciate his father's willingness to touch the Cyrillic script and the tobacco of the oppressor for his sake.

Their next, a boy, arrived in 1973, in the middle of the best of the Gierek years—suddenly bananas and television sets appeared in the stores, color came to the streets, and in the summer, the Beatles wafted out of open windows. Strangers smiled at strangers, as if, for five, six years, the ice shelf of fear retreated, and the former SB informants could now be trusted. So little it took to make the human animal happy.

By 1976, the run had come to an end. Bananas and TVs made an exit; ration cards made their return and remained a fixture. Gierek hiked the prices 60% overnight—and 100% on meat—and made more work for men like Roman. People would go on to remember Płock, Ursus and

Radom, with their dead, but Gdańsk had its own June events to squash. Roman acquitted himself well. So well, in fact, that he never went back to the beat. When he started ZOMO militarized Milicja training, learning to use riot gear, shoot a grenade launcher, and drive a personnel carrier, his mother and father stopped speaking to him again. This time for good.

He tried to be angry at them but couldn't manage it. Mostly, he just missed them. He also began to miss Bernadeta, who, now with three children—the last an accident—and attempting to get back to making art, started to vanish from his life, too. So he threw himself into work. By the end of 1977, Roman Stelmach made full lieutenant.

But his big break came the next year, when, one average afternoon, his major called him into his office. When Roman entered, the major was standing, and another man sat in his chair, behind his desk. "This is comrade . . . Kowalski," the major said.

"Names on need-to-know basis," said the man whose name was definitely not Kowalski. "At ease, Stelmach."

Roman allowed some slack in his knees. He kept his brain churning. With his self-important air, and the fact he'd decided to take over in the commander's office, the man had to be one of the two: either a Soviet "consultant," or Bezpieka security services. Since the man spoke without a trace of a Russian accent, Roman bet on the latter.

He wasn't unfamiliar with SB, or Służba Bezpieczeństwa, or, colloquially, Bezpieka. These were the men who started shooting first last June, and who loaded some of the wounded into their own cars and left without an explanation. Chameleons, they wore Milicja or military uniforms, or, more often, a shirt, a pair of slacks, and a gun. Now you see me, now you don't. They made Roman's stomach contract and his mouth wet as if he couldn't decide if he was afraid of them or admired them. Likely both.

"Tell me something," Kowalski said. "Last June. There in the street. When you held your rifle, did you aim?"

The strike had been a quiet one, a sit-in, and only three thousand or so picketed in front of the shipyards' directorate. They must have remembered the dead of 1970 because none lifted any of the rocks littering the scattered construction spots around the headquarters. Some yelled about the price hikes. Most only stood with faces wiped away by fatigue and fear.

Roman's ZOMO unit had taken root a hundred meters away, with their shields and AK-47s, together with a few dozen Milicja men armed with batons and pistols. He felt sweat wind down his back in the afternoon sun. The air tasted of plastic, gun grease, and his own bile. Or of everyone's: heartburn hung around him as if each of the men behind the riot shields were a hair away from vomiting all over their face masks. Roman swallowed, but the rock in his throat persisted.

Most of the picketers made a point of not looking in his direction. Their faces were turned toward the directorate's entrance. But some, on the edges, threw glances at the armed wall a hundred meters away. A few, like animals on guard, deer or something, stared.

Roman looked through his sights. The cross made by the two thin perpendicular lines fell on a man wearing a work jacket, but, instead of matching pants, a pair of blue jeans covered his legs. Probably not a line worker, then. An engineer, perhaps, but hands-on enough to need a company-issue top. He wore his dark, almost black hair cropped short. Roman's finger tingled on the trigger. The metal felt immovable like a boulder, but all Roman could manage at the moment was to resist the urge to pull. Instead, he focused on his heartbeat, on the cooling sweat on his back. He could pull the trigger and change the world.

"We never got orders to fire, comrade Kowalski," Roman said to the man in the commander's chair.

The man's eyes remained fixed on him for a few seconds, then Kowalski nodded as if he'd received a passing answer. "You're getting a promotion."

It took Roman—in the service of the Fatherland and of Ustrój, the social order—almost four more years to change the world and discover his point of no return.

CHAPTER THIRTEEN

GOOD SAMARITANS

Sunday, July 4–Monday, July 5, 1982. Zygmuntowo.

Emilia tried to lead Kalina while embracing her by the shoulders, but all the windsurfing made her back too muscular and wide. Instead, she held Kalina by the arm and directed her as if the poor thing had been blinded. The pair gathered one or two strange looks, but if anyone had said anything, Emilia would have told them to go to hell.

Once in the apartment, in her room, Emilia sat Kalina on the bed and went to the kitchen to boil water for tea. When she returned with two steaming cups, Kalina had curled up and was puffing, either asleep or more likely pretending to be. Emilia took the tea back to the kitchen, sat, and resigned herself to having to drink the stuff alone. Good for the nerves, but she wasn't a fan of tea unless she loaded it with sugar and lemon juice. She hadn't seen lemons in months. Sugar had just run out. If it wasn't vodka, beer, or vinegar, it was tough to get.

Waste not want not. She sipped the yellow, bitter water through gritted teeth. She imagined punching Zalewski. She looked at her puny fists and accepted that the man likely wouldn't have noticed it had she tried. How does one make someone who doesn't care about anything feel pain? From over the rim of the cup, Emilia studied her mother's collection of kitchen knives sticking out of the old pickle jar in which they lived. Sharp. Especially the serrated ones.

The front door swung open, and Mother walked in with a canvas tote bag. She pulled a small brown-paper-wrapped bundle and put it in the refrigerator.

"Sunday. We'll be eating meat tonight." She smiled.

Mother used to smile more before Father had left for Germany six years back. Before the letters and the money had stopped coming, and they lost all contact.

Emilia wanted to return the smile, but her lips refused. "I hope there is enough for three," she said. "Kalina will be over for dinner."

"Sure, even if she eats like a wolf."

Emilia cocked her head. Mother was being downright cheerful.

The woman seemed to read her thoughts and pulled out two perforated sheets of paper from her purse. She dropped them on the kitchen table with a flourish.

"How did you score extra rations?" Now, Emilia, too, managed a smile, if a little one, in the corners of her lips.

"Magic."

"Black or white?"

"Gray. The only kind there is." Mother sat on a stool and sighed. "Be a good girl and peel some potatoes?"

Emilia pulled the bag from under the sink, where, in the dark behind the cabinet doors, the potatoes kept the propane bottle company. There were six, all sprouting. She pulled three out and put the rest away. Out of habit she made sure the valve was shut; the range's burners tended to leak gas intermittently. She picked a paring knife, too short to gut Zalewski. Instead of carving into that pig, she made potato peels serpentine into the trash bucket.

"Lettuce?" she inquired, once she'd cut up the potatoes, dropped them into a pot of salty water, twisted the propane tank's valve open, and lit a burner.

"What are we? Rabbits? I got pickles." Mother pulled the jar out of the tote bag which now lay deflated on the kitchen counter.

She tried to turn the lid, gave up, and wedged a butter knife under the cap to break the seal. Once she had removed the cover, Mother drew a breath over the jar. Then extended it to Emilia.

"Want one?"

Emilia crunched a pickle, then another, as Mother took the pork loin out of the fridge and slapped it onto a cutting board. Once she had carved off three two-centimeter-wide cutlets, she put the remaining sliver in the freezer and proceeded to pummel each slice with a wooden mallet until tender and as thin as one of the stapled Saint Mary devotionals Mother used to pull out every night.

"Get the frying pan ready," Mother said.

Emilia had anticipated the order and was already pulling it off its shelf. She poured a bit of oil and turned on another burner while Mother coated the first cutlet with egg, salt, pepper, and flour. Once it crackled on the pan, Emilia attended to it, while Mother prepared another.

"Can Kalina stay with us for a while?"

Mother paused as she flipped the cutlet in its coating. Then she started back up and said, "She still have that job? Waitressing?"

"Yes."

"Why?"

"Zalewski," Emilia said. She took the cutlet off the pan and transferred it onto a paper-lined plate before it burned.

Mother replaced it in the frying oil with the next one. "Would she sleep with you or on the floor?"

"We'd figure it out."

Mother flipped another sheet of raw pork into its dish of flour. "If she helps with the co-op fees and throws in her rations."

After Emilia cooked the last of the pork cutlets and dropped it onto the short pile, and as Mother started to mash the potatoes, she walked out to check on Kalina. She crouched down and touched her shoulder. Kalina's eyes fluttered open.

"Dinner's ready," Emilia said.

A few minutes into the meal, Emilia wanted to take Kalina by that thick neck and shake her. Why did the damned woman have to be so stubborn?

"It's too much. I can't take advantage of you two like this." Kalina had already said the same thing at least three different ways and hadn't even finished her cutlet.

"But we want to do it." Emilia also repeated herself.

"What are you thinking of doing?" Mother finally entered the conversation as she got up for another pickle.

"I could rent a room," Kalina said.

"Rent? How much hard currency do you have? Rent, she says." When Kalina gave no answer, Mother continued, "I don't know what happened there. Emilia didn't say a word. But I've heard things. Walls are thin and people talk."

"People can be fucking dumb."

"They say he's been fucking *you*."

Emilia threw her mother a look, but it was too late. Kalina dropped her fork. Her chest began to heave. If she bolted out, *then* what?

"Since Mama left for Greece. For work. Every time he drinks. He's strong. I don't fight anymore. He hits anyway but hasn't broken anything in a while."

Emilia stepped over, leaned, and drew Kalina's head to her chest. "Shhh," she said.

Mother's crisp voice came from across the table. "Stay here," she said. "As long as necessary. This is a stupid time to let your pride lead the way. If it makes you feel better, pay one-third of the fees and utilities. We'll go get your things together when that asshole is out."

Emilia felt Kalina nod. Then she held her friend while the rest of their dinner grew cold.

* * *

Emilia's shift on Monday started at seven. When she walked out, Kalina still slept, curled up on a spare comforter on the floor. Mother would leave a few minutes later and spend the day managing the bookkeepers at the City Hall. Running meetings as the vice-chairperson of the local committee. And making sure the local ZOMO had the money for enough riot gear and ammunition. Kalina had an alarm clock and knew where to find breakfast. Instant ersatz coffee, too, if she could drink it without sugar.

Right outside the building, Emilia imagined Zalewski's bulk emerging from behind the bushes and scolded herself for being an idiot. As if there weren't enough real problems. Still, she maintained vigilance and looked over her shoulder more often than usual until she walked up to the telephone station.

Once the director buzzed her in, she climbed the stairs and crossed through the door into the station's heart. Frania was already sitting in her chair, adjusting the headpiece to cause the least amount of disturbance to her thin, permed hair. They exchanged polite greetings, but Frania remained typically taciturn. Instead of words, the woman gave Emilia a long stare, finished with a wry, sad smile. Emilia had no idea what to do with that. Perhaps the woman really had nothing to say? Or was going mad? Both?

Emilia masked her thoughts by adjusting her own headpiece and fidgeting with the microphone. When seven in the morning arrived, she stuck the first plug of the day in its blinking hole. "This conversation is being controlled," she said. The cigarette factory in the Koszary district placed a coal order. Why anyone needed coal to make cigarettes stumped her.

"This conversation is being controlled." The Most Sacred Heart of Christ parish got a call from the bishop. A gruff baritone, he kept clearing his throat as he monologued on the importance of the vows of celibacy. Emilia suspected she knew why this call had been necessary. People talked. The bishop hung up, having taken no questions.

"This conversation is being controlled," Emilia said for the hundredth time, soon after two o'clock.

"I have a kilo of smoked eel for sale," a woman's voice said.

"I'll take two kilos, but only if they're fresh," a man answered.

"As fresh as December. Tomorrow's mass in the intention of Antoni's soul is canceled. Contact has been lost."

"Fuck," said the man. "What now?"

Emilia couldn't hear the woman shrug but could almost feel it in her ears. "We'll regroup."

The man exhaled. "Fuck," he repeated. The connection clicked off.

Lights on her console blinked at Emilia as she sat, working to put her thoughts together.

She wrote down the local number—again a pay phone—and the time on a paper scrap and put it in her pocket. There would be no report this time, or ever again, but something made her want to keep the information.

Emilia connected the next call, saying nothing. Frania turned, raised her eyebrows, and gave her one of her rare open smiles. At three, Emilia left and headed downtown to bug Kalina at work.

Two kilometers later, she looked up at the neon sign: *Restauracja Albatros*. The fanciest place she'd been. The fanciest in town. Linen tablecloths, matching tables and chairs, full-service. She climbed the wide concrete staircase to the entrance. The day had become overcast, but the murk inside still forced her to pause and adjust her eyes.

Most of what had to be at least three dozen tables stood lonely, useless. The mid-day rush had just ended. Snow-white cloth draped the tabletops as if they announced their surrender. If a table had a mind, what would it feel? Emilia shook her head. A bad time to start going mad. She spied Kalina in one corner, attending to a group of three men. Emilia took a seat at another table she judged close enough to be in Kalina's section.

Kalina turned and sauntered over with her athletic gait. She put her palm over Emilia's shoulder and squeezed. Not hard, but enough to anchor her in this time and place and make her suddenly feel all right about having just wondered about the inner life of four-legged inanimate objects.

"Thank you," Kalina said.

"What for? I haven't paid yet."

"Alright then, what will you be having, my princess?"

"Tea, the best you have."

"The chamberlain has procured one kind. It could be tea, or it could be dry pine needles. In any case, it comes in white paper bags, and it'll curl that one hair on your left nipple."

Emilia giggled, breaking character. "How about tea with lots of sugar and lemon?"

"That can be arranged."

As Kalina danced away, Emilia tracked her friend's figure with admiration. Then she settled in and contemplated the clouds outside the window.

Kalina came back with a steaming cup of water, a tea bag, and a thin lemon slice presented on top of a saucer. She reached into her pouch and dropped four sugar cubes on the table next to the cup. "Shhh," she said, with a finger to her lips. "Don't let anyone know I gave you double. I'll come back once I've gotten a tip from those drunks." She walked back over to the three men who were snapping their fingers in her direction.

The clouds had darkened. Come to think of it, Zygmuntowo was overdue for a nice storm. The National Primeval Forest bordering the town had slammed a fire ban in place. The river Netta ran low in its banks. The water in the lakes flanking Zygmuntowo—Necko, Białe and Sajno—usually cool and clear, had turned into a hazy, lukewarm bath. Emilia didn't mind the heat, but no one wanted a forest fire.

The heat happened to be one of Emilia's favorite things about summer. Throughout most of the year, she couldn't get warm enough. Didn't seem fair. If anything, the folds around her hips should provide plenty of insulation. In the summer, one of Emilia's favorite things to do was to lounge on her balcony and catch sunlight while reading poetry. Reading *and* writing. This year, she hadn't written much, but the summer had just started.

Kalina came back, sat, and reached out a hand. Emilia clasped it in both of hers. Kalina placed her other hand on top.

Emilia considered communication one of her strengths; now, she found herself empty. All she could do was swallow again. But their palms, intertwined, felt like enough for the moment.

CHAPTER FOURTEEN

TRINITY

Monday, July 5–Tuesday, July 6, 1982. Zygmuntowo.

Emilia watched Kalina work until five o'clock; her friend lacked the seniority for the late shift when the real drinking and tipping happened. She pocketed the sugar cube left on her plate when she saw Kalina approach, dressed in her street clothes.

"Go hang out at Agata's?" Emilia asked. Kalina nodded.

It looked like rain when they set out for a two-kilometer walk to Agata's Borki District apartment. A quarter of a house, really. Agata, or her daddy, owned the lower northern part of a gray walk-up. From outside, it looked like a perfect cube, marred only by a gently sloping, corrugated-tile roof line.

The first raindrops caught Kalina and Emilia a couple of blocks from their destination, but the clouds wasted no time, and when the women ran up to Agata's place, the air had become so full of water, Emilia imagined fish swimming around her soaked, cowering head. Kalina got there first and rang the bell.

Emilia couldn't tell how long it took Agata to answer the door. Kalina yelled, "We're drowning here!" and mashed the buzzer again.

Agata unlocked the door, opened it, and Kalina and Emilia slipped in.

"I'm going to have to mop this puddle up," Agata said.

Emilia looked down at the rivulets landing on the scratched-up parquet.

"This stuff rots worse than tripe." Agata rushed away. She trotted back with a few towels over her arm. She handed one each to Emilia and Kalina and threw the rest on the floor around them. "Come in," she said, once satisfied the water had been contained. She herded them into her apartment, then closed and locked the hallway door. Emilia wondered what Agata had worth stealing that she always made a point to throw her two bolts shut.

"I have told you. Daddy insists," Agata said. "But maybe he'll relax a bit once the phone line gets installed tomorrow."

"I didn't say anything. Wait, a phone? Finally! That's wonderful."

Agata beamed. "Daddy stopped by today to let me know. I'll get you wet hens some more towels. And shirts." In less than a minute, she reemerged from her bedroom with an armful of textiles. The two women grabbed the clothes and towels and filed into the bathroom to change.

Emilia and Kalina wrung out their hair, put on Agata's shirts—baggy but too short on both of them—wrapped the towels around their hips, and hung the wet clothes on the line above the bathtub. They padded out barefoot and met their friend in the kitchen.

"Ta-daa!" Emilia presented herself with a flourish.

"You look better in a towel than I would in a ball gown." Agata had opened a couple of bottles of beer and was splitting them between three glasses.

"Nonsense," Kalina said. "Having all those guys falling all over one another to get you makes you a liar. Or at least much too modest." She sat down next to a full glass.

Agata froze.

"Oh my God, I'm so sorry." Kalina sprang back up and squeezed Agata in a bear hug. "I was such a bitch the other day. Please forgive me."

Emilia thought Agata might have said something, but her height placed her face right in the middle of Kalina's chest.

"I'm sorry," Kalina said and slid half a step back. "What did you say?"

"I said get your boobs out of my face, and I forgive you. Now, drink your beer."

Neither Kalina nor Emilia had to be asked again.

"Let's hang out in my bedroom," Agata said. "I'll put on some music. I scored a tape with that Depeche Mode album."

"The one all over the radio?" Emilia couldn't help the excitement.

"You took English in high school. How do you say the title?" Kalina asked.

"Speak and Spell," Emilia said, doing her best to do the weird English *l* consonant justice.

Agata pressed play, cracked a couple more beers and poured. Kalina folded down on the rug like a machine. Agata plopped. Emilia groaned as she bent her knees to lower herself to the floor. The women lounged and listened.

"You really ought to stretch," Kalina said to Emilia as soon as *New Life* ended.

"Shhh," Emilia said. *I Sometimes Wish I Was Dead* had started.

"What's this song's title?" Kalina asked.

Emilia translated.

"Sometimes it does sound like a good idea," Kalina said.

"Kalina!" Agata put a palm on the other woman's knee. "You don't mean that. You have to believe. Things do get better."

Emilia looked from one friend to the other but kept her mouth shut.

"They do. I live at Emilia's now," Kalina said.

Now it was Agata's turn to stare at her friends.

Emilia pursed her lips.

"She walked in on my father sticking his cock in my mouth," Kalina said. "Same as he's been doing since I was eleven." Kalina nodded over to Emilia. "I'm sorry," she said. "I lied to you." She turned back to Agata. "I've lied to you both for years. My mother . . . She told me not to resist, that it wouldn't hurt as much that way. He said he'd kill me if I let anyone know. After she left it did get worse . . ." Kalina grimaced and began to blink. "Fuck," she said. "I'm going to cry again. I hate that."

Agata sat across her friend, frozen. Emilia tried to hand her a half-full glass, but Agata's open eyes appeared blind, as if too busy with seeing something inside the woman's mind.

"Kalina," Emilia said. "I wish you had told us, but I understand. When my father was hitting me, I didn't want anyone to know, either, just you two. And this is . . . different. You have the right to hate, and don't worry about the crying. Cry away."

Agata began to move. "We . . . , *I* should have asked. I'm so stupid! The bruises? Not all of them sports injuries?"

Kalina nodded. Now it was Emilia's turn to feel dumb.

Agata had by now reanimated and drained her beer. "Fuck," she said. "What do we do?"

"What do you mean?" Emilia said.

"What do you mean what do I mean? Justice."

"What justice? Who's going to care? Milicja? Priests?" Emilia choked up, too.

Agata lifted her finger, asking for a pause, then left and came back with three more beers. "Tonight, we get drunk. Tomorrow, we sober up at work. Planning meeting right here at five-thirty."

Kalina nodded.

Emilia rubbed her cheek. "Absolutely," she said. She thought she might have caught the scent of an idea but needed to follow it and understand where it could lead.

* * *

Emilia's hangover ranked at about six or seven on a ten-point scale. Then, at mid-morning, it picked up to an eight before it began to subside. She stuffed blinking holes with plugs and clicked off after she'd made each connection, communication control be damned. Headache. Too much pain to listen to blather. If a small animal weren't chewing on her brain right behind her forehead, she might have defied orders anyway, as she had during the prior shift. Feeling as she did made the decision for her.

Frania sat a couple of meters away, smirking. Damned woman. Awfully happy the last couple of days.

Emilia drank water. Then coffee; four cups. She switched back to water when her left eyelid began to flutter.

By noon, the liquids and the food—she'd brought a pork sandwich—seemed to have done the trick. The headache receded to no more than a gray noise. Listening and speaking no longer made her want to squeeze her eyes shut.

Emilia made more connections. Once, as a little girl, she had swiped a lollipop from a vendor outside of church after mass. Staying silent and clicking off after each call made her remember that feeling. No one saw, but someone's eyes seemed to touch her all the same. At least the lollipop was sweet. Why take this risk? She did it anyway.

Kalina served Emilia tea at *Albatros* at three-thirty, and they left together for Agata's at five. Emilia arrived soaked with sweat rather than rain this time. Inside, the shade and a fan helped a little. Agata's beer helped more. Emilia watched as Kalina pressed her chilled bottle to her forehead. Hard and precision-built as it might be, her body wasn't made of metal after all.

Soon, the three women sat in a circle on Agata's floor, beers in hand, plates of bread, pork, and cookies between them. They made short work of the meat and the bread, and quickly put a dent in the cookies, too.

Once the beers were gone, Agata made tea. "Let's keep our heads clear tonight."

Emilia wouldn't have said no to another beer but nodded.

"Look, I don't know about all this," Kalina said. "I don't want to think about it. Do you understand? Let it go."

As if in a Baczyński poem, Kalina seemed to have pressed her tears under the surface, behind a gray wall made of a steel gaze, pursed lips, and gritted teeth. Emilia wanted to embrace her. Kiss her. Touch her skin. Wrap Kalina up and encompass her within Emilia's body as if inside a shell. Like a child. Like a lover.

But instead, Emilia grabbed a cookie so that chewing could obscure a tremor in her jaw.

Agata seemed ready to argue. Then she nodded. "You should move here," she said. "I live alone, and this place is bigger than Emilka's."

"Nonsense," Emilia said. "We're fine."

"I don't want to offend Pani Sokołowska," Kalina said. She glanced at Emilia. "Having accepted the hospitality. Seems rude."

"Fine. The offer stands if you need it." Agata got up, disappeared into the kitchen, and returned with a couple of wide tin cans and three beer bottles. "You'll need some more food, then," she said. Then she cracked the beers open.

Emilia took a long draw. "There was a weird call I heard," she said.

She'd never spoken to anyone about her controlled conversations. Not to be done, one of the officers had said in training. Arrest and imprisonment. Emilia didn't remember for how long, but two years or twenty . . . Not sure why she had spoken up, she found herself glad she had, as if she'd just popped a particularly annoying zit.

"Aren't you supposed to stay quiet about that?" Kalina said.

"You're not going to rat me out, are you?"

"Who do you think I am?" Kalina glared.

"Never," Agata added her assurance, an open palm over her heart.

Emilia glanced at both of her friends and rubbed her chin. Then she recounted as much as she could remember about the odd calls about eels for sale. She added the bit about the holy mass even if she couldn't see how it fit.

"Weird," Kalina said. "Maybe someone is just fucking with you?"

Agata shook her head. "Cipher. I'm pretty sure. The first part is how they know they are who they think they are. You know, a code, an answer, a counter-answer. The part about the mass is the real information, but it sounds like they've masked it."

"Agata, you should give the rest of your beer to me," Kalina said. "You've had too much."

"Sounds crazy, but she might be onto something," Emilia said. "It rings true. They sounded . . . frightened? Imagine a mouse trying to talk as it's stealing one of these cookies." She reached out and illustrated her words by stuffing a whole cookie in her mouth.

"If it happens again, you'll know something is going on," Agata said.

"I don't listen. Not anymore."

Agata picked up another cookie and presented it to Emilia like a holy host.

Kalina put her fingers on Emilia's knee. "What if they find out?"

"Frania Nowak never listens, and she's still not in prison. And my mother . . ." Emilia failed to find the right words to explain her mother's privilege. Not that she really had to. Her friends nodded. She blushed.

"You do what you can," Kalina said.

Emilia nodded; her throat suddenly constricted. Did the desire to kiss Kalina make her a freak? As if the missed masses and holy communions had accumulated to mount a set of devil's horns on her forehead. Horns or not, if she had any money, she would have given all of it to

Kalina just to see her smile. They'd leave this place together. For Japan. Or France, Italy, America. Somewhere where a telephone operator's job description didn't include listening in and reporting. Somewhere without old Zalewski.

***

Emilia and her headache took a detour on the way to work and knocked on Agata's door at six-thirty in the morning. The door cracked open, and a face appeared. The face wore eye makeup that failed to conceal the dark circles and a grimace. Agata's headache had to be at least as bad as Emilia's. That her friend hadn't met her with a curse proved it.

"Let me in," Emilia said. "We've got to talk. Now. I only have a few minutes."

"Tea?" Agata asked once Emilia had settled at the kitchen table.

"God bless you."

Agata put the kettle on the stove and sat down. "Yes?"

"I've been thinking all night," Emilia said. "I know how to put that pig Zalewski in prison. Hear me out."

Agata listened. By the time Emilia finished talking, Agata had developed a scowl but nodded. "I'm in," she said, "though I'd want to tweak a few . . . most things. And we can't tell Kalina."

CHAPTER FIFTEEN

IN NEED OF A MURDER

Tuesday, July 6, 1982. Zygmuntowo.

Of the five Polish United Workers' Party's powiat-level transportation committee members, one owned a car. As such, he had long ago trained himself in the art of saying no and was known for it. Emilia knew well that his son would often take it into the woods and park there with his girlfriend. God alone knew how both fit in the back seat of the Fiat 126. How they managed what they undoubtedly attempted there, in the back of a maluch, could hardly be explained by science.

"Emilia," the man said on a sweltering summer afternoon. "This thing's in pretty poor shape, needs a new gasket."

"I'll wash it," she said, and gave him a quarter of an eyelash bat. "And I promise I'll come by an extra petrol ration."

"And then sit in the petrol line for three hours, breathing fumes? There is a reason I've practically given up driving."

"Seeing St. Mary's Sanctuary at Studzieniczna on Sunday would mean the world to my friend. She's of fragile health."

That seemed to stop him dead. He swallowed. "Which one? The athlete or the sturdy meat plant girl?"

Emilia found it was her turn to pause. To blush. She hadn't expected as strong a reaction. But perhaps she should have, from a widower whose wife had died from the flu. She needed to reel the conversation back. Back to the maluch. Back to getting to use it for a couple of days. Back to The Plan.

She played her trump card: "Life's so fleeting, isn't it? How about we get together for coffee? Or something stronger. Talk."

He scratched his scalp. He was cute in a forty-year-old, receding hairline kind of way. Bright blue eyes. Strong chin. His wife had seemed happy. Still, Agata would owe her for this regardless of how non-gross he might be.

He sighed. "Fine. Pick it up on Saturday."

* * *

The Plan rested on several pillars. After Emilia returned to Agata's, they worked for hours to flesh it out. In the end, it bore little resemblance to Emilia's simple original idea which was to report Zalewski for listening to Radio Free Europe. Which he likely did not do. But that probably wouldn't have mattered.

First, Agata pointed out the obvious. "Not durable enough. So they'll arrest him. He may get held for a few months. He'll still be back to make Kalina keep looking over her shoulder. And you, too. No, we need something more permanent."

Emilia had to admit the point was valid. Had he been someone deep within Solidarity, the smallest pretext might have been enough to put him away for years. Maybe even make him disappear. But the pig had no interest in much besides eating and fucking, definitely not politics and least of all risk.

Agata got up and paced back and forth on the other side of the coffee table. Emilia watched. The pacing had taken on a mechanical aspect, a rhythm, as if Agata expected to keep pacing until the Earth cooled and stopped and all souls stood muster in final judgment. A perpetual-motion pendulum.

But it had only taken minutes, not an eternity, for Agata to raise her index finger and, without breaking her stride, say, "A murder. We need a murder."

Emilia's heart reared up and galloped. The pounding made her see splotches, and tremors marred the surface of the beer in her glass. And yet. "I know," she said.

"Question is how."

"I have thought about it. I don't think I can do it."

"He rides a bicycle from work, doesn't he?"

Emilia nodded and emptied her glass.

"Right. Mental note. There is also the fact he lives on the top floor. A balcony. A concrete staircase."

Step. Step. Step. Step. Turn. Step. Step. Step. Step. Turn. Agata kept it up as if in a military parade. All she needed was a rifle slung over her shoulder.

"We can't wait for the winter, or ice over the lakes would have been convenient." Step. Step. Step. Step. Turn. "Something messy, bloody will be best."

"How are you so calm?" Emilia asked, her voice, she knew, held less shock and more admiration.

Agata stopped, thank God, and faced Emilia. "I was eleven. The three of us over at Kalina's for a slumber party. We had so many of those, I know. No reason for you to remember that specific time."

Emilia closed her eyes. Remember?

"I was eleven. He gave you a few złotych and sent you out to get him cigarettes. Made Kalina go with you."

A slaughter of a thousand geese sounded between Emilia's ears, the noise grew in intensity, threatened to deafen her, and yet Agata's alto, little more than a whisper, rose above it all.

"I was the first of the three of us to get boobs. Hips. Really, face it, I'm the only one of the three of us to have any now." Agata's smirk was gone quicker than lightning. "He started by telling me how pretty I was."

"Agata." Emilia forced the air through a scrunched-up windpipe. "You don't have to—"

"But he didn't wait to hear what I had to say. Locked the door. Took my skirt off, my shirt. My bra and panties. I stood there. Naked like the day I was born. And I froze. I didn't move. I didn't speak." Agata's voice now came out cold, itself frozen.

"Agata . . ."

"He. Did his thing. And I was still frozen. He dressed me like a rubber doll."

"I didn't know. Why . . . ?"

"When he put me out, he said he'd hurt you both if I was still there when you came back. He'd hurt you if I told you. So I moved. I made my legs move."

"Let's kill the son of a bitch," Emilia said.

Silence made Emilia open her eyes and seek Agata's. She found Agata staring right back, her jaw shut hard enough to jut her cheekbones out like elbows. But there were no tears on those cheeks.

"No. We won't kill anyone. He will."

* * *

The sun had long fallen when Emilia left Agata's home with a can of lunch meat in her fist and a dust storm in her mind. Her eyes and ears must have registered something since she eventually made it home without tripping and falling or getting hit by a bus. When she tried to remember, though, all she could recall of her walk back was saying bye to Agata and climbing the staircase of her apartment block—the two kilometers in-between had left no conscious impression.

And yet Emilia knew that she hadn't simply blacked out. Her thoughts never stopped boiling. *This is crazy* was a refrain she started before leaving Agata's and continued to repeat. *Can't possibly work* took its own place in the rotation early. She didn't know whether she'd made it as far as Sacred Heart Cathedral before wondering about the length of the prison sentence should things not work out. She couldn't have made it much further before making the firm decision that everything would definitely go terribly wrong, and she'd have to talk Agata out of her insane idea.

Mother was likely sleeping or wondering where her daughter was with the curfew an hour away. Kalina wouldn't yet have come back from strength training that she attended as religiously as some might mass every Tuesday and Thursday night. Emilia eased the door back into the frame to prevent that crypt lid from slamming shut and sending an echo off the concrete walls, making the glasses in the cupboard ring. She shouldn't have bothered. No one was home. She took off her shoes, wiggled her toes, and shuffled over to the kitchen. *This is crazy.*

She put water in the teakettle, opened the valve in the propane tank under the sink, and ignited the burner with Mother's lighter. Then she sat and rubbed her thighs, which felt sore enough to make her think she'd run for an hour instead of walking back from Agata's.

The loose-leaf Russian tea swirled in the glass like black snowflakes. Two tablespoons of sugar would have made it taste less of leather. Emilia put the glass aside and let it steep. A tightness in her back joined the sore legs, and she felt a twitch between her shoulder blades, too. She took a breath, then another, telling her lungs to compress and expand no faster than the waves in Lake Sajno, but no use—her ribs fluttered instead.

Suddenly, Emilia couldn't tell if the muscles in her chest were about to snap or if her heart was trying to burrow out. She moaned and called out for Mother, but what left her throat was no more than a whisper. She thought she was still blinking but could move no other part of her body. *This is what death feels like. Rigor mortis.* But no, it wasn't death quite yet because when she slid off the chair, sideways, and met the linoleum-lined concrete with her shoulder the impact squeezed a groan of pain through her tight throat.

It hurt like hell, but, somehow, the agony helped, and Emilia managed another whimper. She was able to roll onto her back and focus enough to try corralling her racing breathing. She called out again, a bit more volume this time, and, before another attempt at a scream, she saw a beautiful face and half a meter of blond hair hovering above her.

Kalina shushed her attempt to speak. *Dumb to find so much comfort in a hiss of air.* Dumb? That didn't matter. Kalina wouldn't let her die. Emilia's heart still trundled like the rolling skulls from the poem by the poor, tragic boy, Krzysztof Kamil Baczyński. Kalina's hair fell on Emilia's face, and she could no longer tell if she was still having a heart attack or was simply in love. She inhaled lavender. Her arm rose, as if of its own, and ran the tips of its fingers across Kalina's suntanned cheek, their touch light enough that it wouldn't have left a mark on a butterfly wing.

"Am I dying?"

"No, stupid, you just had a panic attack," Kalina said.

Then Emilia found a moment of delight in the musk of a day's worth of waitressing and weightlifting sweat before Kalina's face obstructed everything, and a kiss stopped her heart. She couldn't care less if she'd ever breathe again. Her shoulder and clavicle felt just fine. She locked her lips on Kalina's and locked her arms around her muscular shoulders.

CHAPTER SIXTEEN

ALBATROS

Tuesday, July 6–Wednesday, July 7, 1982.

Kalina's Tuesday shift began at ten in the morning. *Albatros* always opened at noon. She helped set up the dining room, touched up her makeup, and then spent the next hour bored out of her mind. *Albatros* always opened at noon, she had been told, and so it always would. Don't question the wisdom of the directorate.

She needed the job, so she quit asking.

The first couple of people stopped by at around one in the afternoon. By two, the dinner rush started. If she were to make any tips today, the next two hours were the time to do it. She was always polite to everyone but reserved her best smiles for men in clear need of alcohol.

Last night, she had slept on the floor. When she opened her eyes, both Emilia and Pani Sokołowska had already left. The women usually started work at seven. Kalina had spent hours listening to Emilia puff softly in the dark, imagining touching her shoulder, her cheek, her hips. Slipping in under the covers with her and holding Emilia while inhaling the linden flower shampoo in her hair. What would her kiss feel like?

She cleared her throat and approached a table. "Pani Jadwigo, Panie Leszku, welcome to *Albatros*," she greeted the director of the tobacco fermenting plant. And his mistress. "The usual?" The man seemed not to have heard, but the woman nodded her brick-red perm. This table carried little upside. They never tipped, but one whisper from either could cost her the job. At least she could forgo smiling—one look from Jadwiga through her plum, droopy eyelids had put Kalina in her place as soon as she had tried a smile on the couple months earlier.

She made her jaw relax. Once Jadwiga nodded, Kalina turned back toward the kitchen. A new guest sat in a corner of the room. His torso protruded above the table like the swollen stem of a tree fungus; a small, pale head with drooping jowls sat on top, neckless, as if plopped from the sky without regard to proportions. Kalina changed directions and sauntered toward the fellow.

"I'm Kalina. Welcome to *Albatros*." She beamed, showing her teeth, and dropped the menu she had carried down onto the white cloth. She even turned up her shoulder in the way she knew made men swallow and clear their throats.

The flesh over the fellow's invisible Adam's apple bobbed up and down, and he coughed. "Good day," he said once he could. "A beer?"

"Coming right up." Kalina turned and walked away. When she in turn swallowed, it was her pride that went down. She called the director's order into the kitchen. As she headed behind the bar to retrieve a half-liter bottle of Dojlidy, she could still feel the mushroom-man's eyes glued to her ass.

Kalina stopped by the fellow's table and poured half of the bottle into a glass, using its inside wall to control the head. Once she was done, she had a perfect centimeter of foam on top. She set both vessels down. *Smile*. "Something to eat?"

He turned the menu's pages this way and that. "Everything sounds good."

"We wouldn't want to overwhelm the kitchen," Kalina said and regretted it immediately, not sure how the man might take it. But he smiled faintly and relaxed his shoulders, making his breasts fall further. *C-cup, at least*. He looked up. The moisture in his eyes was probably sweat.

"How about cucumber soup? And gołąbki. With new potatoes, not mashed," he said.

Kalina nodded. "Another beer?"

"Why not. And, kindly, please add some ice cream for dessert."

At that, he grimaced and turned to stare through the glass door, his index finger, as if of its own volition, drawing a never-ending figure eight on the tablecloth in an invisible ink of skin diluted in perspiration. Kalina shuffled back to the kitchen.

Why the hell would the fat man's beady eyes make her want to cry? This was ridiculous. She wished Emilia were here. That girl got people. Once the order was in, Kalina ducked into the bathroom to check her mascara. She sniffed and looked into the mirror.

Everyone kept saying how stunning the face staring back at her was. Whatever. If it was so pretty, why hadn't it made life easier? More often than not, people, especially men, would let their gaze slide off her face and speak to Kalina's hair, shoulder, or some point in space next to her ear. *Talk to me*, she'd want to say but never did.

Only here, at *Albatros*, could the curse ever appear a blessing. Once their owners had had enough to drink, men's eyes would find her. She'd feel them on her cheekbones, breasts, hips, ass, and they took out their wallets and ordered more vodka. Even only one of those tables made for a good day.

When the big man's soup was up, she brought it and set it down. "Good choice. Simple, but delicious. One of my favorites."

The man picked up his head and, again, looked into Kalina's face. His eyes didn't roll off her, but neither did he swallow or skip a breath. He might as well have been looking at a sister. "Zenon. My name. Zenon Drobina. Please call me Zenek."

"Pleased to make your acquaintance, Panie Zenku."

"Just Zenek, dear Pani Kalino."

"Oh, I'm no Pani. We don't put on airs here. Just call me Kalina."

As she walked back to the kitchen, Kalina realized that she'd relaxed her shoulders, allowed herself her usual, non-work athletic slouch, and that her lips carried a smile she had made no effort to put there. She looked around; two more tables had filled up, and through the glass in the doors, she could see a small school of heads bobbing ever higher up the stairs, about to swim in. It promised to be a busy afternoon.

Zenek's gołąbki came up twenty minutes later; the seasoned meat and rice wrapped inside cabbage leaves and slathered with rich tomato sauce steamed. Kalina tasted the air over the plate. Stuffed cabbage was another of her favorites. But her dinner would have to wait until after five. Two plates to a hand—the other three filled with pork cutlets and a knuckle—she navigated the floor. Zenek first. She smiled as she put the plate down. He said thanks, nodded, and blinked his eyes, and there was no doubt a tear rolled down one of his cheeks. Her throat tight, Kalina delivered the plates of pork.

People usually waited until a fifth or sixth drink to start weeping, but someone would shed tears at a table every afternoon. Usually more than one someone at more than one table. Kalina brought them food and drink. They'd have to find somewhere and someone else to nourish their souls. But the sad fat man was getting to her, and it was becoming annoying.

Kalina put a dish of simple vanilla ice cream in front of Zenek and perched on the edge of the opposite chair. "Everything alright?"

He snorted. Kalina almost got up right there and then—that's what one got for a moment of human concern, a snort—but didn't, and the irritation melted when the man's breasts sunk as his chest deflated. He cleared his throat. "Fine. Just fine."

Kalina swallowed her next words. Instead, she put the bill on the table. "I work this shift most days. Please, come over if you need to talk," she said. "Next time, dessert on me."

The regular Tuesday night weightlifting session couldn't come soon enough. The sweat and the necessary focus would help her make sense of her mind.

* * *

Zenon Drobina came back to *Albatros* the next day. Kalina saw him push through the door and take the course for the same table he'd taken the day before. Yesterday, she hadn't watched him leave; today, seeing him upright, she had to revise her estimate. Yes, the man wobbled with folds, but she had to subtract at least twenty, thirty kilos. Zenon's gait resembled that of sea lions—while swimming, not on land—inexorable with inertia, smooth, like a planet's orbit.

Kalina gave the man a minute. Service must be prompt, but thoughtless eagerness devalues it; every waitress knows this. Then she danced over to the table just as he began to look around, trying to attract someone's attention.

"So, not just passing by," she said, having handed him a menu. "A beer?"

"I'll stick with tea for now. Work." He opened his hands in a gesture of apology.

Kalina went about getting the tea. That the man was drooling over her she did not find surprising or unusual. Most men did. And a good thing, too, or she'd be looking for a different job. But she found these men and their interest in parts of her—her ass, her tits—unworthy of more than momentary notice, as if they'd all drowned and lain in the depths of an artificial lake she'd built and filled to the brim with her contempt. She could just make out the outlines of their minds resting on the bottom.

Compared to the others, Zenon's boy-like awkwardness was endearing and lent him buoyancy. None of the men, including this one, could know she found them . . . irrelevant. She'd always kept busy, so few people asked how such a beauty never managed to hold onto a boyfriend.

Albatros served whatever tea they had. Usually, it came in teabags shipped and stored in cardboard boxes labeled *Herbata Popularna*. It tasted as if it had been rejected by a tannery for not being quite caustic enough to break rawhide.

Kalina had used the last bag from the current batch for another customer. Now, she reached up to grab a new box from the shelf. Her eyes widened. *Madras, Herbata Indyjska*, this box said. Now, that's a treat: a real tea flavor, and without doing to the tongue what salt does to leeches. Kalina opened the box, glanced around, and pocketed two teabags. Then she placed another one on a saucer, poured hot water into a teacup, and headed back out.

"And for dinner?" she said, having placed the steaming cup and the tea on the table.

"How good is your tripe?"

"The best. Soft and spicy. And we just got fresh bread."

Kalina was soon putting in the flaczki order—it wasn't going to take long; the thing had been pre-cooked and just needed heating, ladling, and garnishing. She next cut a few slices of bread and delivered them to Zenon. Then she produced a few more smiles and waited on the other two populated tables. A slower afternoon.

She would have preferred a busy, sweaty one. One to keep her mind occupied.

Kalina could hear her own heartbeat. She attempted to go at least five minutes without thinking about the kiss. She failed. Emilia hadn't pulled away. She'd opened her lips and probed the tips of Kalina's teeth with her tongue. Her eyes fluttered and fixed on Kalina's. Emilia's arms embraced Kalina with a crunching power. A kiss and then a sound of the front door. Kalina had recoiled and jumped up, breathing as if she'd been about to come down with her own panic attack.

Now, she was standing in the back of the room at *Albatros*, hoping the blood her heart pumped didn't show too brightly in her cheeks.

When it came up, the flaczki bowl appeared close to overflowing, and Kalina swore under her quickened breath. The pork stomach lining, simmered for hours in brown, peppercorn broth, had come to a boil no more than a minute earlier. The cook had left no clearance for her fingers to grip and lift the dish. She pictured dipping her thumbs into it, the pain, then sucking on the burn and the salt.

Yesterday evening, Emilia's mother had come in, and, heart beating as if after a race, Kalina covered up for her flushed face by grabbing Emilia by the shoulders, acting out an effort, and pulling the girl to her feet. The kiss. "Poor Emilka was feeling faint," she told Zofia Sokołowska and immediately worried whether she rushed the explanation.

But now Kalina stared at the overfull bowl, the liquid in it hot and viscous enough to toss from ramparts and considered her options. She decided to dispense with professional pride and slid a tray out from under the counter. To make the trip worth her while, she opened a bottle of beer and placed it on the tray next to the stew. Might as well get in front of the request which was definitely coming because few things went as well with flaczki as cold lager.

As she rounded the corner to enter the floor, holding the tray with both hands, her elbows out, Kalina caught the edge of the bar hard with her right forearm. She swore, out loud this time, as the tray tilted, but her windsurfer's instincts kicked in and she recovered her balance before more than a drop of the stew landed outside the bowl. All of the beer remained in the still upright bottle.

Kalina unzipped her pursed lips and exhaled. She could feel the throbbing in her arm and knew she'd find a bruise there tonight. She smiled at the thought—this bruise felt honestly earned. Kalina approached Zenon's table on ever so slightly bent knees, using them like a set of shocks to cushion her steps. She rested the tray on the next table over and presented the beer to the man.

"Have I read your mind?"

He nodded and showed his bright teeth.

Then she lifted the bowl filled with hot stew and carried it over to Zenon's table. She felt a twitch in her bruised arm, with the flaczki carried in both hands only a few centimeters away from the white tablecloth. One side of the bowl's rim slipped out of her fingertips, the world tilted, and Kalina's reflexes took over.

Her right hand shot down to support the falling plate. The hand swerved like a pendulum and missed, its only profit a coat of scalding tripe juice. It was too late—it had been too late back in the kitchen when she hadn't insisted on a new serving.

The brown erupted. Like a mud volcano, it covered Zenon and Kalina in hot peppercorn-flavored sludge. Zenon, the sea lion, swerved with the grace of one on land. In the middle of her own fall—to wrap herself around the hurt on the floor, to embalm the burn within her body—Kalina saw the big man tip and fall back over his chair.

Having done its violence, the din fled, leaving behind not so much as ringing in her ears, and all she could hear was her shaking breath as she lay curled up, and Zenon's murmurs: *fuck, fuck, fuck*.

The profanity stopped, and through vibrations in the air, Kalina felt a bulk approach. She curled up tighter and put her good hand over her head to shield it from blows. She brought her knees up to her breasts to cover her stomach.

What felt like a set of tongs made of two frankfurters picked her hand off her head. "Hurry!" Came Zenon's breathless voice. A hand slid under her left arm and Kalina opened her eyes. "You need to get these clothes off you and rinse with cold water." The hand lifted her off the floor as if she were a mannequin made of papier-mâché. Running across the floor, Kalina registered the other guests, all on their feet, none moving to help. A couple walked toward the exit. Without paying.

Zenon shoved her into the ladies' room and shut the door from the outside. Kalina tore the blouse off—it had been white—kicked off her skirt and slid out of her underwear. She ran the tap and started to splash her skin with handfuls of cold water as if bailing the Titanic's rescue boat. She let the liquid run down to her feet. Some of it pooled and some continued to the drain grate in the middle of the room. Pink splotches stood out on Kalina's stomach; on another day that might have meant she'd forgotten to reapply sunscreen.

She bathed in cold water until her belly felt as frigid as her spine. It might have grown cool to the touch, but the skin above her navel and below her breasts now looked livid like raw cow's tongue. Kalina bent over the stinging, picked up her clothes and washed them as well as she could with hand soap and cold water. She wrung them out and put them back on, sucking in her middle to lighten the pressure of the skirt's waist against it.

Then she faced the door. There she stood, stained, shivering, dripping water the color of early spring's melt from the hem of her skirt. She was going to open this door, walk to the business office, and beg Pani Elwira, the director, to let her go home *and* keep this job. She was going to walk to Emilia's place and, if they had no aloe ointment, call Agata to ask for some. Then she would slather it all over her abdomen, take a couple of pain pills, maybe three or four, and close her eyes.

And what would happen if she stayed like that, eyes closed, if she refused to acknowledge the world? If she denied it, could it force her to accept the pain waiting to pounce from all around? As simple as that. Could she just refuse to see and move?

Well, this was an idiot's thinking. She reached out and opened the bathroom door.

Kalina saw Zenon's face first. His clothes clung to his folds, the hems of his pants dripped; he must have done what Kalina had, but next door, in the men's restroom. The other face—wrinkles around raspberry lipstick—was Pani Elwira's.

"Pan Zenon here is very sorry for this." Pani Elwira looked up at Zenon Drobina's face. "He'll pay for the damage."

Kalina said nothing, her plan had fled.

"Go home Kalinka, dear," Pani Elwira said. *Kalinka? She'd never called Kalina that or anything else endearing.* "Come back when you feel better." Then Elwira stomped off to her lair.

"What did you do?" Kalina asked.

"Bought her two bottles of Żubrówka."
"Are you alright?"
"I'll live. You?"
"I'll live." Kalina couldn't help but smile at the fat man. "Need to get some ointment. I'm a windsurfer. I'd prefer to avoid scars all over."
"Let me walk with you."
Kalina nodded and they moved toward the exit.
"Right, so, a windsurfer?"
"A bronze in the Polish championships last year." She failed to keep a note of pride out of her voice. "Look me up in the papers if you'd like. Kalina Zalewska."
"Wow."

Cracked cement tiles paved the sidewalk from this point on for a good kilometer, and Kalina diverted some of her attention to making sure not to trip. She knew exactly what was on her left—a general store and, in half a block, a pączki bakery—and to the right, across the street—an optometrist's followed by a full block taken up by the Sacred Heart Cathedral and the parish. They'd need to cross the street and might as well do it here since people tended to slow down in front of the church.

The asphalt had softened enough to give. It felt like putting her weight down on a windsurfing board. She expected to make imprints in the road, but the impression she'd left behind seemed no deeper or clearer than the Christ picture on the Shroud of Turin. She glanced sideways. Zenon's black leather lace-up walking shoes sunk halfway down the sole with each step.

"Ye of little faith," she said and giggled. When the man's lips pursed in confusion, she giggled harder. "Hold onto me, I won't let you drown." She offered Zenon her arm. His expression changed little, but he accepted it and lifted the corners of his lips just enough to tell her that he had no clue what was going on. *Do I?* Kalina thought. But then all that fled when she saw something in a church column's shade. Another large man, taller and wider than Zenon Drobina. Her father turned around and walked into the church before she could be sure whether he'd seen her.

She wasn't giggling when she stepped up onto the curb on the other side. She was no Jesus walking on water. Closer to the Magdalene before she'd given up whoredom.

"Are you well?" she heard and realized she'd stumbled on the curb. Zenon had held her arm, though, and they now stood on the crumbling sidewalk.

"I'm fine," she lied. "Just lightheaded." She strode away from the church and made Zenon exert himself to keep up.

Less than a block down the street, Kalina heard the man's voice, "Wait, I know this place."

She turned around.

"This?" she said. "This is our local pig pen." She pointed at the Milicja Obywatelska plaque.

"I'm working out of an office in here these days," Zenon said.

***

Why she'd slapped him, she couldn't say, precisely. It just happened. It was too much. The spring had stretched too far. Two blocks down, almost to Śródmieście Street, Kalina glanced back and saw the man's sea lion bulk fewer than twenty meters behind.

I'm not going to run. The turn leading to Emilia's apartment approached. But she couldn't very well lead Zenon Drobina home, could she? No, if she were to confront him, it had to happen here. Kalina used her thighs and calves to stop in place as if she'd run into a sheet of bulletproof glass. She swiveled and came to a rest.

She went on the offensive: "You're a fucking pig. See, I'm not afraid to call you by name. Functionary Drobina!"

"I don't like it any more than you do," the man said, once he'd taken a slower breath.

"Quit following me."

"My father insisted. People don't say no to my father."

Kalina scrunched up her forehead. "What the hell does that have to do with anything? Just leave me alone."

"I even got into the Academy of Fine Arts, the one in Gdańsk." Drobina dropped his head. "But my father burned all my sketches when he found out. A few weeks later, I was in ZOMO training."

"So just stop following me, and we can both go on with our lives. I need to get some ointment on this burn and start cooking supper; and you . . . go beat someone up, or something."

"I hate seeing pain. Just wanted to make sure you were alright."

Kalina exhaled. She took a course down Śródmieście Street toward the pharmacy. The man fell in next to her.

"Why me?" she said.

"What?"

"Why open up to me? What makes me the lucky one?"

"You didn't treat me like a useless pile of shit. The way most people do."

Kalina cursed her ability to smile professionally at just about anyone. That Zenon Drobina might be a useless pile of shit had in fact crossed her mind. It did not make her proud.

Kalina could think of no perfect response. The last thing she wanted to do was to say something personally sappy. So, instead, she took an even tone and said, "How long has it been since your last confession, my son? Squint and imagine I'm your priest."

Zenon's face remained straight and pointed down. Kalina couldn't tell whether he had drowned himself in vigilance for stray edges or in regret. She sighed and turned her attention to her own steps.

She halted a quarter kilometer later and pointed at the lead-colored stucco of the building in front of her. *Apteka*, said the sign above the white-painted metal door.

"Pharmacy," Zenon said.

"Yes, that's what the sign says."

Inside, Kalina had to stop for a few seconds and let her eyes adjust to the murk. At least two air fans droned on somewhere close. The room began to settle into contrast, and Kalina moved toward the counter before it fully resolved. She'd been here often enough. Mostly for ointments, compression bandages, and aspirin.

A grunt floated over the shelves and a second later a woman came into view. She stopped on the other side of the counter, scratched her temple, and fixed an invisible wisp of hair over her left eye.

"Yes?"

"A tube of Aloe Vera. And some topical antibiotic. Please."

The woman disappeared between the shelves.

When she shuffled back out, she dropped two cardboard boxes on the counter and pecked a few keys on the register. "One thousand, nine hundred and eighty złotych."

"What?"

"The antibiotic is a hundred, but the Aloe Vera is imported."

Kalina took her hand out of her purse, leaving her wallet inside. Useless. Nobody made this kind of money without turning tricks. So the burn would need to wait a little longer.

"Change your mind?"

Kalina opened her mouth to answer just as Zenon's hand dropped down a wad of bills on the counter. They fell like rotten, wet leaves. They stayed right where they thwacked down onto the laminate. "No," Zenon said. "We'll take both."

Kalina moved aside. She could have protested, should have. But she was tired. Too tired to say another hard word.

The woman behind the counter counted out a few coins in change. "Bag?"

Zenon shook his head, grabbed the boxes, and gestured toward the exit. Kalina moved into the space he offered and opened the door but made sure to hold it for him. She wasn't some princess.

Outside, she moved to stand by the wall. "You should not have," she said.

"Please, just take it."

Kalina stared at the box with the ointment while an anthill burrowed beneath the skin above her navel. Her arm floated up, but instead of scratching the itch, the pain, she closed her hand around the box. Before she went back up the steps, she grabbed the other box, too.

Inside the pharmacy's bathroom, she took her blouse and bra off. She ran cold water from the single faucet, and tsked as she wiped the dust and sweat with a waterlogged hand. She expected no paper towels or toilet tissue and found none. Instead, Kalina turned her blouse around and used the back to dab the skin drier.

She opened the Aloe Vera tube, squeezed out enough to cover her fingers, and tsked again as she smeared it over the skin. Placebo or real, she felt immediate relief. She breathed in and out. She repeated the process with the antibiotic cream.

The sun, pinkish now, seemed cooler when Kalina left the pharmacy. Zenon waited where she had left him.

"Please wait a moment. It won't take long," Zenon said and went back into the store.

Kalina took his spot by the wall. Really, she should leave now. Why was she standing here, waiting for a man she didn't know—a Milicja functionary, a fingernail attached to the Soviet arm hanging over the country from the east—to, likely, take a piss? And yet her feet remained fixed to the cement, and Kalina watched the reddening sky.

Ten minutes later, the door banged open and gave birth to Zenon Drobina. Before she could ask him what the hell had taken so long, he raised a hand, and Kalina noticed a couple of sheets of notebook-sized paper. He must have asked for that, too. "Please read these," he said and kept the hand extended.

Suddenly, she felt worse than she had before the Aloe Vera. Little blond hairs on her forearms stood straight up. She looked at the paper in Zenon's hand like it was a shit-encrusted venomous snake.

"I don't think I should," she said.

"Have you ever felt like you had an opportunity to escape your shitty life? And that you'd never have one again?"

An escape. Kalina took the papers and stuck them in her purse.

"Are you working tomorrow?" he asked, eyes on the ground.

"Yes, the dinnertime shift."

Zenon Drobina nodded, said goodbye, and shuffled away, back up the street in the direction of downtown. Whether he was heading to the Milicja headquarters or somewhere else, she didn't know. She turned, too, and set off toward Emilia's apartment, trying to guess what was in those handwritten pages.

CHAPTER SEVENTEEN

A TURN

Wednesday, July 7–Thursday, July 8, 1982. Zygmuntowo.

Emilia liked afternoon shifts the least. A layperson might think the nights would be the worst, but she didn't mind those. Being at the station alone at night, overhead lights dimmed, the console lights blinking red, green, and white, made her think of outer space. Sometimes she felt weightless enough to float. The blinking would lull her to sleep, and the buzzer would wake her up to connect a call. Each night, no more than a few of those. Decent people used nights to sleep.

Time before the morning shifts became compressed. She'd rush to shower, get to work by seven, and it'd be mid-morning before she knew it. She'd have her sandwich while juggling cables. The last hour stretched thinner than facts on daily news, sure, but once it dripped away, at three o'clock, Emilia still had half a day to breathe, live.

But the afternoon shifts were imperious. They spread all over and swallowed the day whole. She went in at noon to join the morning crew to cover the peak hours. She would envy the women who got to leave at three and suspected they felt the same on the days when their shifts passed each other in the opposite direction. Emilia and Frania shared the rotation. The older woman ignored the departing morning shift; Emilia would watch them get up and pack, and she wondered what plans they had, what they were cooking for dinner, and when had they last seen their lovers. Then the tap of Frania's fingernail would return her attention to the console's lights.

Today, Frania didn't need to tap. Emilia stared at the blinking lights and made the connections. She flitted from plug to socket, to socket, to socket, as if the plugs might blow up if she stopped. During the few moments the lights failed to illuminate, when no one reached out through the copper, thus denying her a legitimate reason for activity, she drew the cables and stuck them in holes anyway.

If she kept talking, if the words maintained a flow, she wouldn't have to think. But by five o'clock most of the lights dried out, and only one or two, every few minutes, pulsed like sunlit water nibbled from underneath by a fry. Push back as she might, Emilia felt Kalina's lips on hers.

Emilia's heart raced, but it wasn't the beating of a panic attack. She wanted to taste Kalina's salt and feel the contrast between her tongue and teeth. She squeezed her eyes shut to drown the image in black. She squeezed her legs together to chase away the spreading warmth and forced her hands to remain above the console's edge.

It didn't help.

"I have to pee," she said, and trotted out without waiting for Frania's response.

She locked the door to the control room behind her and ran to the bathroom at the end of the hallway. She made sure to lock this door, too, and dropped her skirt and underwear. Her mind filled up with Kalina's face, her eyes. Kalina's mind and her bitchy sense of humor. The pressure of soft, dry lips.

Emilia had no idea when she became aware of time again. Her heart still kept wanting to jump out of her chest, but the curtain shielding away rational thought began to lift. Her panting slowed down. She made sure to squeeze out some pee since she wasn't a liar. Once she cleaned herself, Emilia washed her hands and face. She fixed her hair.

The person in the mirror was staring back at her with wide eyes. The mascara had smudged a bit, and Emilia used a scrap of toilet paper to coral it back. Her lips looked and felt dry, and she regretted not having grabbed her purse with its lipstick. And with the mints. She could really go for a mint. She must have breathed through her mouth, since the air reflected off her palm made her nose scrunch up.

She judged the reflection presentable enough. On the way back to the control room, Emilia practiced slow, deep breathing. After Frania buzzed her in, Emilia popped a mint before taking her seat at the console. The hard candy was mostly sugar, nothing like fresh peppermint, but it did enough to remove the stink from her throat.

"Are you well?" Frania Nowak asked.

Emilia nodded and pointed to her mouth, lips puckered out around the hard candy.

"Take your time," Frania said. "Slow evening."

An occasional light in front of her would quickly wink out as Frania took care of all the calls from her station, her swivel chair creaking every so often a couple of meters to Emilia's right. The woman never said much, and Emilia had made no more than a few perfunctory attempts at conversation in the years they'd worked together. Frania was thirty to forty, short like a child, had two kids, and smoked a pack of *Sport* cigarettes a day. She never mentioned a man in her life. Emilia knew little more.

She had sucked the mint down to a flat blade and crunched it up when it began to threaten to cut her tongue. "Thank you, Pani Franiu," she said. She gave the woman a smile, a large warm thing she usually rationed out.

"I'm proud of you," Frania said.

The shock of the statement short-circuited her thinking and, for a reason she couldn't explain, sent a jolt of adrenaline into her solar plexus. It appeared Frania had taken Emilia's bug-eyed, hyperventilating silence for a flood of gratitude. She reached out and patted her cheek. The hot blood in Emilia's arteries made the gentle touch feel like a thousand tiny electric pins.

In moments, her anxiety had fallen, and if Emilia's cheeks were red now it was due to embarrassment at least as much as to adrenaline. *I need to get a fucking grip.* Her body had become like a monster in a horror movie, one you know is there, ready to jump out any moment now, any moment... now. If she couldn't trust it, what could she trust? Kalina. She could trust Kalina.

Emilia turned to the other woman. "Thank you. But why?"

Frania pursed her lips. Not for the first time, Emilia wondered if the woman was wearing dentures. Something in the way she set her jaw, self-conscious, reminded Emilia of watching Soviet cosmonauts on television putting on spacewalk suits. Words made it through Frania's airlock only once they'd been brought to ambient pressure. Never before that.

"I have a brother in Warszawa. He's been in an internment camp since December," said Frania.

"I am afraid," Emilia confessed, surprising herself.

Frania nodded as if that response made sense. "Your mother?" She poked a hole under a blinking light, sideways, scarcely looking. "How is it?"

Was she asking if Emilia was concerned for her mother? About her? Mother came and went. Took phone calls. *Five years' prison sounds right*, Emilia had heard her say to the receiver last Friday. That same night, Mother sat in the kitchen, smoking, slack-jawed, a bottle of vodka by her side.

"Some days she's just a bookkeeper, then on others a Party Commissioner. She's not a bad person. She just does what she has to do."

Another nod from Frania. The sideways angle of her head expressed caustic mockery better than any words could. Emilia's pulse quickened and she grimaced. Before she knew it, she was snarling. "She raised me all alone!" *Fuck her! Damn this woman.*

Which one?

How had she ended up here, defending her mother? It was true; the beatings were Father's main contribution to her upbringing, and then he left. But having to stand up for the bitch made Emilia's eyes water in frustration. Before she knew it, grief gripped her windpipe and she let out a sob, then another. Emilia hugged herself, squeezed, and reminded herself to breathe.

"Hard to find a good man," Frania said and gave Emilia half a smile. "My brother is one of those. Now, he's in prison."

"She got Marelski out. After . . . after I'd filed a report."

"I know."

"I'm sorry." Emilia couldn't have stopped the sobs that followed and didn't try. "So sorry."

"I know." Frania sidled her rolling chair over and wiped Emilia's cheeks with a rough, nicotine-yellow palm. "I know."

Emilia leaned into the caress. Frania made another connection, then rolled even closer and hugged Emilia's head to her chest. "I know," she whispered.

"What do I do now? What do I do?" Emilia couldn't have said if she'd meant the question to refer to Pan Marelski, Mother, or her soul.

Frania cleared her throat and pulled back. Silence made Emilia raise her head and make eye contact. The woman's lips were pursed, her jaw clenched. Then she exhaled with enough force to leave behind a corpse. "You could help," Frania said. There was nothing unusual in the woman's voice, but her eyes narrowed and her nostrils flared up. If Emilia didn't know better, she would have said Frania was suddenly frightened of her.

"How?"

"Not here. Come to my apartment tomorrow afternoon." Frania smiled. "I'll make tea and cookies. We'll talk." She picked up a paper scrap and scribbled down an address. Just a couple of blocks away from Emilia's place. "Let's say five-thirty. Does that work?"

Emilia nodded. That seemed to be enough. Frania swiveled over to the console, then used its edge to propel her chair sideways to her station. She made a connection.

* * *

Thursday morning's sunlight woke Emilia before she would have preferred. She liked to sleep in on her days off. She propped herself up on an elbow to check out the blankets on the floor where Kalina had already snored when Emilia returned from work last night. The floor was clear, and the blankets and pillow were stacked on a shelf by the opposite wall.

Emilia sat up, rubbed her eyes. She rose and dressed, then smoothed down her hair which bounced right back into a pillow-perm. She sighed; it would stay ratty until she washed it.

The clinking of a teaspoon reached Emilia from the kitchen, and she went to investigate. Kalina, dressed in a loose, long T-shirt, sat at the kitchen table, sipping tea. Her face split up into a sunny smile when Emilia walked in. "Good morning, princess," Kalina said. "You look so cute when you're asleep."

Emilia said nothing. Instead, she walked over and kissed Kalina on the lips. The other woman raised her arm and cradled Emilia's head while she responded, sloppy and enthusiastic. Emilia broke it off. "Where is Mother?" she asked.

"Out. Left soon after I woke up."

"So, what are we?"

"Friends?"

"Just friends?"

"Best friends. I love you, Emilka."

Easy as that. So easy that Emilia giggled. "I love you, too."

After another kiss, Kalina rose. "Sit, sit, I'll make you tea."

"I prefer coffee."

"Coffee, then. Your Highness."

"Hey, you offered! Why up so early? The sun's just come up."

Kalina shrugged and smiled. Emilia contracted the smile and stared at Kalina's form as the other woman made instant coffee and cut bread for toast. Her face. The face she'd loved since elementary school. What makes love change, evolve?

Emilia's smile slipped. "What do we do?"

Kalina's arm paused mid-stroke. A drop of soupy jam ran down the knife's blade. It missed the bread and bloomed on the off-white counter.

Kalina glanced at Emilia for a moment, but her eyes fled and landed on the jam. She licked her finger and swept it across the blemish on the countertop. She placed the jam dollop on her tongue and sealed her lips around her finger.

"I have an idea," Kalina said, once she'd taken the finger out of her mouth.

"Quit it."

But Kalina refused to quit. She picked Emilia out of her seat and, straining, grasped the jam jar between two fingers. Then she carried Emilia to her bedroom and applied jam liberally. For about an hour.

Emilia had used her fingers to return the favor at some point, she was pretty sure—it was all a blur. With time she might work up to what Kalina had done.

A little shiver ran down her side. The sweat had cooled, and her heartbeat had slowed down. Emilia pulled a blanket up and shut Kalina's gaze away from her hips.

"Mother might have come back."

"Next time we'll lock the door." Kalina parked one butt cheek on the edge of the bed and leaned in for a kiss.

Emilia intercepted her with a raised palm. "Please. Be serious."

"I'm so fucking tired of being serious." Kalina sat back. "You and I. Why can't we be just . . . not serious, and seriously together?"

But that couldn't be, could it? Loving this woman was the scariest, most serious thing Emilia had ever done. Pressure pricked Emilia's eyes. She wiped them with her fists and knew the water on her skin would be salty.

"Let's lock the door and take a bath," Emilia said.

Kalina saw to the logistics. When Emilia walked into the bathroom, she couldn't see the water beneath thick, steaming froth.

Emilia scrambled over the edge and lowered herself to the enameled bottom. The water felt comfortable enough, but she would have preferred hotter. Kalina gathered her shirt around her and lifted it over her head. An archipelago of blood-colored stains covered her chest and stomach. Emilia's breath caught, and she pushed a foam-covered palm against her face.

Kalina looked down. "A work accident," she said. "Hot flaczki. It almost doesn't hurt anymore. I slathered it with aloe. Top-notch imported shit."

Nude, Kalina stepped over the edge. Before Kalina's knees bent to sit, Emilia knelt up and embraced her hips. She buried her face in the curly, blond hair. Breathed in. Felt her blood heat up the water like a radiator. Any moment it would start to boil.

Emilia pressed in with her mouth and reached in with her tongue. Kalina's taste made her own hips writhe. But she persevered until she heard a moan from above and Kalina's thighs quaked as if she were about to collapse. Emilia pulled away.

"Don't stop," breathed Kalina and pushed Emilia's face back between her legs.

A few more moans later, Kalina half-fell into the foam, and water sloshed back, splashing out a puddle. Her eyes widened.

"No worries, I'll wipe that off," Emilia said.

"Hurts like hell."

Oh. Right. Lukewarm the water might be, still probably not terribly pleasant on the burns.

"Getting better," Kalina said.

"Alright, turn around. I'll get your back. You have to tell me about this work accident."

"Tripe. Like I said." She paused. Before Emilia could nudge her for more, Kalina took a breath and told her a story about a bowl of flaczki, burns, Aloe Vera, and a fat Milicja man named Zenon, including what turned out to be his love letter scribbled on two loose sheets of paper. "All one hundred percent true."

Emilia stared. Kalina cleared her throat.

"Right," Emilia said. "Damn."

"How was your day?"

"Got a tea date with Pani Frania from work."

Kalina's eyes narrowed.

"Nothing like that!" Emilia said. "You should come with me. She won't mind."

Emilia blinked when she saw Kalina's cheeks redden. "I'm sorry," Kalina said. "I'm not going to be a jealous idiot. I'll tag along if you'd like, but I do have to make it to training by six-thirty."

* * *

Frania's was a clone of Mother's apartment, only a kilometer away. Emilia met up with Kalina as the latter walked back from *Albatros*, and they now meandered on hardened dirt paths between apartment buildings until they got to block 19a. They climbed the stairs to the third floor, and Emilia knocked on the door marked with the number six above the nameplate.

The peephole darkened. A bolt scraped open on the other side a second later. Then another. And what certainly sounded like a third. Kalina and Emilia exchanged eye rolls. Might they come to regret accepting the invitation? Emilia resolved to make an excuse and get them both out if the quiet Pani Frania turned out to be paranoid and crazy.

The door swung in. Frania smiled and said, "Dzień dobry."

The younger women returned the greeting, and, at Frania's gesture, filed in. As Frania closed the apartment door, Emilia wondered how the woman had managed to peek through the spy hole—its plastic aperture cleared the top of her head. The woman stood no taller than Emilia's shoulders. Kalina, at a few centimeters more, towered over Frania, and discomfort was showing in the taller woman's face. They shuffled from foot to foot in the hallway.

"Please, come in, come in," Frania said after a moment, washing her palms and appearing unaware of it. Her eyes darted.

"This is Kalina," Emilia said. "She is my best friend. I would trust her with my life." Agata's disappointed face flickered in the back of her mind as she said this, but it was the plain truth. What had happened between Kalina and her would change things. Agata's place in The Trinity would change. Would The Trinity survive? *Focus!* She'd deal with Agata later. For now, Frania appeared less jittery and repeated the invitation.

In the living room, a coffee table stood in front of a sleeper sofa. An armchair flanked the table from the opposite side, the side of the standard wall of shelves—in this instance shining with light-brown lacquer and with a nook for a television set. Frania pointed in their direction.

"Sit, please, sit," she said. "On the sofa or the chair. Feel right at home. I'll start the water for tea."

Kalina and Emilia glanced at each other and perched on the sofa as one. Emilia wanted to scoot closer but maintained a few centimeters' distance. Kalina ended up on the far end of the sofa by the glass door to the apartment's balcony, while Emilia sat by the living room's door and with a clear view of the kitchen. Frania busied herself there; she'd put the kettle on the stove and emptied a box of cookies onto a plate. Every few seconds she'd shoot a glance over her shoulder. After she'd caught Emilia looking once and smiled, Emilia made sure to watch from the corner of her eye. She couldn't say why. It felt dumb to sit here, afraid to be seen looking.

Frania carried in the plate—the painted pattern made it a Bolesławiec original—and placed it in the center of the table. The cookie mix included gingerbread, shortbread, chocolate-covered wafers, and butter biscuits. The woman must have stood in line for hours, maybe overnight, to score this. And she put it on an heirloom piece of pottery. Next to the cookies, Frania placed two smaller bowls, lemon wedges in one, sugar in the other. *Lemons*, and cut into hefty wedges, no less.

Emilia glanced at Kalina and caught her eye. She seemed to have noticed it, too. Not a casual afternoon tea. Emilia had expected a conversation about politics, something Mother forbade, and had anticipated a taste of a forbidden fruit. Instead, something bitter and biting rose in her throat.

When the whistle went off, Frania trotted into the kitchen and soon came back with three steaming glasses, placed each on the table atop a doily, and took the chair.

"Help yourselves, please." She gestured at the spread.

Kalina nodded and took a wafer. Emilia studied the cookies a second longer, then opted for glazed gingerbread.

"This is very kind," Kalina said.

"My children are staying on my sister's farm for the summer," said Frania.

Emilia nodded. It hadn't occurred to her to wonder. She watched Frania's hands, the palms back to their washing movements, seemingly an unconscious habit, the skin dry and cracked enough for winter. Frania stopped fidgeting with her hands, made fists, relaxed, and rubbed her right palm on her shirt. Where she'd touched it, the fabric seemed darker. She reached out and grabbed a gingerbread cookie.

The women chewed. They sipped tea. Frania tapped her foot.

Kalina's face had reddened a few minutes ago but she'd kept her mouth shut. Emilia found herself impressed. She drew in a breath. "Is there something wrong, Pani Franiu? Do you need our help?"

Frania glanced at Emilia and gave her a bobblehead-doll nod.

"Yes. If I told you something. . . . I haven't done anything wrong. Haven't hurt anyone. I only want some dignity . . . for all of us."

"Pani Franiu, I won't tell anyone. Whatever it is." Emilia meant it. She glanced at Kalina. "She won't, either, or I'll kill her."

"Is your mother still with the Party Committee?"

"Yes. But just for the *powiat*. She might have some pull here in Zygmuntowo and the countryside around, but no more than that." Emilia's pulse quickened, and her damned chest tightened. Frania was about to ask a favor, possibly request an intercession on someone's behalf.

"Is she in good standing?" Frania asked.

"She keeps getting calls in the middle of the night. I don't see much of her. Always working. So in as good graces as anyone, I suppose."

"I need you to keep some money at your place for me. It's not safe here."

Emilia blinked. So it wasn't about a relative in jail. Money?

Kalina still hadn't said anything but stopped fidgeting.

Emilia slowed her breath, cleared her throat, and said, "I'll need to know more."

"Right. It's Solidarity's money. I'm in the union, like eleven million others used to be, but I couldn't stop, couldn't do nothing. So now I suppose I'm part of the resistance. Me, can you imagine? Someone is coming to get the money from Gdańsk, but we lost contact. Something's not right, and now too many people know it's here."

That might have been the longest speech Emilia had heard from Frania, and she began to purse her lips, started a head shake, as soon as the woman finished.

"I print a resistance newsletter," Kalina said, and Emilia's neck whipped sideways, instead. "I do." Kalina met her eyes. "I should have told you sooner. Almost did." Kalina grimaced. "I am sorry. I had to do something. And with what your mother is . . ."

As tears welled up in Emilia's eyes, something solid wedged in her throat. But of course, she couldn't be trusted. Who would trust her? A bitch who eavesdrops for a job and rats people out?

"If it came up now, I would have told you," Kalina said. "I swear to God I would have." She reached out and patted Emilia's hand.

Emilia swallowed, then turned to Frania. "Why can't the money stay here," she asked.

"There is a Bezpieka major in town. With one of his henchmen. Could be a coincidence, I know. But it doesn't feel right."

"Why me?" Emilia asked.

"Because you've stopped listening." Frania sighed. Then added, "And you came to that on your own. And because I already knew about your friend's work with the paper. And, to tell the whole truth, I can think of no place less likely for anyone to look."

Emilia stared at her own hands until Kalina's cleared throat prodded her. She looked up, swept her eyes toward Kalina and attempted a smile. Then she turned to Frania. "I will take it and keep it safe. How much is there?"

CHAPTER EIGHTEEN

EMILIA'S CHOICE

Friday, July 9, 1982. Zygmuntowo.

Yesterday, when she had sneaked back home alone—with Kalina on her way to the marina—relieved that Mother hadn't returned, she had to sit down and force her breath to behave. All this with twenty thousand American in a plastic bag on her lap. It felt wrong that so much wealth should take so little space. Emilia multiplied: twenty thousand dollars equaled roughly two million złotych at current black-market exchange, equaled a 200-square-meter house. No, that's a palace or two houses. On her lap, Emilia Sokołowska was holding real estate. It should have felt heavier.

Real estate investment wasn't this money's destiny. On Emilia's lap had rested printing presses, paper and ink, radios, and who knows what else. Had Kalina used a printing press? She must have. Ask her later. The stack of green bills, small, heavy, felt holy somehow.

"Under the mattress?" Kalina had asked as they parted.

Emilia had shaken her head then—she'd already planned what to do.

Their iron bathtub had been ensconced inside a wooden box fitting tightly under its lips and covered with linoleum tiles. An expected aesthetic. The design provided for one of the tiles and the plywood square holding it—one close to the wall and the drain—to be removable in the event a need for repair arose. If she shoved the money in the opposite direction, away from the drain, and snug to the inside wall, no one would find it; it might still be there when World War III was over.

Emilia sat in the kitchen and couldn't bring herself to face the bathroom door more than necessary. She'd kept her pooping and peeing to the minimum. But she couldn't go without a bath and still keep showing up at work. People would start asking questions. She glanced at the clock again. Two hours until her shift.

She'd need to get in there soon and turn on the water.

She peered into the cup. The tea was almost gone.

She'd eaten. She'd laid out an outfit. She had vacuumed and dusted.

Emilia rose and washed the cup, then walked over to the bathroom before she could change her mind again and locked the door. The tiled walls imprisoning the tub appeared entirely innocent, as if they weren't holding a secret. Perhaps there was a lesson to learn there. She turned on the tap, checked the water's temperature, stripped down and stepped in.

Bathing on top of a couple of houses, or twenty Fiats, should have felt special. The off-white enamel should have reflected gold. Rose petals should have fallen out of the faucet together with water and rust.

But water was what came, and the rust appeared light today. No roses. The paint remained the color of Mother's teeth.

The warmth had risen above Emilia's breasts, and she turned the water off. Now there was a choice to make. One she'd made thousands of times: would Emilia's legs or her torso have to grow cold? The tub was too short to cover all of her with water.

She hadn't kept count, but if forced, would have said she'd opted for a warm chest most of the time. Today, she felt contrary. Emilia sat up straighter and let her knees submerge. The hair on her legs danced like hornwort at the bottom of the lake. That required attention.

The razor in Emilia's hand could have been a stone sculpture. If it shook, the human eye was too poor an instrument to detect it. Emilia found she enjoyed each stroke. She would usually curse while shaving and usually cut herself. Today, the razor glided with a cosmonaut's confidence. To think she'd usually avoided thinking about shaving her legs.

She'd avoided something else. Agata. Kalina had become Emilia's world, upended it in a week. What will Agata think? What would happen to The Trinity? Their tripod had always relied on no preferential treatment. Emilia made a decision. She hurried the shave—not a drop of blood!—soaped up and rinsed, then washed her hair.

A plan it was not, sure, but it was a resolve and fed Emilia energy.

* * *

Agata had sat her on the sofa and offered her a beer. Emilia declined. A fruit tea seemed a better idea at a quarter after nine on a work night, and she'd been preparing for this conversation all day while she mechanically connected the calls. Agata nodded, put water on to boil, and cracked a beer bottle open for herself. Then she sat on the floor opposite the sofa and stared at Emilia without a word, taking an occasional sip.

"Quit weirding me out," said Emilia, once the irritation had grown enough.

"Me? Weirding *you* out? You're the one coming over at night. Not even an hour before curfew. Calling first to make sure no one else was here. What the hell's happened? Did you kill someone?" At this she paused. "Did you off that pig Zalewski?"

"God, no."

Agata gave a little air puff of relief, but the teeth biting her lower lip spelled out disappointment. "What then?"

"Can I have a beer?"

"Now we're talking."

Once a beer bottle sat in her hand, Emilia inhaled its aroma, stalling. The story seemed to be missing a beginning. Oh, what the hell.

"I love Kalina," she said.

"Right."

"I mean love love."

Agata sucked in her lips and broke eye contact before pausing. But what she said once she exhaled again was, "I've seen how you've been looking at her since sixth grade. You might just be the last to find out."

Emilia took a swig. "That obvious? You don't mind?"

Agata shrugged, but her teeth kept pinching her lip. "I love both of you. As friends. I'm no dyke."

Emilia skipped a breath. "Is that what I am? A dyke?"

"If it's got a cooch and it eats a cooch, it's a dyke. I don't care. Really. I've always known."

Emilia wanted to believe it. But she knew Agata's tells, too. That lip. "Do you think anyone else suspects?" she asked, though, instead of confronting her friend's discomfort. Facing simple jealousy would have been better.

"No way. You may never have kept a boyfriend, but you've both had them. That's good enough for these people. They'd rather not see what's uncomfortable."

Emilia found herself stuck, unsure how to respond. How does one go on in a strange city, in the dark and without a map?

Agata took a swig, then stretched her lips. "Look, you've always been the closest I've had to a sister." She sighed. "I grant you, this is weird. I'm not dumb—"

"No, you're not."

"Don't interrupt. And flattery will get you nowhere."

Emilia managed a smile, and her courage grew when the other woman's return smile reached her eyes.

"As I was trying to say," Agata continued, "there is no way for things not to change." Emilia wanted to disagree, protest that it wasn't true, but couldn't. The Trinity was broken, and the shards hurt like hell. "I can't be to both of you what I was before. A sister," Agata said. "I know you won't let me become a spare bicycle tire." There, the lip, the anxiety, again. "How about an old, frumpy aunt?"

The only response Emilia had to that was to get off the sofa, lie down on the floor next to Agata, with her head in Agata's lap, and begin to cry. Agata said nothing. She lifted her arm and stroked Emilia's hair. She made no soothing noises; she uttered no words. Emilia's gratitude for the touch and the silence, both, made her cry harder. There would be a distance between them now. There was no way for things not to change.

Inside her grief time passed at its own pace, and by the time exhaustion made her stop crying Emilia felt as if days had ticked by. She lifted her head and sat up. Agata still hadn't said anything, just sat by the wall and wiped her own tears with the back of her hand.

"You've made me look like I pissed my pants," Agata said.

Emilia embraced Agata and squeezed. But no more crying. Then she let go and crawled on all fours back to her beer. She brought it back and clinked it against Agata's. "Here's to Aunt Agata, the greatest of aunts."

"I can live with that," said Agata and chugged down the rest of her beer. She licked her lips. "Now, what does all this mean for Operation Pig?"

It took Emilia a second to catch on. "Right. It is on. That isn't just about Kalina."

Agata swallowed. "Thank you," she said.

"Didn't know we've given it a name."

"I have, now. Not terribly creative. You'd have done better."

"It's yours to name," Emilia said. "I should go. I'll have to run to make it back before curfew."

They both rose and hugged, Agata's embrace hurried and softer than usual.

"Are you going to be alright?" Emilia asked on her way out. The distance was already there, and she hated it.

"I'll be fine. Don't you worry about your old aunt," said Agata and shut the door.

CHAPTER NINETEEN

MARRIAGE

Friday, July 9, 1982. The Train to Zygmuntowo.

Antek stood in the corridor of the train to Białystok. There he would have twelve minutes to hobble over two platforms to catch a local connection to Zygmuntowo. He patted his pockets, and when he realized what he was doing, he clasped his hands together. Dorota didn't approve of his smoking, and he'd refrained from mentioning her apartment's sooty curtains. Antek instead turned his face into the rushing air and drew a breath. Moisture coated his lungs. The dark sky promised rain.

The pressure in his bladder reminded him to stop by the lavatory before going back to his compartment. He shuffled the length of the train car with barely a twinge of discomfort in his side. Whatever Dorota had done, and the antibiotics, seemed to be working. The thing no longer looked furious, boiling; instead, a neat wound rested under a layer of antiseptic cream and sterile dressing.

He shut the door behind him and, knowing well what to expect, made sure to draw shallow breaths. That made the stink almost tolerable. The toilet consisted of a metal tube, flaring out at the top, with no seat or cover. Its lumen, crusted brown, blurred in the middle with the rushing of the tracks like a kaleidoscope of shit. Antek unzipped and let go, leaving a trail of three or four kilometers. *What do stray dogs make of the scent of trains?*

He knew the futility of trying the faucet and ripped open a packet with an alcohol towelette. Dorota had stuffed a few of these in his pockets. He rubbed his hands making sure to cover every square millimeter, then used it to unlock and open the door. He dropped the towelette in the trash bin hanging opposite his compartment and slid open the door.

"I was starting to think you jumped off the train or fell in the toilet," Dorota said. She had put down her book on a lap covered by a floral, knee-length skirt. The old woman sitting across from Dorota—her hair gray and her shoulders covered by a cardigan despite the summer—smirked but kept her eyes on the landscape. The lady had already taken a seat in the compartment when Antek and Dorota boarded, but the others were even fuller. They had exchanged hellos, but the woman appeared content to sit, silent, seemingly deep inside her thoughts.

Antek's head still swam a little when he thought about how he'd ended up riding to Zygmuntowo with Dorota and, every once in a while throughout the trip, on the receiving end of her sass. He had missed her humor. He had known from the beginning that though he lusted for her body, it was her mind and her wit that had snared him.

Two days earlier, as he lay on her couch, it had seemed more likely that he'd be riding alone, and that Dorota would keep cheating on him with someone random. Cheating? Technically correct, but it didn't feel fair to call it that, even to him. Oh, fuck fairness! But he couldn't, dammit; wanting things to be fairer was what got him into this confusing mess to start with. Dorota had called him her noble knight more than once. Her eyes would grow soft each time, and they made his heart lift, and his ears redden; happiness was feeling the flushed burning in the ears. That is when she didn't accuse him of having a hero complex. That happened more than once. But not as often as the other thing. A net win.

The stupidest thing did it. The sound of Dorota's steps returning from the kitchen, after he'd heard her toss his plate in the sink and crack another beer, had reached him right before she swept into the room and sat in the chair. Her first pull on the beer bottle emptied a solid third of it.

Her face tensed, then she backfired a belch loud enough to spark. She giggled and covered her mouth.

Oh, fuck this! "Come with me. Please," Antek said in response to the belch. He wanted them back, as soon as the words had left his mouth, yet he was glad he had let them fly, all at the same time.

Dorota blinked. She took a sip and watched the bottle sitting on her knees.

"I'm sorry," Antek said. "That was selfish. Unfair."

Dorota's knuckles grew white around the beer bottle.

Then she shot out of the chair and drew her arm back, as if to throw the bottle at him. But she never let go. When her arm completed the arc, she sprayed Antek with malt foam. She stalked all the way to the couch and shook every last drop over his hair. Her lungs sounded metallic, like the accordion connector on a modular city bus.

"God!Damn!It!" she heaved. "Be selfish! For me! Be selfish for me!" She blinked, and a couple of tears started down her cheeks. With a wheeze, air went out of her, and she whispered, "Be a little more selfish."

Beer continued to drip off Antek's hair, off his nose. The aroma, herbs mixed with pub, matched the green of Dorota's glistening eyes.

"Come with me?"

"You need another bath," Dorota said and marched off to the bathroom.

Now, as Antek took the seat next to his wife, the two of them irrationally together again, he made sure his shoulder touched hers. He still didn't know if it would be alright to hold hands.

* * *

The old woman stayed with them all the way to Białystok. The train trundled into the station, its undercarriage sighing in metallic relief. Dorota had lowered their suitcase from the overhead shelf, rising as soon as the first apartment buildings came into view, while Antek attempted to ignore the judgment boring into his side from the old woman's eyes like lasers. He had found the bag manageable at floor level, but Dorota would have killed him if he had opened his wound by lifting a suitcase. Chivalry had to wait.

They waved the gray-haired woman ahead, using their manners. As they followed a few steps behind, Dorota glanced at Antek. "Never mind her," she whispered. When he felt her hand touch his, he grabbed it and didn't let go until he needed his arm to drag the bag off the train. By a miracle, the train had arrived on time, and Dorota and Antek walked down the platform holding hands. Antek kept his eyes ahead and on the cracked pavement but hoped her grin matched his.

He remembered the trains from Białystok to Zygmuntowo as clotted with humanity. Finding a seat would have been an impossibility any given summer among the masses destined for lakes, camping, and pristine forests. This train, this summer, made him question if he'd gotten on the right one. Dorota gave him the look which said he was being an idiot when he'd asked a conductor.

A half-empty train to Zygmuntowo in July was unnatural. A sin. A waste.

But Antek wasn't going to complain about not having to stand in the corridor for three hours. They found a compartment all to themselves—dirtier than the last one and funky with some alien smell—and sat by the window, facing each other. Antek had been starting to get hungry, but breathing the compartment's atmosphere took his appetite away.

"Everyone's first class when there is no class," he said.

"Oh, this isn't so bad. I just wish we'd have brought a bite of something to eat."

"Mhm."

Dorota squinted at Antek. She sniffed, a curious puppy picking up a scent. "Are you feeling well?"

"I have the best nursing care in all of Poland."

"Shut up." But she smiled.

Dorota had put her glasses on to change trains. Now, she took them off and used a fold in her green silk blouse to buff off a smudge. She turned the frame around. She swiveled it. Then Dorota shoved the glasses back onto the bridge of her nose and grimaced. She may have pinched it—in proportion to her entire body, her nose was just large enough to offer room for pinching—or finally smelled the stink.

"I love you, Antek."

Antoni Piekarski grew suddenly lightheaded, and his throat became too tight to speak. He looked away from Dorota but couldn't avoid seeing the clothes on his body: the shirt sleeves and the pant legs of his wife's lover. His eyes swiveled back to her.

Dorota took her glasses off and put them on the table under the window. Antek watched her eyes—green slits, flickering, as she watched the landscape, blinking every few seconds. The train crawled at no more than thirty, forty kilometers per hour, and Antek joined his wife in studying the grays and greens outside.

He couldn't remember when—it may have been in '78 or '79—they'd gone to see a film, an American one, one of the dozens that the later Gierek years had brought with borrowed money. He remembered the title: *The Graduate*. And the conversation. *What if I met a Mrs. Robinson*, he'd asked. *I'd have your balls*, she'd answered. He had no balls to reverse the question, and she hadn't volunteered.

Dorota had been no virgin when they'd first met. But the only time he had to think about the men she'd had was when they had run into one at a fancy Gdańsk bar. Stocky, not particularly tall. Balding in his twenties. Dorota introduced them, and they shot billiards for an hour. Antek had chosen to remain silent on the walk home and would have stayed that way if Dorota hadn't said, "You know, he played rugby for a while."

"Mhm," Antek said.

In response, she had grabbed him by the elbow, made him stumble and look her in the eyes as she continued, "You're twice the man he'll ever be, sweetheart. He got kicked in the crotch once and ended up with a single testicle." Then she play-kneed him in the nuts and smothered him with kisses while she tickled him until his grunts turned into giggles.

The compartment's funk wasn't lifting. He needed air. Antek tapped on the table under the window until Dorota's eyes swiveled toward him. He pointed at the door and nodded. She nodded and turned back to the view, now fields of wheat, beyond the scratched-up pane of glass. Once Antek stepped into the corridor, he made sure to slide the door shut behind him. Then he unlatched the window and let it slide down as far as it would go. The rushing air tussled his hair, but the wind was far from a hurricane. The breeze cooled his face. He wished he could unzip his chest and vent the heat radiating through his bones, flesh, and skin. Antek hadn't studied biology since starting at the polytechnic all those years ago—mechanical engineers scoffed at such squishy things—but knew it wasn't coal but adrenaline. Fight or flight. His hormone-driven brain was the same instrument that designed and pieced together oceangoing moving parts as big as this train car. And they worked. Every single time.

Since his chest remained tightly sealed—something Antek would never again take for granted—he settled for undoing the top two buttons of his shirt. He stood there until his heart calmed down and the bear sitting on his lungs got up and trotted away. A headache was coming on. Antek closed the compartment door after stepping back in and turned to Dorota, whose face, trained at the window, didn't move.

Antek stopped in front of her and slid to his knees. He rested his cheeks on her thighs and clasped his hands behind her back. In the darkness, her warmth cooled him down better than the breeze had. Antek knelt in front of his wife, his face buried in her skirt, and felt the adrenaline drain, leaving behind space. When his shoulders began to shake, when Dorota bent down to rest her face on his neck and began to stroke his back, the space began to fill back up. When drops fell on the skin of his neck, Antek stirred, rose, and sat next to Dorota. Then he embraced her with gentle intent, but she cleaved into him so tight that science couldn't have declared where one body ended and the other began.

Dorota and Antek held onto each other, afraid to let go, until the train managed to slow down further and came to a stop at a station. They wiped each other's tears with the palms of their hands, kissed, kissed again, and rested, hoping that their compartment would remain undisturbed.

***

No luck. The man who joined them wore a flat farmer's cap and a checkered short-sleeved button-down. The folds of his face, well-aged, had cured to the color and thickness of a leather wallet's hinge. If he'd noticed their red faces, he said nothing about it after offering a curt good day. He sat by the compartment door, leaned his head against the glass wall, and closed his eyes.

Dorota and Antek sat shoulder-to-shoulder, hands clasped. After a few kilometers, the train hit its top speed of fifty. The clouds still carpeted the sky, but a worn-out hole here and there let through an occasional stray ray of sun. Dorota rested her cheek against Antek's shoulder and, a minute later, began to purr in deep sleep. The warmth spreading throughout his body made Antek's eyelids fall, too.

The thud of air compressed under a bridge jolted him awake. Soon, a lake danced by on the left—with tents set back from the beach and bodies bobbing in the water—before the tracks cut back into deep forest. Another lake revealed a similar scene on the right, across the hallway window. The land of a thousand lakes, he'd heard it called. Antek didn't know if that was a formal designation. He'd made a habit of camping outside of Zygmuntowo every year and kept it up with Dorota. The lake count might have been inflated, but not by much.

The bridge and the lakes had meant they'd be getting into the station in a few minutes. Antek stirred his body to bring Dorota out of her sleep slowly. His sleeve had grown damp with a mix of sweat and his wife's drool. She blinked, appearing halfway back to the world of the living, and Antek kissed her on her sleepy lips. "Almost there," he said.

She blinked again, shook her head, closed her eyes, and tried to burrow back into him.

Given no choice, Antek kissed her, then kept on kissing.

"Not fair," she said.

"We'll take a nap later. Promise."

The old man was gone, either off the train at one of the villages, or smoking in the corridor, perhaps preparing to get off.

Something else was missing, too.

"Dorota."

"What?"

"That old fucker stole our bag."

With a hiss, Dorota jumped up and hurled her pocket-sized body into the hallway. She pushed through people leaving their compartments in one direction. Antek followed out but turned the other way. He ran through the car door, onto the landing, where a woman with a chicken in her hand and a duffel at her feet gave a startle and crossed herself. He nodded in apology, then ran back. That's when he heard Dorota scream, a shriek without words—one of fury or pain, he didn't know which—but it made his wound disappear from his mind as he sprinted, trampling over anything and anyone in his way.

A short, red-headed tornado had hit the other landing. The suitcase lay splayed open on the ground, while Dorota was half-sitting astride a man right next to it and windmilling her fists into his face, neck, and torso. Antek registered a few other passengers huddled by the walls but wasted no time and lunged.

As he arrived, Dorota's head flew in the opposite direction, trailed by her hair like a comet, and her body followed. This was not the farmer. This fellow was no more than thirty, skinny, and he met Antek with a fist. It might have delivered a sting rather than a wallop, but Antek's field of view darkened anyway. His nose grew numb and his side hot. He felt the hardness of the steel floor underneath his knees.

Antek scrambled over, stretched out his arm to catch the man's ankle, but the fellow had risen and was wrestling with the door handle. It swung open, the stale air on the landing changed little as the train had slowed down to a crawl, and Antek watched the man jump and run across the dozen or so tracks and into one of Zygmuntowo's outlying neighborhoods.

When he turned back to Dorota, Antek tsked under his breath. She was zipping the bag up, silent, but her left eyebrow dripped a trickle of blood. He glanced around. The people had relaxed, now murmuring to one another, but continued to ignore the couple and their luggage. Antek shook his head. A year earlier, someone would have come up, done something. Helped.

He sniffed, surprised not to have a bloody nose, and put his hands on Dorota's arms.

"Are you alright? There is a little blood."

She looked up. Then she gave him as wide a grin as he thought her lips could manage. She giggled. "I showed this motherfucker!"

CHAPTER TWENTY

LOVE AND WAR

Friday, July 9–Saturday, July 10, 1982. Zygmuntowo.

The taxi was a well-cared-for Fiat 125 with a blanket over its back seat. The driver had cracked the trunk open without getting out, and when he swiveled back to greet Antek and Dorota, his eyes narrowed.

"We were attacked on the train." Antek got in front of any questions. He had a little trouble breathing and was glad when the man seemed satisfied. Dorota gave the address to the rented room, and the car jerked into motion making Antek stifle a groan. He glanced at Dorota, who was watching the trees while nursing a slow smile. The water in the station's bathroom was out, but she'd used an alcohol towelette to both disinfect the scratch and clean the dry blood off her cheek. She could do little now about the swelling threatening to shut her left eye.

The damage to his face stopped at redness and a bit of puffiness, but that wasn't what bothered Antek. His side hurt like hell and felt increasingly moist. But when he watched Dorota's pride, he couldn't stop a grin.

A ten-minute ride got them to the destination. The cottage stood in a row of similar 1930s' cottages on a side street, a Partisans Avenue tributary. Dorota paid, they got their bag, and climbed the two concrete steps to the door. Antek pushed the doorbell. A high-pitched yapping announced a small dog before the door opened just a crack, and an eye, set under a gray eyebrow, took their measure.

As many times as Antek had visited the region, he'd never used a room-letting broker. The right way to experience the Zygmuntowo lakes was a tent, a campfire, beer, and, if his luck ran hot, a few links of sausage for grilling. This time a tent was not an option. Instead, Antek forced a smile and nodded his respect in the eye's direction. Dorota said, "Good day," and a hand collaborating with the eye unfastened the safety chain. The door swung in.

"Dzień dobry," the woman to whom the eye and the hand belonged answered.

She wore a long, toucan print dress and a pair of thong sandals. Her graying hair had been pulled back with enough force to give her a facelift.

"We're the Kowalskis," said Antek, just as Dorota smiled and said, "We spoke about the room. Pani Maria? Maria Prusak?"

Maria Prusak nodded and waved them in. A few dollars changed hands at the bottom of the stairs, and Maria climbed the steps. Dorota and Antek followed.

"The room and the bathroom are all yours." Maria pointed to a door off the short hallway. It led to a wide space with a bed set against one wall and a bookshelf by the other. Most of the third wall looked out over water through a bay window. Antek saw another smile bloom on Dorota's face.

"This is gorgeous," she said.

"If you don't mind my asking, what happened to your faces?" Maria said.

"A man tried to steel our bag on the train," Dorota answered. "We got it back. Together."

The woman's eyes narrowed. Then she rubbed the bills in her hands together without seeming to realize it. "Since my husband died, I've been staying downstairs," she said.

"We appreciate it."

"We do," Antek added, at a prompting from Dorota's waving palm.

Maria's features relaxed. "Feel free to use the kitchen," she said. "But keep in mind I turn in by nine. You'll find ice for that face in the freezer. And remember I'm not the cleaning woman." She stabbed the air with a finger. "Ah! Here's your key. Almost forgot."

"She seems nice," Dorota said, after Maria shuffled away.

"Her?"

"Let's unpack."

It took Antek about thirty seconds as he dumped all his borrowed clothes in a drawer. Dorota used the hangers in the wooden wardrobe for her blouses and skirts. The T-shirts and the underwear, all folded, went in another drawer. She stepped out of the room to the bathroom and arranged their toiletries, including Antek's brand-new razor and toothbrush, on the glass shelf over the sink. Then she went downstairs, brought back something in a towel—ice, Antek guessed—and disappeared into the bathroom for another half-hour.

Antek took the opportunity to lift his shirt and check on his side without alarming Dorota. It hurt less now. The liquid he'd felt earlier was likely sweat cooling off, because the skin, while still red and slightly puffed up, seemed no worse for the recent wear. Still, it would probably be good to avoid any further wrestling and fistfights for a few more days.

After Dorota strode back into the room, she took Antek's hand and said, "How about a walk to start?"

Antek left the job of procuring a couple of umbrellas from Pani Prusak to Dorota. He waited by the front door, peering through the glass pane at the darkening clouds. A soaker, likely, and no later than in an hour or two. But if Dorota wanted a walk, she would get her walk no matter how wet it got.

When he heard footsteps, Antek glanced back to see his wife brandishing an umbrella in each hand. She had tied her jean jacket around her waist in case it got cooler with the rain but now had another set of sleeves embracing her, these brown rather than the jacket's navy blue. She handed Antek the black umbrella, keeping the red. Then she untied the sleeves of what appeared to be a brown corduroy blazer.

"For you," she said, "from Pani Maria. Used to be her husband's. She worried about you catching a cold." Dorota's face remained straight throughout.

Antek cleared his throat and accepted the jacket. "How about we take a stroll up the river?"

***

A hundred meters up the banks of the Netta, while the rain hung above, the humid air had grown cooler, and both put their jackets on.

"I got that wrong, didn't I?" Antek said once he'd tugged at the bottom of the blazer to seat it around his shoulders. It fit perfectly in the chest, but he would have preferred it a bit longer.

"Hmm?"

"About Pani Maria."

"You get a lot of things wrong."

He kept his eyes ahead and only sought Dorota's hand for his answer. Not speaking felt right. Tight. Just the right kind of snug.

Holding hands, Antek and Dorota climbed the steps leading to the sidewalk over the bridge. Partisans Avenue, which paralleled their walk to the right, just across a block's worth of houses, took a ninety-degree left turn, as if bouncing away from the city cemetery across it, and led toward the river under a new name: the Avenue of the Red Army of the Union of the Soviet Socialist Republics. The locals didn't bother with the tongue-twister and neither did the tourists. They all called it the Reds' Street.

"Ice cream?" Antek asked. "If that place by *Albatros* is still open?"

Dorota pursed her lips. "Fine, you've talked me into it."

Antek glanced up. Good thing they had umbrellas. He envisioned melted ice cream soup dripping over his wrist, dairy mixed with rain and coal dust, the latter occasionally drifting over from Belarus on prevailing winds. As if by magic, he felt a drop on his forehead. Dorota must have sensed the rain, too, for she unfurled her umbrella into a red stain against the sky. A couple of wires protruded through the fabric, but the thing held up well enough to make it worthwhile. Antek opened his umbrella, and it obstructed the sky without a blemish to its spiderweb shape.

"Take mine, yours is broken," he said.

"I would, but I prefer red."

And that was that. Antek knew better than to insist.

Raindrops the size of blueberries materialized mid-air as if waiting there for Antek's face. Water hung, suspended, motionless, a ripe drop every few meters. Dorota turned to face him with a grin the size of the Panama Canal and her umbrella askew. For once Antek knew for certain that the rivulets running down her cheeks were not tears.

"Still want ice cream?" he asked.

"Hell, yes!"

Explosions of dust underfoot became a layer of slick as the sidewalk saturated. Soon, they arrived at the town's premier restaurant, and, tucked in next to it, a kiosk with a sign proclaiming "LODY" over its window. The ice cream place was open and without a queue. The awning in front allowed Antek and Dorota to close and shake off their umbrellas.

"How many scoops?"

Dorota pursed her lips. "Two?"

"Just two?"

"As many as will fit between the wafers?" Dorota turned to the window. "Two orders. Four scoops each," she spoke into the opening and stepped back, leaving Antek by the window alone, apparently considering her part of procuring ice cream accomplished.

A boy reading a periodical with a soccer ball and photos of players on the cover stirred from his stool. Right, a World Cup was going on. How could he have forgotten? Antek used to kick the ball around before his hamstrings grew too brittle and counted himself a Lechia Gdańsk fan. A World Cup, with Poland in it, and no one talking about it. Only so many things a mind could handle.

The first ice cream sandwich went to Dorota. Antek took the second and struggled to pay while keeping the indulgence safe from splattering on the concrete or his feet. He exhaled in relief once he'd put the change in his pocket and could focus on the loaf of ice cream in his hand.

"We should have gone with two scoops," he said.

"Mhmmm." All of Dorota's attention seemed to have turned to the weight in her hand. "Aaaah," she moaned, dropped her umbrella, slapped the top of her head with an open palm, then rubbed her scalp as if applying a medicine. "Crap." She paused her industrial ice cream consumption.

"Brain freeze?"

"Let's stay under the awning to finish," she said, letting the umbrella lie where it fell. While she kept massaging her head, she brought the ice cream sandwich back to her lips.

"Take a break, maybe?"

She shook her head. "Haven't had ice cream in months. I'll be careful."

Ice cream: sugar, cream, vanilla, and eggs. Most of those rationed; all hard to get. The price for the two sandwiches almost emptied Antek's pockets. In earlier times, what felt like decades ago, he'd developed a habit of taking Dorota out for ice cream once a month on payday. Far from an original idea, it meant they'd had to stand in a queue not much shorter than the Sopot pier. Neither of them minded. They talked about their day, Lechia Gdańsk soccer, and remedies for indigestion. They exchanged ideas about human nature and God. About the Church and the state, about the Bolsheviks and the Mensheviks. They imagined the faces of their children. Dorota's words would animate her entire body, while Antek would eventually find himself with a stiff jaw from grinning.

Antek listened to the raindrops on the awning's corrugated plastic and felt the familiar sensation. A feeling he'd given up. He licked his ice cream while his jaw hurt. Dorota had slowed down, but now paused and watched Antek's face. She moved in and pinched him against the wall, burying her face and forehead in his chest. The top of her head, hair matted from rubbing, smelled of hops and sage. Antek kissed it.

"Let's make it work," Dorota said.

Antek kissed her head again. "Let's make it work."

Humid, raining, and yet each drop carried a sun's worth of warmth. Then something cold started to crawl down his palm.

Ice cream. Let it melt.

Over Dorota's head, the houses on the other side of the street appeared as if through the static of a poorly tuned television set. Silhouettes with umbrellas moved across the street. On this side, the downpour's haze hadn't obscured the world as much, and Antek could more easily make out the figures and faces of the few fools who hadn't sought cover.

One was a tall, fat man whose gait struck Antek as familiar. The sight tightened Antek's shoulders and made the back of his neck tingle. He bent his head down, to the side of Dorota's. "Stay as you are and don't look up." At this, her body froze in tension. The arms around him had been soft, now they'd grown wooden.

"What's going on?" she whispered.

"Don't look. The ubek who shot me just walked by not ten meters away."

"Are you sure?"

"He's damn hard to miss. Alright, let's just walk slowly back. Keep the umbrella low."

They'd left the ice cream sandwiches where they'd fallen, already turning into puddles, and Antek banished the guilt about the waste as soon as it started. Dorota sauntered more casually than he thought he could manage, as if she'd just enjoyed some ice cream, looked forward to a hearty walk back, and nothing alarming had happened. He had trouble keeping his eyes on the pavement ahead. The big man likely kept walking, with no reason to do anything else. But an image of the Milicja man setting himself to shoot—one he had caught at a glance over his shoulder—kept intruding; he could feel a bullet rip his flesh, but that he now could imagine one piercing Dorota brought on panic. Antek glanced over his shoulder, hoping he appeared casual. The man—he was the Bezpieka agent, no doubt—was climbing the long stairs to *Albatros's* entrance. When Antek jerked his head forward, his heart beat hard enough to make the rain mottle in his mind before he forced himself to slow down his breathing.

***

It was a good two kilometers to their rented room. Antek thought they must have walked at least five before doubling back. Once inside, they both sat down on the bed and took a few minutes to breathe. Dorota rose and returned a minute later with a couple of glasses of water. She handed one to Antek, and he gulped half of it down after a nod of thanks.

"Take this," Dorota said. "I found some aspirin. Expired, but will still work." Then she popped a couple herself. "How did they follow you?"

"They must have been on the train."

"You know what doesn't make sense? Nothing about this makes sense." Dorota asked and answered. "If they want you, why follow? Why not just . . . boom . . . and be done?" She winced. "Sorry."

Antek looked up. The rain, undaunted, was making the dusk's job easier, and the streetlamps had already come on. Stupid. He had let the miracle of Dorota's love for him distract him. "We'll need to be more careful now," he said. He straightened, but his head felt heavy as reinforced concrete. "Let's get some rest. Let's sleep, and maybe things will look brighter tomorrow."

CHAPTER TWENTY-ONE

A BEHEADING WOULD BE NICE

Friday, July 9, 1982. Zygmuntowo.

Zenon Drobina had few doubts. The guy pretending to be making out next to the ice cream kiosk was staring right at him. When he wore his own uniform, he expected stares. More than one old woman had made an evil eye. He'd seen men's fists tighten. Sure, he wasn't small, but the uniform made Zenon, the man, disappear; in uniform, he embodied Bezpieka. He was another ubek; to be feared, not to be trusted.

He walked down the street in soaked civilian clothes with a waterfall over his face. The only reason he had noticed the fellow was the petite redhead he was hugging. The man's eyes never left Zenon from under the black umbrella. This was strange, and strange made him uncomfortable, especially now.

Zenon had paused at the top of the stairs despite the rain. He wasn't going to get any wetter and wanted to get his breath under control. Not that he was going to flirt with Kalina. She listened and spoke to a person when she spoke to him. A regret about letting her know how he felt about her rose like bile in his throat. Stupid. He entered the foyer and took off his jacket. Not sure what to do with it, he finally decided to wring it. An even larger puddle collected around his feet. He swept his hair back to clear his field of view, sending more rivulets down his back.

He spotted Kalina through the glass in the inner door and decided to enter. She saw him immediately and raised a finger while listening to something from a woman sitting at a table and holding her fork like a director's baton. Zenon knew what to do by now and picked a table by a window, far enough from everyone else, but still in Kalina's row. The cloth seat absorbed the water from his pants and helped to improve his mood. He watched the rain fall.

"Panie Zenku," Kalina said once she stopped by the table. "So sorry. We're swamped and a waitress short."

Zenon Drobina swallowed a sudden flash of gratitude. If she'd read his letter, her face wouldn't let on. He knew what to do with being ignored by a woman. He waved the apology off and smiled. "A beautiful day we're having, isn't it?" Dammit! No, no flirting, that never ended well. The women would usually stare at his folds instead of his eyes, make an excuse, and leave.

"We're all about water in these parts. I promise, though, it'll be sunny and warm tomorrow."

"Magic?"

"No, a weather forecast on channel one."

"Thank God, then. How about a Dojlidy Mocne?"

Kalina nodded and danced away, and Zenon forced himself not to watch.

He knew the man with the stare was going to bother him. He'd done this hideous job long enough to be wary of the unexplained, ill-fitting parts, and having a man consider him steadily but with what felt like an even mix of fear and hate certainly counted as strange. If he'd only thought faster. He should have followed, seen where the fellow ended up. Perhaps even called out, confronted the man. But Zenon had done none of that; he was sitting at his white-clothed table, waiting for a half-liter of lager to show up.

Not many reasons anyone would remember his face. Family would, sure. Father usually looked like he wanted to blow his nose these days when they met and tended to make an early excuse to leave, but he'd still know his son. Anyone from the Gdańsk security organization; they'd smirk but would recognize him. And Major Roman Stelmach; Zenon had been spending most of his days with Stelmach these last few months. But the man in the street was none of the above. *Who was he?* Someone for whom the fear Zenon saw in the man's eyes was a rational reaction. *Who?*

Drobina found himself wishing he'd worn his service P-64 in a breast holster today and shook his head in surprise. He'd made sure to leave the thing behind whenever he could get away with it. He had no desire to shoot anyone else, after he'd hit Piekarski by mistake. He'd aimed—since the major would see him aim—a meter to the right of the man but should have given himself more space.

Something had made goosebumps crop up on his forearms; whether it was the damp clothes or feeling suddenly spooked, he couldn't say. Probably both. He'd put the gun in the breast holster and wear it tomorrow. As per the regulations.

"Here's the beer."

Drobina's neck jerked.

Kalina tried to stifle a giggle and failed. "Didn't mean to give you a fright. I see no white hair, not to worry." She poured part of the bottle in a glass, succeeding at crafting a head as pretty and dense as frosting.

Zenon took a long pull. He put the glass down and grimaced. Might as well be licking dirty coins. The brew had gone skunky, and it now tasted of metal and musk. He sought Kalina with his eyes. She was busy smiling at tourists, with beards and unwashed hair, three tables away. Her eyes scrunched, the smile engaging the entire face. When she'd taken everyone's order, she nodded and walked away with a sway of her hips.

Zenon looked down at his bottle. He poured enough to fill the glass back up. Then he took a breath, brought the glass to his lips, and gulped it down, trying not to taste. He swallowed as much saliva as he could. Really, this way, the thing wasn't so bad. Zenon transferred the rest of the bottle into the glass, collected himself, and slammed that down, too.

When he could catch Kalina's eye, Zenon pointed to the empty bottle to ask for another.

He tasted relief along with the hops when he found the second bottle perfect. A miracle of balance between bitter and sweet. Ha! Goosebumps had left, and the clammy cold had given in to the dry, warm interior and to the alcohol. If he were to guess, alcohol more so than the warmth and hospitality.

Zenon ordered a third half-liter bottle of strong lager. Nice. The bad one was certainly an accident. Not worth mentioning. Glad he hadn't bothered Kalina with it. She seemed to be plenty busy, especially for a rainy night. But that made sense. Who would want to cook over a fire, at a campground, in this weather?

He looked around again. The greasy bunch Kalina smiled at earlier wasn't an exception. A few other tables hosted men and women who looked like their last real bath might have been a few days earlier. It appeared that he had surmised correctly. The investigation business might be rubbing off on him after all. It's not that anything Stelmach had him do called for complex thought, but Zenon was the kind of artist who drew what he saw. He'd always had a mind for patterns.

He poured the second half of the third bottle into the glass and took a drink. Stifled a belch. Right, patterns. Why then refuse to see what's so plain? Well, yes, the answer to that was simple: because Stelmach had a way to make him want to lay his ears flat and cower. If he said sit, you sat. This was no regular mission. Either the major played a higher-level game, or . . . or he had gone rogue. The next belch took Zenon by surprise.

Hiccups followed. He needed something to drink. Zenon caught Kalina's eye and waited while she smiled at other people.

"Any food?" she asked once she stopped by.

"Not flaczki. How about a schabowy with potatoes and beets?"

"Good choice."

"And another Dojlidy Mocne."

"Is that wise?"

"I've done dumber things. I keep doing them all the time."

Kalina pursed her lips. "Fine," she said. "But I'll check on you before you go. And if I decide you need a taxi, you get a taxi, agreed?"

Zenon nodded and put a clenched fist to his chest. "On my honor."

The beer took forever—Zenon's suspicions fell squarely on Kalina—and arrived together with the food. The dish was delicious. The breaded pork loin, pounded down skin-thin, danced in his mouth adding the salt to the malt's sweetness and the bitterness of hops. A perfect three-way balance.

It was over too soon. Zenon chased the last of the breading around the plate with the final forkful of potatoes mashed securely between the tines. He hunted down all the crumbled bits until the bottom of the fork became encrusted with flavor. Once he'd lifted the remainder of the meal to his lips, Zenon made sure to slow down, chew it, and taste it.

If he'd had bread, he would have mopped the plate dry. As it was, he let a busboy take it away before Zenon could decide whether he cared enough for his dignity to resist licking it clean. Instead, he poured the rest of the beer in a glass and sipped it. His eyelids felt heavier than usual, but the world had now slowed down. The sounds and colors had mixed up and he couldn't tell blue from a giggle. The giggle wasn't his, probably. The room, presumably stationary, had assumed a flux and an internal pulse like old cartoons where the animation made everyone and everything on the screen fidget.

"Right. You're not walking back. You'll just land on your face somewhere. We don't want it to get torn up. It's ugly enough."

Kalina had stopped right in front. She bobbed up and down and sideways a little, too.

"Woa, stop moving."

"How much cash do you have?"

Zenon pulled out his wallet and pressed it into her hand. "Take it. All yours."

She rolled her eyes, and it made Zenon's stomach lurch. "I don't want your damn money," she said. "No more than you owe." She opened the wallet and rifled through the banknotes. "Should be enough."

"Got to tell you something. Secret. Psst." Zenon rubbed an eye with the finger with which he had just poked it.

"I'll call the taxi. Then you can tell me outside."

"I'll have another Dojlidy."

Kalina danced away like a fairy. When she came back, she put a glass of water on the table. "Drink this. The taxi will be here in ten minutes."

Zenon followed the orders. That was something he could do. Excellent at following orders.

"Up. Lean on me."

Despite the cartoon around him prancing in every direction, Zenon led Kalina to the door like a first mate in rough seas, and as gallantly. "After you, madam," he said, then realized he'd already made it outside. The rain had stopped, and the glowing sunset revealed plumes of steam going to heaven.

There were only fifteen steps to the bottom, he could have sworn, but it must have been higher because a spell of vertigo bent his knees and sat him down on the top step. A sigh came from his left, and a woman alighted next to him like a butterfly. He squinted: it was almost certainly Kalina.

"We'll eventually have to make it all the way downstairs," the butterfly said.

"Have you been to the Tatras?"

"What?"

"Mountains. Make your head swirl round just like this."

"Two liters of nine-percent reinforced lager are making your head swirl round."

"Secret."

"If it's about the letter, thank you. It was sweet. You're a very nice man, but it's impossible."

Zenon did his best to steady his neck and the finger he'd brought up between them to make a point. "If one works hard enough, anything is possible. Or something like that."

"Love is work, but falling in love shouldn't be. The crush will pass like bad gas, I promise. I have a secret, too, and you'll forget this whole conversation tomorrow, anyway. I like girls. Get it? Nothing personal."

"For real?" Zenon asked, and for some reason Kalina's jaw tightened. Then she sighed.

"I wouldn't lie about something like this just to make you feel better. Or any man."

Zenon nodded. That was fair. Now he really owed her his secret. Only once his lower back met the edge of the step behind him with some force, did Zenon realize that the nod had made him sway forward, and he would have likely tumbled down the stairs if not for Kalina.

"By God . . . just wait for the taxi."

Thank goodness, she didn't sound upset, just annoyed. "I'm with Służba Bezpieczenstwa," Zenon said. "Not just a run-of-the mill Milicja functionary. Nope. Not Zenek. Zenek the ubek. Zenek the shit."

No answer came.

"The major is sick. The flu or something. Getting better, though. Watch out, mister. Watch out. Bezpieka will get you. Peefpafpoom! Hmm. He'll probably shoot me, too, when he's done."

"Zenek?"

"Huh?"

"Shut up."

"Alright. But he always gets what he wants. He'll get the Solidarity dollars, too. And then he'll kill me." Zenon found a grin wander up his face. The grin slipped. "Or he'll kill me before. Can't think."

"I'll help you down."

Arms embraced him, strained. Gave up. A car pulled up. Honked. Then someone pulled at his legs and Zenon Drobina slid down one step, then another. Something heaved him up, and when Zenon's face met the back seat, he found it just about as downy as the concrete steps. The door shut. The cartoon faded to black.

CHAPTER TWENTY-TWO

BIGOS, TONGUE, AND EELS

Saturday, July 10–Sunday, July 11, 1982. Zygmuntowo.

Sunshine in his eyeballs woke Antek. He glanced around. Dorota's eyes were shut, and she puffed softly. She'd punched him a couple of times throughout the night and told him to stop snoring. Hopefully, he hadn't kept her up much. He swung his legs out of the bed and padded over to the bathroom in his underwear. Once he'd emptied his bladder, he noticed a vertical rod rising above the tub to which one could attach the normally hand-held showerhead. Grabbing a shower rather than a bath, standing as if under a tropical downpour, seemed like a good idea. He couldn't remember his last shower. He couldn't even remember if he'd brushed his teeth the night before. He'd meant to, but then his eyes closed.

He made sure to brush now. Today, hygiene also included peeling off the dressing from his side. Pink and slightly tender. Dorota's hands had done magic.

The shower got only as warm as yesterday's rain and no stronger. Perfect. Antek let his head loll forward so that the lukewarm water could gently massage his sore neck. He'd have to ask Pani Maria for an extra pillow.

Dammit, think about the problem at hand instead of daydreaming about pillows! It was nice to get a full night's sleep, sore neck or not, but the fact remained: there were ubeks in town who were after him, and they didn't grab him on the train when they had a perfect chance.

Antek inhaled and held his breath to run water over his face and hair. He resumed breathing to squeeze out a dollop of coconut-scented shampoo—he hadn't brought his own, like Dorota—and lather it on his head. He closed his eyes to rinse it. If there was a palm tree outside, he could easily be taking this shower in Fiji.

Why follow him all the way here? Why not arrest him or throw him under the train and be done with it?

Antek kept the water running while he soaped up, making sure not to miss a square centimeter, especially the sweaty bits. He even managed to reach between his shoulder blades and felt no more than a tug from the wound beneath his ribs. The one in his calf had closed and was now well on its way to a scar.

Why Zygmuntowo? What's here?

Antek took his time rinsing his body and, once the water started running down the drain clean, he gave himself another minute to close his eyes and clear his mind.

"Oh, fuck," he growled and shut the water off. Of course.

He mopped the wettest parts with a towel, wound it around his waist and trotted back to the bedroom. Dorota's eyes were still closed and her breath slow and even. Antek touched her elbow, then gave it a little shake. "Dorota." She buried her nose in her pillow. "Dorota!" he stage-whispered. Her eyes fluttered open, still filmed over with the haze of deep sleep. "Dorota." She blinked, blinked again, then exhaled with a huff.

"I know my name."

"They're after the money."

Dorota's eyes focused, and she propped herself up with an elbow. "Wait. That doesn't seem right. If they thought you had twenty thousand American, they'd have sent a battalion after you, not one or two ubeks."

Antek said nothing, uncertain, not sure whether he entirely stood behind his guess or was afraid it'd become real if spoken aloud again.

Dorota slapped her forehead. "Renegades!" She fell back onto the pillow and stared at the ceiling. "But of course, they would have to be.

Nothing else makes sense." Her middle compressed like a piston, and she sat up while throwing the covers to the side and scooting over to the edge of the bed at the same time. "Thinking about bailing?"

Antek nodded.

"That's the smart option," Dorota said. "We could go back to Warszawa, make a life there and forget all this business."

"I don't think Solidarity has ever executed anyone. I could be the first if they think I grabbed the cash and ran."

"There is that, but they wouldn't kill you. At the most they might rough you up. More likely, they'd just give you a stern talking to. But the ubeks *will* kill you once they have what they want."

Antek rose and began to dress. A moment later, silently, Dorota followed. A shirt, jeans, and shoes on, Antek sat on the side of the bed. Dorota sat next to him and grabbed his hand. A minute ticked away, then another.

"I can't. I can't do it," Antek said.

"Next time you need help simple nursing care might not be enough. And the nurse might need help, too."

"Look, I have twenty dollars left. Sell it. It'll get you home and through a month, maybe longer. I'll come back."

"I've heard that before. I'm staying here."

"If something happens to you, I will never forgive—"

"Shut up! This is my life, my body. I get to decide. You're such a fucking idiot." She sighed. "I love an idiot."

Better not to question one's good luck. Antek decided to stop arguing.

"Fine, but let's lie low today," he said. "You won't mind coming with me to see a woman about some eels tomorrow?"

* * *

Sunday morning had been brisk, but it quickly grew warm, and Antek could feel a rivulet of sweat cutting a valley across his back and collecting between his buttocks. Half an hour into the walk, Antek wished he'd worn jeans. His green slacks were going to show the wet stain in the back.

"Let's slow down. I'm sweating my ass off."

Dorota made no response, but she adjusted her pace, and the churn of her legs no longer reminded Antek of a ship's screw at maximum

RPMs. Except, while the screws he'd helped build could get up to three, four meters across, Dorota's legs were little longer than a rabbit's. A large one. And incredibly sexy.

They rounded the photography studio on the corner and left crumbling concrete slabs for a stretch of asphalt-paved sidewalk. The black had grown soft, like burned caramel, and a few steps after the church had come into view, Antek began to feel his Achilles tendons burn.

"Let's cross," Dorota said.

Once they had, Dorota put her arm through his and pulled him along toward the steel gate to the church's grounds. It stood open, unlikely to ever be barred, just as at least one of the cathedral's doors remained unlocked at all hours. The grounds spread for the length of one city block in each direction. Trees stood alongside the perimeter: sprawling, gnarly oaks and smaller mixed specimens.

Dorota moved toward the church's dark wooden door, made it as far as the first granite step up the stairs, when Antek stopped, still holding onto her arm. Instead, he gently pulled his wife around the front and turned down the pavement on the building's eastern side. Dorota allowed him to lead. She tightened her grip.

The far corner of the grounds housed a small graveyard; the parish's pastors, priests, and perhaps others, rested there in a few neat rows. Across a walkway from the headstones, a narrow path led to a red brick building. Antek walked up to its door and knocked as soon as his feet stopped and before he lost his courage.

A shuffling announced life on the other side. When the door opened, the life turned out to be a middle-aged woman—her skirt conservatively gray and her blouse white with a touch of lace in the collar—who stationed herself in the center of the opening.

"What can I do for you?" she said. Then added, before they could respond, "Keep your voices down. Father is resting between holy masses."

"Please, kindly, take a note. I'd like to make an offering for a mass. For six in the morning. In the intention of Antoni's spirit."

The woman blinked. The silence stretched, Antek shifted from one foot to the other. The woman cleared her throat.

"That'll run you a kilo of smoked eel."

"I'll give you two."

"If they're fresh."

"As fresh as December," Antek said.

"Right," the woman answered. "How do we find you?"

Antek gave her Pani Maria's phone number.

"Go back and wait there," said the woman with the lace collar. "I'm glad you're alive. When the call from Stefan came that we'd lost contact, the father worried." Then she swung the door closed.

The entryway had stood in the shade, but Antek's temples tickled with drops of sweat. *Stefan?* It seemed that Maria Prusak wasn't the only person he had figured wrong. "What she said," he murmured.

"What was that?"

He shook his head and led Dorota away, beginning the slog back. He glanced around and could think of no place less likely to harbor eavesdroppers or microphones. Not breaking his stride, Antek said, "This cloak and dagger bullshit sounds more ridiculous face-to-face. Embarrassing. Wasn't sure I had done it right until she mentioned the eel."

"Stupid boy," Dorota said.

Antek had no idea what she meant by that. But she kept holding on to his arm as if it might flee if given a millimeter or two, and he decided all he needed to do was squeeze back. Once they'd returned to their room, he'd take a cool bath and then talk his wife into taking her clothes off.

***

Antek had climbed into the tub when there came a knock on the room's door. The bed sighed as Dorota rose to answer it.

"Phone call!" Dorota called out.

Antek scanned the space. There was a towel. A fresh pair of underwear hung off a peg on the wall. He calculated how long it'd take him to jump out, dry off and get dressed. Uncomfortably long.

"Take it!"

"Jesus!"

"Please!"

He hurried up anyway.

He had squirmed into a pair of white briefs when Dorota charged back in. She closed the door and squinted at him. Antek expected her to throw something snide in his direction, but she only sighed and thrust a piece of paper in front of his face. Antek took the note, unfolded it, and stared.

"What is it?"

"It's where we're supposed to be in thirty minutes."

The one line was an address. "How far is it?"

Dorota shrugged, then danced over to her suitcase and slipped out a shiny, red packet, which she then unfurled to reveal a lacy negligee. "You'll never know what you've missed."

It was Antek's turn to sigh. "Rain check?"

"We'll see. Hurry up."

As they arrived downstairs, Dorota turned and knocked on Pani Maria's door.

"Thought we were in a hurry?" Antek said. Dorota seemed not to have heard.

Shuffling preceded the scratch of a bolt, and half of Maria's face appeared in the chain-limited crack. "Yes?"

"Would you be so kind and tell us how to get to ulica Hoża number four? *Bar Popularny?*"

"You could walk all the way, but you're better off taking the number three bus. Get off at the movie theater. Then it's a block away."

Dorota thanked the woman more than Antek thought the information deserved. He followed his wife out of the house and across the street to the bus stop. She descended upon the shelter's bench and Antek plopped down next to her.

Dorota's hand found his and squeezed. He squeezed back and didn't let go until the bus pulled up five minutes later.

"We don't have tickets," Antek hissed.

"Nothing we can do now."

The driver continued to stare ahead as they embarked, then yawned and pulled the lever to close the door.

"Let's hope there is no ticket control," Antek whispered.

Dorota shook her head. She smiled at an older man in a fatigued suit sitting over the wheel well. "Dear sir, would you happen to have two spare tickets we could buy?" The man smiled back, pulled out a stack, and peeled off two. Dorota rummaged in her purse and gave him a couple of bills in exchange. Then she slid each ticket into a slot; the machine's snaps sounded like gunshots. She handed one of the tickets to Antek.

If he strained, Antek could make out the date, July 11th, embossed in the paper. The ink had run out. Oh, crap. He'd already missed seeing Poland play France for the third place—didn't even know the score—and was likely to miss the final today. Really, he should care more about that. In a different, better world, he'd be chilling beers and waiting for friends to show up. Hopefully, they would be celebrating yesterday's victory while warming up for Italy versus Germany.

"Probably just a waste of money," he said, as they settled into their seats, and regretted his suddenly gruff tone as soon as the words left his lips.

"Want to have to hand over your ID?" Dorota asked. "Do you?" she repeated once he'd said nothing. His forged Adamczyk identification would stand up to casual scrutiny, but having his presence recorded here, even for a minor infraction, was a different and more dangerous matter.

"No," he grumbled.

By then, the bus reached the cemetery and stopped to let out a couple of old women with handfuls of candles. A few young people got on, their hair wet, probably on their way back from the beach.

As the bus prepared to cross the bridge over the Netta, a voice rang out, "Ticket control!" Antek glanced back. The distinguished gentleman from over the wheel well started down the aisle, a cardboard ID extended in his hand. The driver slowed down to a crawl. The doors would not open until the man had had a chance to check everyone.

The passengers continued to stand or sit, but all conversation ceased. The man took his time with the work, punching a hole in each ticket, having first checked that it had been properly validated. The process went on as expected until the man came to an older woman with a basket on her lap.

"I'm so sorry," the woman said. "I just ran out."

The man said nothing and pulled out a pad of paper. He scribbled something on it. "Identification?" he said.

The woman handed it over.

Having scribbled some more, the man tore out a page off the top and returned the woman's document together with the paper. She glanced at the slip. "Ten thousand złoty!? Jesus Christ and His mercy! That's two months' pension. What am I going to eat?" She rummaged in her basket and came up with a couple of banknotes. She presented them to the man together with the paper slip, and he pocketed them without a word.

The rest of the inspection went without incident, and then the bus stopped across the river and the door opened. The distinguished gentleman put a hand on the old woman's shoulder. "Out," he said. "No riding without a ticket. I don't make the rules." The woman voiced no argument, and they both got off, along with a couple of other passengers. A few people got on.

Antek had found he'd been squeezing Dorota's hand hard enough to hurt and let go with a groan. "So sorry! Are you alright?"

Dorota worked out her fingers. "I'm fine," she said. "Who's a genius?"

"You are."

* * *

Dorota and Antek got off at Śródmieście Street, right past the movie theater. The eatery would be a block or two down. They had five minutes to get there.

"Do you think they'll leave if we're late?" Antek asked.

"Let's not be late."

Dorota put her legs into top gear and set the pace. Her hips approached the unnatural seesaw of an Olympic speedwalker, and even that made Antek hotter than the weather. He trotted to catch up, making peace with the fact he'd be streaming with sweat in a minute or two.

It took six wordless minutes of huffing to get to the eatery's stairs. Dorota hopped up, and Antek followed. Once inside, Antek's eyes refused to see, needing to adjust to the darker interior. He breathed in the suddenly cooler air. His ear caught a hum he had trouble placing.

"Sonofabitch," Dorota whispered, the timbre of her voice impressed. "This place has an air conditioner."

Antek filled his lungs to bursting and exhaled as if enjoying a cigarette. He now began to make out the room and the patrons. And the air conditioner in the window to the left. The far end of the room housed a chest-high bar counter. Above it stuck out a gray female head with a perm. The blackboard on the wall behind the server listed the day's offering: cow's tongue in mustard sauce with mashed potatoes, and hunter's bigos, also with mashed potatoes. Antek hadn't been hungry, but the idea of sour and savory bigos flooded his mouth with drool.

Dorota zigzagged to an open table and sat down with a sigh. Antek stood right by and said, "How about some bigos and a couple of beers?"

Dorota squinted at the board, then grinned. "Tongue! And a beer." Antek nodded and went up to the bar to place the order.

"What now?" he said, once he sat down.

"The lady said to make a paper airplane and put it on the table," Dorota said and pointed at the folded napkin. "Hope this counts. I'm no mechanical engineer."

Antek considered it and decided to put his schooling to use. He put another folded napkin on the table. "How about this?"

"Looks like a cow." Dorota offered her critique. "I thought an engineer would have done better."

"Good enough considering the circumstances."

"I bet the fellows who made the Titanic said the same thing."

"Really?"

Dorota bit her lower lip, then allowed the smile to spread and said, "I've been thinking. I'm going to give you that rain check. Feeling better now?"

"All better." Antek meant to reach out and squeeze Dorota's hand, but a shadow fell on the table. It was a small shadow cast by a small woman, but Antek couldn't ignore it because she placed her palm next to the toy airplane.

"I have a kilo of eel for sale. Interested?"

The smile fled Antek's face. "I'll take two," he said. He looked up and into the woman's face. She was younger than she first appeared, probably not even forty. She blinked, but her eyes seemed to be waiting for something more. "But only if they're fresh," he added.

"As fresh as December," the woman said, pulled back a chair opposite Antek's, and sat down. Just then the bartender called out, "Antoniak!"

and Antek jumped up to get the food, having given a manufactured name, accompanied by startled blinking of the woman's eyes.

When he returned with a full tray, he found Dorota and the older woman frozen like wax figures in their seats. He placed the plate with the tongue, prepared in khaki-colored sauce, in front of Dorota, and the bowl with the sauerkraut and pork stew over potatoes in his own spot. He sat down, then glanced from one woman to the other.

"She said that bullshit about eels again," Dorota finally hissed. "Then refused to—"

Antek raised his hand and, for once, Dorota didn't seem upset at being interrupted. "Pani Frania?" he said. The woman said nothing. "This is my wife. Dorota. I trust her with my life."

"I am terrible at this," the woman said.

"It's difficult for everyone," Dorota said, having first exhaled and stretched her neck, and tried to touch the other woman's hand to offer comfort. The woman jerked her fingers out of the way.

"No!" The woman looked around. "No," she repeated in a whisper. "I mean I should have used the code on the phone. I screwed up. I could have burned everyone. Even the pastor, Christ have mercy on my soul!"

"Christ does since you haven't," Antek said.

"Are you hungry?" Dorota said.

"I could eat. But I haven't brought any money."

"My sweet Antek will treat you."

"He will," Antek said. "Tongue or bigos?"

Soon, Antek brought another plate of cow's tongue in mustard sauce with mashed potatoes and placed it in front of Frania. She inhaled. "Thank you," she said. "Smells delicious." Then she tucked in without further comment. Dorota and Antek glanced at each other, then continued to work on their food. It seemed Pani Frania wasn't going to chew and converse at the same time.

Frania thanked them again when she pushed the plate away, then, seeing they had finished, too, she stacked everyone's plates and took them to the *Plates Return* window. Once back, she sat down, took a drink out of the water glass, and whispered, "There is an ubek in town."

"I know," Antek said. "We've seen him."

Frania stopped halfway through the sign of the cross. "Devil take him!" she hissed, then she covered her mouth with a palm of her right hand. Her cuticles had dried into fissures, in the middle of a summer. She certainly used these petite hands to work. A job, or everyday laundry and dishes? Either one could do it.

"I'm sorry," Frania said.

"No, no need to apologize."

"No, not for that. I don't have the money anymore." She must have seen Antek's face freeze because she continued: "I put it somewhere safer where they won't think to look."

Antek took a breath and exhaled. "Tell us more."

"I was a card-carrying, pin-on-lapel Solidarity member. Keeping the money at my place, with that . . . man on the loose, wouldn't have been safe. I did what seemed best. Please believe me."

Dorota reached for Frania's hand, and this time the older woman let herself be comforted. "We do, Pani Franiu. We do."

Antek squinted at his wife but decided to let it go. "How do we get to the money? I'm the treasurer. If it disappears. Well, I don't know, but I don't think it will go well for me."

"The last place they'll ever think to look. It's in the apartment of a local PZPR commissar."

"Kurwa," Antek said, and planted his face in his palm. "Fuck, what in the name of the fucking plague is this supposed to mean?"

Frania's sharp cheeks seemed to jut out further. "You will not speak to me this way."

"He will not," Dorota said, then punched him in the shoulder with a quick, knuckle-full jab. "Please forgive him. He's been under great pressure, and that ubek shot him not two weeks ago. Right in the belly, and he's still recovering. He still should know better."

"Mother of God. Shot?"

"Yes. One straight through the side. The other bullet grazed his calf. He's lucky his wife is a nurse. But next time I'll let his ass fall off from gangrene if he doesn't learn to behave like a civilized person."

"I haven't been shot in the ass." Antek corrected the record.

Frania looked from one face to the other, and after a few seconds Antek was forced to admit Dorota's approach worked. The woman's face relaxed.

"I work with her daughter. She has a good heart. The old witch doesn't know anything." When neither Dorota nor Antek spoke up, Frania continued: "I'll ask her to meet you. She's working the morning shift on Monday, and if you visit her early enough in the afternoon, the mother should still be at work. I'm going to make it fifteen hundred thirty hours." Pride entered Frania's voice in the end. "Here's the address." She slipped a hand in a pocket of her pants, then pushed a folded piece of paper across the tabletop toward Dorota.

Antek knew that if he'd said something, he'd have sputtered. Instead, he chose to withhold his opinion about this plan. Dorota patted Frania's hand after she'd palmed the paper and said, "Thank you. All this is so brave of you." Dorota let Frania's hand go and patted the table. "Time for us to go. You should stay a minute and leave after us."

Once they reached the bottom of the stairs, Dorota said, "Forget the bus, let's walk."

Antek nodded. A walk, no matter how sweaty sounded like a good idea. As he attempted to dispel his misgivings about the meeting they'd arranged, a slice of his mind continued to wonder whether Dorota would honor the rain check.

CHAPTER TWENTY-THREE

ON THE TRAIL

Sunday, July 11, 1982. Zygmuntowo.

Roman Stelmach couldn't remember the last time a summer cold laid him out like this. Rendered useless. It had hit like a bus and kept him pinned down for a few precious days. Waking up yesterday without a headache and a fever had surprised him, but he'd decided not to question his good fortune. It might not be too late.

Roman had spent much of the day yesterday at the local HQ going through files and drinking mineral water. Food still hadn't felt like a good idea. He'd lost track of Piekarski in Olsztyn, but it didn't mean he'd lost everything.

Enter the local Bezpieka files. One might think a small town wouldn't have many. That person would be an idiot. Where the good folks in the Middle Ages had turned in neighbors as witches, nowadays they reported "suspicious activity," "imperialist sympathizers," and "enemies of the Polish United Workers' Party." Labels abounded. Human nature persisted.

Today, Roman found himself at a desk with three stacks of files yet to be reviewed. He'd been drinking water but had added coffee to the repertoire and was beginning to feel brave enough to perhaps procure a real meal come mid-day. Most of the papers contained annoying and pointless garbage. Average men and women of the town informing on other mediocrities. Roman murmured a bit of thanks. Without everyday spite, his job would have been more difficult.

In some cases, things came up in more formal ways. Take this one, for instance. A Pan Marelski: subversive behavior, possible treason. Reported by a phone monitor. Arrested, jailed. No record of trial or prison. Stelmach smirked. He'd learned to read these tracks. Someone pulled some strings to get the fellow out. Curious, but beside the point. Roman tossed the file over to the done pile.

Solidarity came up in most reports, but he couldn't chase them all any more than the central committee could chase all eleven million Solidarity drones all throughout Poland. He could stop any two adults in the street, and one of them would have once been a union member, even if now they'd deny it like cursing, spitting Saint Peters.

Allegations of membership were irrelevant. He was looking for something else. He couldn't quite define it. He would know it when he saw it. The money was here somewhere—the dread in Grażyna Duńczyk's face made him certain—and in a town this isolated and small twenty thousand American should make more noise than twenty thousand honking geese if one knew how to listen.

One file after another, the remaining three stacks became one, and the last one then began to melt. Then the final file. He shut the cover. Whatever it was he needed, he hadn't seen it. Chewing on disappointment, he lifted the phone and told the secretary to refile all this trash.

Passing the woman in the hallway, he said, "I'll be back after dinner." Then, on impulse, he stopped. "Leave the Marelski file." Clearing his throat, he added: "And please pull the files on all the Party officers in the district. Make sure to include the commissioners."

* * *

The reception boy at the AFR had said *Albatros* was the best restaurant in town. Roman ordered a kotlet mielony with dill potatoes and red cabbage slaw and enjoyed every bite, but if this was the best this glorified clearing in the forest had to offer, he didn't think he'd be going anywhere else. This was serviceable; all the other places must be serving inedible crap.

While the food might have been unremarkable, his server was anything but. A stunning blonde with a strong, muscular body, she glided like a phantom, appearing to no more than skim the floor. Roman chewed the meat and feasted his eyes. So different from Bernadeta.

Bernadeta. Objectively, yes, attractive, if increasingly plump, Bernadeta no longer made his chest tighten and his ears catch fire. A mother of three children, two living. A wife to a father of three children, two living. Two children living because of the grief for the first.

The blonde had disappeared. Now, all Roman could see, clearly, was a bedroom upstairs. He'd painted it in rainbows and fluffy clouds. Eliza had just outgrown her crib and seemed lost in the middle of her big-girl bed. At three, she already spoke fluently, her Polish sophisticated and literary. So much so that Roman, over the last few months, had made her into a party trick. *Eliza, dear*, he'd say. *Recite a poem for the lieutenant.* For Comrade Secretary. For whomever. They'd then expect a few lame lines of rhyme. And Eliza would open her thin, pink lips and let flow some Różewicz, or even Szymborska, but Roman made sure she steered clear of Herbert. He would then turn to Bernadeta and meet her smiling eyes reflecting his pride.

That night, in her big-girl bed, Eliza was burning up.

She'd been fighting measles for a week. Now, she no longer coughed and rarely opened her eyes. The doctor left not an hour before. He'd grimaced and apologized. Nothing anyone can do. It's in God's hands. If she lives through the night, she'll likely survive.

And that night Roman Stelmach prayed for the first time since high school. He got on his knees and clasped his hands. He rested his forehead against the bed's mattress. He prayed, trying to ignore Bernadeta's weeping. Right then it was so easy to believe in God.

The prayer made him miss the last few minutes of Eliza's breath, and he'd never forgiven God for that.

Roman wiped his eyes with the napkin and, as he squeezed them to clear his view, he caught the blonde looking furtively away. He turned his eyes back to the remnant of his food: a wedge of the cutlet and a spoonful or two of the potatoes. He was tempted to push the plate away—he'd lost his appetite—but he made himself attend to the business of nutrition. His body needed it.

"Is everything in order?" A voice startled him, and Roman felt his anger rise but beat it down as soon as he realized the words came from the blond waitress.

"Yes. Fine."

The waitress swayed on her feet, seeming unable to decide between prying further and fleeing. She rubbed her hands together. Then took a deep breath. "I'm sorry. I couldn't help but notice. If there is anything I can do to help . . ." Her cheeks turned from cream to light pink.

Roman cleared his throat. "No," he said, then opened his mouth again to ask for the check. He closed it without speaking. The blonde hadn't moved. "Yes," he said. "How about a beer?" The woman flashed a smile and floated away.

Roman worked to empty his mind. The fewer thoughts the better. It's a truth he'd discovered years ago. The volume his brain spewed out was much easier to control than the nature and the quality of the emanations. When the thoughts threatened to overwhelm, Roman would focus his attention on a single point, somewhere in the very middle of his head, and feed all of his presence into it. Soon, no space remained for intruders as long as he kept up the mental pressure. It was work, but it beat the alternative, and Roman Stelmach had achieved excellence at it.

This time he let his mind hover just short of clear. He'd let himself remember Eliza's brown hair, freshly shampooed, not stuck into sweaty cords in a sickbed. He could see her thin lips, corners upturned in a smile. She had a plain oval face, but Roman had never held a shred of doubt he'd have no trouble killing the world for her.

Roman Stelmach squeezed his eyes shut, shook his head, and took in a breath. He pushed against the memory. His fists wrapped tight around the skirt of the white tablecloth. He sought out the waitress and raised his hand. When she glanced in his direction, he pointed at the empty beer bottle.

When the blonde returned with the next half-liter of lager and poured it into his mug, Roman lifted his face.

"What's your name?" he asked.

"Kalina. I'm sorry, I left my name tag at home."

"I'm Romek."

"Nice to—"

"Don't be fooled. I'm not nice." Roman took a long draw from his mug and watched the waitress blink. "I'm a son of a bitch. I could kill you like . . . ," he snapped his finders, "this."

The waitress swallowed. "Would you like your bill?" she said.

It sounded like the funniest thing Roman had ever heard. "A bill!" He giggled until he had trouble breathing. "Sorry, a bad joke. Just a bad joke." He worked hard to get the giggles under control. Kalina's tan face had grown gray, and her chest heaved. Roman ran his eyes over her figure in appreciation. "Yes, a bill."

When Kalina had brought him the green, hand-written bill, Roman took his time counting out the banknotes. "This was great. I will come back," he said, and enjoyed the blanching of fear in the woman's face.

***

Roman hadn't planned on having a tall one with dinner, let alone two, and as he made his way out of the restaurant, the world a bit abuzz, he wondered whether he should call it a day early. Go to the hotel. Sleep it off.

Nah. Might as well sober up while doing something useful.

Walking into the HQ, he winked at the secretary. She responded with a grimace Roman chose to interpret as a smile. "The files ready?"

The secretary nodded.

The stack was about the size Roman had expected. Twelve files. Plus Marelski's, sitting to the side all alone. Stelmach sat down and pushed that file even further back. Instead, he took one from the top of the pile. Name, position. Blah, blah, blah. The interesting details were to be found at the end. Buys and sells dollars and deutschmarks on the side. Useful, but there wasn't a person living who hadn't committed that crime.

Halfway through the pile, Roman grew bored and angry. Such small people. Such small imaginations. He gritted his teeth and forced himself to keep going.

The first glance at the next file startled Roman. Last name: Sokołowska. Hadn't he just seen it somewhere? He chewed his lip, cursing the buzzing in his brain. When nothing came, he rose and walked out of the room toward the secretary's desk.

"I'll buy you a whole pack if you let me bum one cigarette now," he said.

The woman sighed. Then she pulled the white paper pack of *Sportowe* out of her purse, advanced one bleached tube half a centimeter, and offered it to Roman. The secretary pulled out her lighter, and Roman leaned over to let her light the cigarette.

Roman walked back and closed the door to the office. He smoked, enjoying a different kind of buzz, coughed, spat, then kept the next cloud of smoke in his lungs as long as he could manage. He hadn't had a cigarette in years and now wondered why. Bernadeta had harped that they were unhealthy for the kids. Well, dammit, memento mori. Carpe diem and shit.

It took only a few moments for the nicotine to wash away the alcohol's bluntness. His brain buzzed the way it should. Sokołowska. Roman studied the rest of the file. The Committee accountant and all-around money woman. Skimming no more than expected. One child, a grown daughter Emilia. Divorced, ex-husband caught up in Libya by martial law while working in an oil field.

Roman could feel the epiphany like a stubborn zit. It was just there but refused to pop. He put Sokołowska's file on top of Marelski's.

"Fuck!" He'd now gone through all of them and nothing.

Roman slid the Marelski file from under Sokołowska's. He opened the covers. Ratted out by a phone operator. "Fuck," he whispered now, slowly, a grin coming over his face. Black on white, the letters spelled Emilia Sokołowska. But of course. Someone had let the man go, probably to spite Sokołowska. Or might it have been the mother herself? The sense of guilt did strange things to people. Limited, small-town people.

And the phone monitors. He cursed himself for an idiot for not thinking about interviewing all the phone operators. Then Roman decided to give himself a pass on account of his illness. Beating himself up wasn't going to solve anything.

This was no twenty thousand dollars; it was a thread, the only one in evidence, and Roman was going to pull on it. He would give it a good yank tomorrow.

Roman Stelmach left the HQ with Sokołowska's address in his pocket. He already knew where the telephone station was.

CHAPTER TWENTY-FOUR

THE PLAN

Sunday, July 11, 1982. Zygmuntowo.

On Sunday, Emilia rose, cleaned up and left for the morning shift at the regular time. No one needed to know that she'd taken the day off. And it wouldn't have happened if not for Frania. When Emilia broached the topic with her shift chief during break on Saturday, the woman took her on a guilt trip with stops at Responsibility, Maturity, and Collectivism, and at the end shut her down cold.

"I can find cover," Frania had then said from behind them, and Emilia saw the old witch was as startled by Frania Nowak's initiative as she was herself. Sure enough, Frania had produced not one but two names for her by the shift's end. Emilia wondered in the moment what favors the woman had called in to swing that, gave her a smile of thanks, but then reminded herself to curb the gratitude—what Frania had done hardly compared in scale to what she was doing for the woman—and pictured the wad of green bills underneath her bathtub. Gratitude had fled entirely after Frania passed her a note later in the shift, and Emilia learned she would have visitors on Monday at half past three.

At eight in the morning on Sunday, instead of sitting in a telephone station or church pew, Emilia sat behind the wheel of an off-white maluch. The tinny Fiat had two doors and, by the sound of it, a rusty coffee grinder for a transmission. It protested the first gear most painfully but didn't seem happy about the second, the third, or the fourth, either. Not that Emilia had a chance to get up to the fourth more than once or twice in the city streets.

After Emilia parked and locked the car, she walked up to Agata's front door. Agata unlocked on the first knock. Peering up at Emilia, her eyes glistened amber brown from behind red bars of broken veins. The dark circling them didn't come from mascara. Her lips were folded back between her teeth, and it made them look just about the regular size for anyone else.

"Rough night?" Emilia asked in lieu of a hello.

As Agata nodded and moved aside to let her in, Emilia realized she'd slept as well as she'd ever had. It felt wrong now, somehow. Aberrant. Thinking about it made her stomach tighten. *I'm turning into Kalina.*

"A beer?" Agata said.

"Jesus. It's breakfast time. How about tea?"

"Breakfast beer."

Emilia exhaled and sat down on the floor, folding her legs. "Fine. If it's breakfast beer. But not a lot."

"Just enough for courage."

"And put water on for tea, too, if you'd be so kind."

After a thumbs-up, Agata disappeared into the kitchen.

It took longer than necessary for a couple of beers, and when Agata reemerged, Emilia understood why. The woman held the beer bottles wedged against her ribcage, and each of her hands supported a plate, one filled with open-face sandwiches, the other laden with pieces of cake.

"Help."

Emilia rose to peel the bottles and plates off Agata. She placed the beer and the food on the coffee table one item at a time.

"I don't know how Kalina does this. Full respect," Agata said, once free to join Emilia on the floor.

"You learn—"

"Wait." Agata scrambled back to her feet. "We need some paper and pens."

"Is it safe?"

"We'll shred it. Or burn it." When she returned, she dropped a few loose sheets down next to the food and handed Emilia a pencil but held onto a couple of sheets already covered with scribbles. "All out of pens. Let's eat first." At this, she drained half of her beer.

One sandwich down, Agata licked her fingers and flattened a page. "I've made some notes."

Emilia took another bite.

"I've got a bucket of pig's blood in the fridge," Agata said.

Emilia swallowed and put the half-eaten sandwich down on the plate's edge. She wiped her lips with the side of her palm. Her stomach rumbled, but the hunger had suddenly fled. Emilia remembered perfectly well what she and Agata had discussed. She nodded. Trying to make Agata stop would have been futile. The woman was always prepared. Enough canned meat stashed to last a deluge. Always a spare case of beer in the closet. A condom on her person at all times. And the need to chew on every detail of any plan more times than a cow. No matter how stupid it was. But this plan wasn't stupid.

Crazy. Probably suicidal. But not stupid. They'd get Zalewski drunk. Back in the shed in his garden plot, the blood and just enough torn underwear would make a convincing crime scene. Emilia had seen Agata rehearse her anonymous phone call to the Milicja: two kidnapped, one murdered. She was forced to help dump the body in a lake, taken advantage of, then escaped once the brute had drunk too much. Simple and not too far-fetched; everyone still remembered the Trojanowski gang that murdered half a dozen people around Zygmuntowo five years back.

Agata paused, then said, "Please. Would you please pay attention?"

"I know," Emilia said. "It's just that talking about this makes me nauseous."

"You'll feel worse if we fuck up." Agata focused her eyes back on the page. "I called Zalewski at work yesterday. The whoreson will meet me. Us. By the canal." Agata kept her eyes steady on the paper. "I took a bath after," she added.

It took work for Agata to convince Emilia that she could keep her cool. That the man would believe what he wanted to believe.

That the girl he'd raped couldn't get him out of her head.

Emilia knew that at least was true. She crawled over on all fours and put her arms around the other woman. Agata's face pressed into the nook of Emilia's neck, and her eyelashes smearing warm, salty water on her skin gave her the saddest tickle in the world.

Agata cleared her throat and pushed away. She sniffed. "Let's make this count," she said. Then she read the next item on the agenda. By noon, Emilia was as well drilled as a French legionnaire, but none of that helped unclench her stomach.

CHAPTER TWENTY-FIVE

THE RENDEZ-VOUS

Sunday, July 11, 1982. Zygmuntowo.

The pinnacle of the 19th-century civil engineering and a boon to the local economy at the time, the Zygmuntowo Canal had grown obsolete. Under czarist Russian rule, it connected the Wisła and the Niemen through their tributaries. Now, under Soviet control, it was a waterway to nowhere, as the Belorussian part was never repaired after the last war's bombing. Besides, the 20th century belonged to trains. Only tourists with too much money and time bothered with river ships.

On its Wisła-facing end, the canal meandered through the Baraki district and out of town, through woods and fields, with a hard-packed dirt road running alongside it. Garden plots granted to loyal citizens by the voivodeship PZPR committee on their bribes' merits lay a few kilometers down the road and took advantage of the canal water for irrigation. The canal's overgrown bank offered shelter to swans seeking romance, *homo sapiens* couples seeking privacy, and parties seeking peace and fresh air in which to drink their liquor.

A quarter to two in the afternoon, Emilia stopped the maluch about a kilometer past the last of the gardens. The stand of willows, offering them shade, would serve as a landmark. Agata clutched one of the two bottles of vodka she'd bought. As closely as she'd held it, the stuff was probably body temperature now. Emilia didn't care for vodka. She didn't see the appeal.

Emilia checked inside her bag. More vodka, in case. Paper plates. Three shot glasses. A bottle of carbonated water. A jar of pickles. Sliced smoked pork belly. Agata had procured the latter. She claimed nothing went as well with vodka as pork and pickles. She would know.

"Agata, would you grab the blanket, please?"

Agata started, then nodded, and scrabbled out. She leaned over the headrest and snatched the cotton blanket from the back seat with her left hand. Her right held the bottle like a Molotov cocktail. Most of this had been her plan, and now she was acting like a ghost. Emilia pinched her lip between her teeth. Then she took a deep breath, then another.

"Do you want to leave? We don't have to do this. He'll feel like an idiot anyway if we're not here when he shows up."

Agata shook her head. "Don't forget to lock the car," she said. With that, she strode across the grassy knoll between the dirt road and the bushes, and soon disappeared in the vegetation.

Emilia locked the car and followed. From a distance, the growth had appeared wild, but up close she could see a narrow path. She held her arm in front to deflect the branches and wound a few meters along the path to the clearing on the other side which almost immediately started to slope down toward the water. If she slipped and rolled here, she would end up wet. Agata had spread the blanket a few steps to the side, high enough up the bank so that it covered enough of the flat to create a table on which she'd put the half-liter of *Wyborowa* vodka. Emilia knelt next to Agata and emptied out her bag, except for the spare bottle. She stuffed the bag under the nearest bush.

Emilia sat on the blanket, pulled her knees up to her chest, and trained her eyes on the woods on the other side. There was a dirt road there somewhere, too, but it had become so overgrown, that few used it now. Most likely, soon it would become more forest. Despite the recent rain, the green of the leaves reminded her most of the sickly and dry hue of an American dollar. A single soaker wasn't enough to break the drought. Funny how something so powerful, the dollar, could be so drab. If she'd had enough dollars to spend, she wouldn't be sitting here, next to Agata and vodka, waiting for old Zalewski by the canal. The right hands would get enough so that soon she and Kalina would have passports and visas. She glanced toward Agata—also curled up, resting her chin on her knees—and felt a prickling of guilt.

But Agata would be fine, no matter what. She always was.

"I know they have their own problems, but now I would trade places with a squirrel," Agata said without lifting her head.

Emilia reached out and squeezed Agata's hand. "Let's leave," she said. "Let's go. Forget about this. This is crazy."

Agata squeezed back but shook her head. And then both of their heads jerked in a quarter-swivel when a sudden clatter of a large animal struggling, pushing, breaking branches, came from the path through the bushes.

Agata's squeeze turned into a death grip before she released Emilia's hand and rose to her feet. Emilia scrambled up, too. She shuffled back a couple of steps. The women stood shoulder-to-shoulder, Agata upslope, and thanks to it at least of a height now with Emilia. When she looked over, Emilia found Agata's face blank, her eyes closed.

An arm stuck out of the twigs and the leaves, and then the monstrous birth canal produced a giant man, one dripping with sweat and holding his palm against his cheek. As soon as he'd noticed them, Zalewski planted his feet and slid a few centimeters before he recovered his balance.

"Fuck," he said, no more emotion in the voice than in the murky water below them. "What the fuck is she doing here?" He pointed his finger, the tip of which had turned purple—perhaps he'd caught it in a door or smashed it with a hammer—and waived it at Emilia. "Are you girlies playing games?"

"No games," Agata said. If Emilia hadn't known better, she would have believed the smile the other woman manufactured. Agata stepped over to the man and put her palm on his elbow. "Please. Sit." She patted him like a pet. "We have smoked pork," she added.

Zalewski blinked but let himself be led. Emilia backed off and perched on her haunches on one of the blanket's top corners. Agata shepherded Zalewski to its center and patted his arm again, and he lowered himself with a grunt. Agata sat on the other top corner.

Zalewski formed a smile of his own. "I could grab each of you by the neck and drown you both in this canal like kittens."

"I let it slip to Emilia that you and I would be meeting," Agata said, as if the man hadn't just threatened murder. "She asked to come along. To apologize."

Emilia couldn't help a sudden shake before she caught herself. "Yes, apologize," she said, and did her best to stretch her lips into what she hoped looked like a smile.

"You should do more than apologize. Stealing a father's own daughter. It's against God. A sin!"

"I'll speak with her about going back. I think she's almost ready."

Agata picked up the vodka bottle and gave the cap a twist. "Let's be friendly," she said and fixed the red bikini strap running parallel to one of her tanktop's shoulder straps. Zalewski swallowed, while Agata began to pour. She passed the glasses around. "To peace and friendship?" she suggested.

Zalewski and Agata knocked their shots back and both reached for pickles. "To peace," Emilia murmured and drank her vodka. She coughed at the sudden burn and chased it down with sparkling water and pork.

"You need more experience." Zalewski nodded in her direction.

"I don't often drink vodka. I prefer beer."

"You'll drink. You owe me." He pulled out a pack of cigarettes and lit one before putting it away.

"Do you mind sharing a smoke?" Agata said.

"Have this one." He pulled the white tube out from between his lips, flipped the cigarette around, planted it filter-first in Agata's mouth, and she made no protest. Emilia reached for a pickle and chewed it in hope that the sour would push back the growing nausea.

Zalewski lit another cigarette. He puffed and studied the canal's other bank. The breeze carried the smoke away from his eyes and into Emilia's. She blinked and cleared her throat, then again as much as she needed to, but made no attempt to remove herself from the smoke's path.

Zalewski had always been the mountain of a man he was now, as far back as her memory reached. He'd always been balding. Always sweaty. His eyes had always been crisscrossed by the lattice of broken veins. Always the malevolence in the smirk of his swollen lips.

The man sighed. "Pour another round."

Emilia palmed her shot glass as soon as it was full and held it by her thigh while Zalewski peered into his, as if divining a future or looking for a bug. Emilia let the glass's contents dribble into the grass and hoped Agata had found a way to do the same, as they had planned.

"To fathers," said Zalewski, and raised his glass.

Agata lifted hers. It was full. Then she poured the liquid down her throat.

Emilia pretended to swallow. The smell, like gasoline mixed with vinegar, made her throat constrict and she didn't need to pretend when a cough racked her chest.

Zalewski shook his head and tsked. "Another round!" he called out.

"Help yourself to some food," Agata said instead of uncapping the bottle.

Zalewski's arm shot out and he wrapped his fingers half the way up Agata's thigh. He squeezed and pushed the fabric of her skirt into the muscle. All of Agata's air seemed to escape her chest too quickly for a scream. Instead of trying to claw at the man's skin, to resist, she twisted her torso and whimpered. A second later, Zalewski let go, and Agata's breath came back in heaves just as tears began to pour down her cheeks.

Emilia hadn't moved. She cursed herself for not bringing a knife but flushed as much from anger as shame as soon as the thought had crossed her mind. Bullshit. Knife or no knife, she would have been as much of a coward.

"Please," she said, willing herself to unfreeze. "I will pour." She took the bottle which had become wedged between Agata's wrist and the ground, unscrewed the cap, righted the other woman's glass, and poured the round.

Zalewski knocked his back and presented the empty glass. Emilia poured. He winked. "Na zdrowie," he said.

With the man's eyes on her, Emilia left the bottle on the ground, raised her glass and poured the alcohol down her throat.

It came right back up. She scrambled the two meters down the bank and threw up into the green water. She lost the capacity for thought as her chest continued to contract against her stomach; she felt particles on her tongue and tasted acid. Her mind had fled into the well beneath her ribcage. She puked long enough that night should have fallen by the time the heaves dried up, but when she felt it was safe to wipe her lips with the back of her hand and turned around, the mid-afternoon sun hadn't moved, and Zalewski sat on the blanket, his arm around Agata, his mouth split by a grin.

"How about some cold cuts? Must be hungry, now." The corners of his mouth turned down, making the grin into a sneer. He squeezed Agata and then let her go with a slight nudge. "Pour another round, little muff."

Emilia watched Agata hunt down the glasses in the grass and retrieve the bottle which was still somehow standing upright. *How could anything be upright?* Agata poured and handed the full glasses to Zalewski and Emilia.

The man sniffed at the glass and paused. When he finally moved, he raised the glass, and said, "This one is to atonement and forgiveness." Then he turned and fixed Emilia with his bloodshot eyes. "You atone. And I may forgive you. Drink." Once Agata and Emilia had, Zalewski downed his shot. Throughout, he kept staring at Emilia. "Take your top off."

Agata lifted her tanktop over her head. "Let me," she said.

Zalewski seemed not to notice and didn't look away from Emilia. "You owe me," he said. "Take it off."

Emilia couldn't have complied had she wanted to. Her arms had frozen, the stiffness extended to her chest, to her heart. Something squeezed her lungs hard enough to pop them like a water balloon. No breath came.

Zalewski's arm pushed her back into the grass. His other arm grabbed her tee-shirt and tugged. Something ripped; it might have been fabric; it might have been her skin. The man's hand then dove beneath the waist of her skirt and pulled.

And then all of Zalewski's weight fell on her. If Emilia hadn't already lost her breath, she would have now. Warm, dark liquid filled her eyes. It stung.

The timeless pain in her chest promised never-ending agony. *Is this purgatory?* She should have blacked out. She dared not open her eyes, but Emilia's neurons continued to fire and force-feed her consciousness.

When she gasped and took a breath, it came as a surprise. She still couldn't see, her chest still felt bound, but the weight on top of her disappeared. Greed for air overtook her. She wanted to drink in all the oxygen everywhere and even that didn't feel like enough.

"Slow down!"

Agata's voice. But somehow both huskier and higher pitched. Emilia counted out seconds. Seven. Breathe out.

Breathe in. Keep counting.

She ran a forearm across her mouth. Her face.

"I can't see."

Something soft mopped against her eyelids. Soft, but it pushed hard enough to make her eyes conjure grayscale clouds, as if she'd beheld a Hades landscape: black earth, gray emptiness above it, and ghosts floating throughout.

When the soft material became wet, and thus harder, Emilia accepted it and focused on air instead. The heart spasms of a panic attack had now subsided, but she kept counting and thinking about her breathing.

"Open your eyes," Agata said, her voice stronger now.

She did and closed them back up immediately. The light burned and made her eyes add tears to the water Agata had used. Emilia turned, then rose on all fours, her face hanging toward the ground. She opened her eyes again, and this time was able to resist the urge to close them. In seconds, she made out the blades of grass. Someone had splashed brick-red paint all around. Emilia tasted iron. Glanced sideways.

A ribbon of red led to a large body resting on the edge of the water. Zalewski's right foot hung above the murk, and his arms, splayed to both sides, must have arrested his roll just as he was about to plunge in. Emilia couldn't see his face. The man's nose pointed into the ground.

Emilia made herself count. Breathe in. Wait. Breathe out. She looked away from the body and fixed her eyes on Agata instead. The other woman's chest heaved hard enough for a panic attack, too. "Slow down," Emilia said.

"It didn't even break." Agata nudged her chin to the left. Emilia made her eyes follow. The other bottle of vodka rested on its side in the underbrush like a drunk who'd lost his way home overnight. "When you can," Agata said, "go and start the car."

Emilia's mind failed to understand, but her head shook "no" of its own accord.

Instead of responding aloud, Emilia crawled toward Zalewski's body, Kalina's father's body. She extended an arm, but her hand stopped a few centimeters away from the striped polo shirt. This bulk had rested on her only a few minutes earlier. Emilia remembered the ripping sound and looked down. Her shirt had split along the left seam half the way up. She lifted it. Scratches she hadn't felt earlier bloomed with tiny droplets of blood. As if the seeing had made them real, their sting made her next breath stutter before she forced it to steadiness.

When she returned her eyes to Zalewski, his nose no longer pushed itself into the ground. Instead, the face rested at an angle. His chest lifted with a shallow breath. "He's not dead," she said.

"We should push him off before he comes to," Agata said.

Emilia's head shook. Agata made no attempt to make her words a fact; she continued to sit on the blanket, her knees pulled up to her chin, without a care for what the pose revealed.

"If we pull together, we can get him into the car," Emilia said.

Agata blinked. Then she rose, stepped down and grabbed Zalewski's right arm. Emilia said nothing and took the left. Tugging backwards, the women leaned away from the weight, making their legs do the work. Emilia was about to give up when the tension broke, and the body moved a few centimeters. Coordination was the trick. "On three," she said, and then gave the count. A few centimeters at a time, they got the man up the slope and onto the flat next to the path through the vegetation.

Emilia expected the job to become more difficult among the bushes, but she found it easier. Somehow, the underbrush lessened the tension, and the body slid like a poorly oiled sleigh. As soon as her head broke the brush line, Emilia glanced both ways. No one.

She let Zalewski's arm drop, trotted over to the maluch, unlocked it, and ran back. She picked the man's arm back up. "We're not stopping until we get him in there," she said and heard no protest.

A stop ended up being necessary. No matter how hard they tried, Emilia and Agata couldn't get Zalewski's torso into the car. Only once Agata suggested they pull him in legs-first and cram the torso folded on top did their attempts eventually succeed.

Sweat ran down Emilia's back, but she didn't dare to stop. She took a moment to drop the blanket over Zalewski in the back seat, then unfolded the coupe's driver's seat back, while Agata perched sideways across from her, the woman's eyes on the bulk in the back, her hand grasping the spare vodka bottle by its neck.

Most garden plots consisted of a shed and a few square meters of arable land, all cut up by wire fencing. But some were more ambitious. The plot size was standard, and sheds could only grow so much, but some functioned as miniature vacation homes, complete with kitchens and TV antennas. Kalina's father's was one such.

Emilia started driving as soon as she'd shut the door, and Agata asked no questions. It took a minute for Emilia to realize she'd set the course for the Zalewski family plot. Exactly as their initial plan assumed. But things hadn't gone exactly to plan, had they? The plan stipulated ferrying a man who'd passed out drunk, or near to it, not one bleeding from the scalp.

"Check his pockets," Emilia said. When Agata made no move, she spoke up louder, "Check his pockets. For the keys."

"I might have killed him."

"He was still breathing last I saw."

"What if I had killed him?"

"Check his pockets."

Agata reached out with the air of a woman using her bare palm to swat a wasp. Sooner than Emilia had expected, Agata sat back on her haunches, a key ring jingling in her fingers.

"He's still breathing," Agata said.

Emilia nodded and stole a sideways glance. Tears stood out on Agata's face and dripped off her chin. Emilia felt anger rise up her spine like a shiver. "Don't fall apart now," she said. "This was your idea."

Silence answered her for half a kilometer, while she kept her eyes on the dust of the road.

"When did you last go to church?" Agata eventually spoke up.

"Before last December. Before people started looking at me like I'd drowned their kittens."

"I go most Sundays. And to confession before Easter and Christmas."

"I know. You're a decent woman."

Silence fell again.

"I think I am going to hell," Agata said.

"You did nothing wrong. You were defending me."

"I was disappointed he was still breathing. I want this son of a bitch dead."

It was Emilia's turn now to say nothing. She had no idea how she felt. Her heart kept thudding hard enough from adrenaline to keep her going. She knew little beyond that. There was no plan accounting for a half-dead Zalewski. For Kalina's father and rapist who might possibly come to any minute, soberish and murderous. Or die, leaving behind a gigantic piece of evidence and guilt. And an impossible conversation with Kalina.

"Fuck."

"What?"

"Fuck! Fuck! Fuck! Son of a whore! Fuck!" Toward the end, Emilia's scream became a whine. At this moment, she would have paid twenty thousand dollars to trade places with a squirrel.

The garden plot came into view. Emilia knew that Zalewski loved his refuge most of all. Among dozens of sheds, his was one of the two or three with a chimney. The chain-link fence had been lined with a thick row of manicured bushes, rising about a meter tall. They fell short of granting the plot privacy, though. That was bad. On the plus side, Zalewski had installed a gate wide enough for a car, since, according to Kalina, he'd always planned to one day purchase a maluch of his own.

Emilia had Agata unlock and throw open the gate, and she pulled the car into the grassy spot next to the shed. When she turned the car off and silence fell between the women, Emilia forced her thoughts into a straight line. A short one. She would worry about the future once they'd gotten the man into the shed unseen.

***

The maluch ought to have had a periscope. Emilia sat with the windows down and listened to birds and a distant hum of machines, likely cars and tractors. She couldn't hear conversations, but a song—wafting in from afar, but strong enough to sound like Czesław Niemen's hippie falsetto—proved that they weren't entirely alone. She wished she could survey the landscape like a submariner or, better yet, a sparrow, and know for certain if any eyes were likely to turn in their direction.

Agata closed the gate, walked over, and pulled the passenger-side door open. She nudged a leg in the back seat. And nothing happened. "Still warm. Let's pull him inside," she said.

"What if someone sees?"

"We'll pull him by the shoulders this time. It'll look like we're doing him a favor."

"Right," Emilia said, "but what if there is an investigation and the Milicja ask them?"

"Let's worry about it one step at a time."

Emilia nodded. Yes, she could get on board with that. One step, one problem solved at a time. Oh, God, what will Kalina say? She might not care that they'd tried to frame her father for murder. On the other hand, she might, very much. Either way, she'll most definitely be pissed off about having been kept in the dark about Agata's plan. *No, you coward, our plan.* Agata might have worked out the details, but it was Emilia's idea, wasn't it?

At least the usual steel seemed to have returned into Agata's back, and Emilia sighed with relief. For the past few minutes, she had felt her mind disassembling, the connections between the now and the future thinning down and disappearing. Just as the body in the back seat rested in the limbo between the living and the dead, she floated in the unknown, the space between plans and fate, and the feeling, as if falling from a tree, made her stomach clench with vertigo.

Agata unlocked the shed's door, solid as any front door, shielded by a corrugated awning, and with "K + M + B" written across the top with chalk still left up from Epiphany months before. Emilia and her mother hadn't chalked their door in years. The carolers had thinned to a trickle after Mother had taken the Party job, and then vanished completely. Mother didn't seem to mind.

Emilia stared at the chalking. What could Epiphany mean to old Zalewski, with carolers unlikely to visit remote garden plots? No one really lived here. Definitely not in January, when the cold made trees crack, and no one bothered to clear the snow off of unpaved roads. *"Kacper + Melchior + Baltazar,"* the three wise men come to see the Lord in the manger. Emilia felt none the wiser for having seen the chalk.

Agata pulled the door open. Then she dropped the keys into her skirt's pocket and rounded the car.

Emilia took a breath. "Ready?"

They tilted the front car seats to gain access to the rear. Then Agata began to pull Zalewski's arms while Emilia did her best to lift the bulk off the seat to break the friction. She couldn't say how long it took, but by the time Zalewski's chest protruded out of the car, sweat dripped from her temples. Emilia took one arm while Agata retained her grasp on the other. They heaved.

Once they got Zalewski out to about his stomach, Emilia and Agata wrapped each of his arms around their shoulders—Emilia the right and Agata the left—and used their thighs to push. By no means was this easy, but being able to push off made Emilia feel that she was no longer about to get a hernia. Once Zalewski's hips and ass squeezed out, the rest of him plopped out like an afterbirth.

Emilia and Agata dragged the body around the car—damn her poor planning—and then into the building. They both staggered as soon as they'd let it drop stomach down to the floor inside. Agata rushed to shut the door. Then she flipped on the light—Zalewski's shed had a chandelier—and slid the window curtains closed.

Agata crouched next to the man and put her fingers to his neck. Some of the tension seemed to melt out of her, and she ran her hands over Zalewski's head, neck and shoulders.

She rose. "Still alive. And the bleeding has stopped."

"What now?"

Agata glanced around, found a bench by one of the walls, and dropped on it like a swan after a heart attack. "I don't know."

Agata seemed to have found something riveting in her toes and all Emilia could see was the top of her friend's head. The cowlick she always fought. And the gray hair, or two, no one ever mentioned, but which disappeared for a few weeks before new ones sprung up. For all her success with men, Agata wasn't one to sit around hair salons or spend a fortune on makeup. She did what she did out of who she was.

Emilia bumped her fists against each other and took a few moments to breathe. Now, in safety, whether real or imagined, she could take the time to study Zalewski. His chest moved with each inspiration and expiration. His hair had clumped with blood and dirt. The path from the door to where he rested appeared clean. He was out, but for how long?

"Where is the vodka?" Emilia asked.

"What?"

"The other bottle."

"In the car. What for?"

Emilia didn't answer. She sneaked out of the door, making sure to open it no wider than necessary, and returned with the other half-liter. She latched the shed door behind her. "It was a good plan," she said.

"What?"

"We can still get him drunk. If he's drunk enough, nobody's going to believe anything he says."

Agata nodded. Almost smiled. Then her lips turned back down. "He can't swallow. You'll drown him. Or just waste the vodka."

Emilia considered it and was forced to admit Agata had a point. She turned round to scan the space. Zalewski kept the place neat. One half of the shed contained a sofa, not large, but large enough for the man to sleep on if he curled up. There was a sink with the drain directed out through a hole, but with no faucets. A pail of water sat on a table next to the sink, and next to the pail rested an electric range with two cooking spirals.

On the other side of the body sprawled on the floor, the man had arranged gardening tools. A shovel, a spade, pitchforks, and a dozen other implements each had its own nook or hook, its own rightful place. Each glistened, no dirt, no rust. If Emilia had in that moment found herself concerned with her looks, she could have fixed her hair using one of the small, chromed hand spades for a mirror. She'd hoped to find a length of hose, any hose, but all that Zalewski's shed offered was a watering can. She'd pictured shoving a hose down the man's gullet and pouring the vodka down. Once she'd given up the search, her stomach suspended between vomiting from the growing panic and the relief at not having to touch more of the man than she'd already had to, she turned and discovered that Agata had undone Zalewski's belt, his zipper, and was pulling his pants back.

"Jesus!" Emilia screamed before she could clamp her hand over her mouth.

"Pull down on the other side."

Emilia crouched down, faced with half of the man's hairy ass continuing to wax ever greater as Agata pulled on the fabric.

"It's got caught! Do something," Agata said.

Tugging at Zalewski's pants on her side seemed easier than finding the right questions.

The fabric gave before whatever snagged it, and Agata and Emilia pulled the man's pants down to just above his knees. "Enough," Agata said. "Hope this works."

Agata rose and stretched her back. Then she picked up the vodka bottle, unscrewed the cap and dropped it to the floor. She stared at the neck of the bottle long enough for a prayer, put the vodka back down on the floor and turned to the toolshed side of the room. Once she located something small—a pair of wire snips, Emilia saw once Agata turned back around—she performed a brief operation after which the metal band which had held the bottle cap, its top edge jagged, fell to the floor.

The woman held the bottle of vodka and stared at old Zalewski's pale ass. Suddenly things fell into place for Emilia. When Agata said, "Spread his ass apart. I don't want to spill too much," Emilia's mind scrambled for a way out, but her hands didn't hesitate. She did as Agata asked but kept her eyes on the wall. One thing she didn't have to do was look.

"Alright, you can let go," said Agata, and got back up with a grunt. Emilia still didn't look. Instead, she drew a few ladles of water out of the pail and washed her hands over the sink. She hesitated for a second, then used Zalewski's dark-smudged bar of soap and washed her hands again.

"Can't see if it's still going down," Agata said, and Emilia turned around.

Zalewski lay on his stomach with a bottle of vodka sticking out of his asshole.

Emilia swallowed. "Much spilled?"

Agata shook her head. "A few drops. I jammed it in there fast."

To Emilia's eyes, the bottle still seemed three quarters full. She swallowed whatever was coming up her esophagus again, walked around the body and picked up the shiny hand spade. She rested back on her haunches next to Zalewski's ass cheeks and held the edge of the spade at the level of the vodka's meniscus.

In another minute or two, she could be certain that the liquid had fallen a couple of millimeters.

"Ha!" was all that Agata said to that.

Emilia put the tool away and stood next to her friend. "How long do we wait?"

Agata shrugged. "When it's all gone down?"

After another hour of staring at Zalewski's ass, when about a quarter of the vodka still remained, Agata rose off the sofa on which they had perched. "This has got to be enough."

Emilia could offer no expert opinion, but the prospect of being able to leave helped make a strong argument in favor. "It must," she said.

Agata plucked the bottle out of Zalewski's butt hole, poured the rest down the sink and threw the glass in the trash. Then she returned to Zalewski, got on her knees and said, "Get off your ass. I can't do this alone."

"Let's roll him over?"

"No," Agata said. "Don't want to waste any of the vodka in there."

Emilia sighed but got up.

Pulling the pants back up proved more difficult than tugging them off had. After each had broken a sweat, the women finally fell into a rhythm: they rocked Zalewski on his long axis, and with each high tide made a centimeter or so of progress. When the time came to button and zip up, their seesaw method failed Agata and Emilia. It created enough clearance around the zipper for a finger, but not for long enough, and they likely wouldn't have been able to maneuver freely enough.

Emilia let go and sat back. "This is good enough."

Agata settled down for a break on her side of Zalewski. "It'll look suspicious."

"There is already a tear. And people do all kinds of weird stuff when they're drunk."

"Maybe," Agata said. "But why take the risk?"

"Roll him over?"

"No, we already discussed it."

"We discussed nothing. You decided."

"I was right. Still am," Agata said, then unfolded up to her feet. She stretched, then stepped over to study the tools in the shed. When she picked up a shovel and a log, Emilia began to guess her friend's plan.

Indeed, Agata used the shovel as a lever while Emilia advanced the log under Zalewski's belly until Agata's smaller fist could fit comfortably between the floor and the man's zipper. With the pants secured, Agata and Emilia put the tools and the log away.

When they returned to the maluch and shut the doors, Emilia could still pick up Zalewski's musk. She'd have to detail the interior before taking the car back, even if the blanket had soaked up the blood. She twitched her nose all the way to downtown Zygmuntowo. There, in the dark, minutes before curfew, Agata fed a coin into the pay phone and made the call: the report as they had planned it, and, *no, I can't give you my name, not safe while the man still walks free.*

When Agata hung up and turned around, Emilia stepped forward and used her palm to wipe tears off her friend's cheeks.

CHAPTER TWENTY-SIX

THE QUESTION OF DROBINA

Monday, July 12, 1982. Zygmuntowo.

Zenon Drobina stopped by the Milicja headquarters after he'd failed to find the major everywhere else. Once he'd made up his mind, it felt right to tell Stelmach first. It's not that he wanted to talk to the man. But calling in his resignation, or sending a letter, would have felt like running away. Even after Zenon had decided to free himself, he still allowed Stelmach to dictate his fears and actions. Looking into the major's face to say *I quit* was going to sear Zenon's throat with stomach acid; he could already feel a touch of heartburn, but he imagined—hoped—that as soon as these words had left his lips he'd have changed his world into one in which a Zenon Drobina did not need to fear what a Roman Stelmach thought or intended to do. The pain of making the cut would dissolve in the relief of freedom.

Of course, he'd do it in public, among witnesses. He wasn't an idiot.

Stelmach hadn't been at the hotel nor at the beach, where he'd taken to strolling, and when Zenon arrived at the HQ, he marched straight to the office the major had commandeered. He stopped before the closed door. His rapping, once, twice, a third time, brought no response. He tried the doorknob to discover it had been locked.

Zenon shuffled back to the front desk and asked about his boss.

"He stormed out an hour ago. Like he was going to hurt some poor fuck," said a young receptionist. "How is it to work for him?"

Zenon would have schooled the private about proper respect up-rank, but the telephone rang, and the man picked up.

The receptionist grunted, snorted, then said, "No shit," at which point he stopped speaking for a good minute. When he spoke up, he asked the party on the other side to hold. "Lieutenant," he said, "you'd better take this."

Zenon pressed the receiver against his ear. He pursed his lips. Something kept him from saying anything for a couple more moments than felt comfortable. There would now be the before and the after this call, and he knew this for certain even if he couldn't say how.

Someone on the other end cleared her throat.

"Yes?" Zenon said.

"Is the major around?"

"This is lieutenant Drobina. I work with the major. Who is this? What's this about?"

Zenon wasn't certain that he'd heard the gnashing of teeth. "I've repeated myself three times. I'm sergeant Morawiec," the woman said. "A call came up through the ladder from dispatch. They referred it before sending out a car, and I think they did the right thing for once."

"Excuse me?"

"Got a call about a rape and a murder—"

"Understood, but what does that have to do with Major Stelmach? Or me? We . . . we don't get involved in local trouble. That's for the powiat Milicja to sort out."

"Last time we had a murder was a few years ago, and then we called for reinforcements and a detective right away. Since you're already here . . ."

"When did the call come in?"

"The switchboard got it around ten, right before shift change. They sent it up at about three in the morning. But then no one wanted to wake up the shift supervisor. Once he got in, he kicked it up to me. I got the notes a few minutes ago. I thought, all things considered, maybe the major would want to take the first look."

"Are you saying no one's been there, yet?"

"I thought best someone with experience handle it. Whoever's dead won't be in any rush. Look, I'm not even on duty today. This is eating into my beach time."

Drobina inhaled and forced himself not to raise his voice. He asked for the address. After that, he gave the receiver back to the receptionist and requisitioned a car.

* * *

In addition to the car, Zenon commandeered the private from the reception. He gave the young man a few minutes to find a replacement—a civilian woman from personnel in a leopard-print sun dress—and huffed out of the building, trusting the other man to follow.

"What's your name?" Zenon asked, once they stopped by the white Łada.

"Józefowicz."

"First?"

"Konrad."

"Right. Konrad, you're driving." Zenon rounded the vehicle to the passenger side and got in. Once Konrad put the key in the ignition, Zenon added: "Stop by *Albatros* for a few minutes first." Konrad shot him a glance but said nothing and pulled out of the lot. Perhaps there was a bit more depth to the youth than Zenon had thought.

At the restaurant, Zenon told Konrad to wait in the car and got his body up the stairs as fast as he could. At a few minutes after ten in the morning, *Albatros* wasn't open to customers yet, but the door was unlocked. Inside, he spied Kalina right away. When he saw that she'd noticed him, too, and watched her face contort in a grimace, he realized that for the first time she was now seeing him in a uniform. Before he could decide whether to press on or to leave, Kalina strode toward Zenon and stopped with her face a few centimeters away from his.

"Are you here to arrest me?" she hissed. "Wearing those rags."

"Was going to resign today. I swear. But then something came up. The major's missing, and we got a call about . . . well, bad stuff. Ugly. Have to check it out. But I needed to stop by and tell you. This is my last day in this uniform."

"Why?"

Zenon shrugged, and as soon as he'd done so, felt guilty about it. Was she asking why he'd decided to quit? Or why he'd felt the necessity to drop everything to tell her?

As for the first why, Zenon was still turning it around in his head. It felt right. It was right. He knew from the start that the role of an ubek was going to fit poorly. If anything, he should have never nodded along to everyone—Father, Stelmach, others—when they dictated what his life would be and what his conscience could bear.

As for the second why, Zenon was perfectly clear on the answer, but couldn't tell Kalina. She might not be into any men, including himself, but that only made things easier in a way. Before arriving in Zygmuntowo, Zenon Drobina had no lover and no friends. He hadn't found a lover. But he quickly grew to care about Kalina and thought she might care a little, too. A friend, then? With a bit more time? She needed not know that he couldn't stop thinking about her. But that she knew now that he could be a good man, would one day be one, made him feel better. In the end, Zenon said, "I just needed for you to know," nodded stiffly, and fled the restaurant.

Back in the Łada, he ordered the private to drive them to the address from the report with haste but no siren. A kilometer later, he told Konrad to slow down after the car slid sideways on gravel spilled on the asphalt.

"We could go faster with a siren," Konrad said.

"Element of surprise."

"But it's been hours since the call came in."

"The perpetrator could still be there," Zenon said and hoped his voice carried more authority than he felt.

The private pursed his lips and said nothing, keeping his eyes on the road. Zenon thought Konrad was about to argue again, but then the Łada turned off the pavement and onto the dirt road which would carry them to the destination, and the young man shut his mouth and seemed to use all his concentration to slalom between the potholes.

By the time Zenon began to see the telltale sheds and fences, Konrad had slowed down enough that Zenon thought even he could have walked faster. The potholes really weren't this bad. He would have complained, but then the young man pulled over to the side and killed the engine.

"Is this the address?" Zenon asked.

"I don't know. But I thought we'd look around on foot. To maintain the element of surprise, sir."

Zenon, a fat man who had been a fat kid, didn't have to be told when someone was having a bit of fun at his expense. This wasn't even subtle. He paused and considered ordering Konrad to start the damned car back up and get them where they were going. The temptation lasted a moment. Then, Zenon nodded and said, "Good thinking, private. Lead us."

The twitch that went through Konrad's jaw could have been guilt. Probably not. But it could have, and Zenon decided to accept it as the best payment he could get. He had never been fast, athletic, or handsome, but necessity forced him to hone other abilities. Making people feel rotten after they had been rotten to him had been one of those skills. He'd gotten good at it. But it never worked on Father. Or on Stelmach.

Zenon reminded the private to lock the car after he'd gotten a couple of paces down the road. Having thus put things in their proper order, he ordered Konrad to consult the report for the address one more time. It was the plot across the street. A little twitch went through the private's face again, and Zenon fake-yawned to hide a smile.

Konrad unclipped his holster's flap, pulled out his sidearm, checked the magazine and slid the safety to off. Zenon lost the desire to smile. He would have checked his gun, too, but hadn't thought to put it on his belt. Again. Despite the promises. It rested, clean and unloaded, in the hotel safe.

"Most likely, there is no one here, and the whole thing was some sort of a joke," Zenon said and padded his chest, as though a concealed piece were hiding behind the uniform's fabric.

"Who'd joke about a thing like this?"

"We're here to find out. Lead us, private."

The thick living fence, lining the chain link from the inside, wasn't tall but obscured enough that all Zenon could see of the garden plot was the upper part of the shed and the tops of two poles with an empty clothesline stretched between them. Konrad approached the gate and put his hand on the handle. Instead of pushing it open, he turned.

"You sure this is a good idea?" he said.

"Open the gate." This was not a good idea. What was he thinking? Responding to a report of rape and possible murder without a handgun and with a boy fresh out of school. But then lieutenant Zenon Drobina had never had a reason to respond to any distress calls from the citizenry. In the line of duty, before Stelmach, he would usually consider his fellow Poles across his shield and his baton. Swinging. Trying to miss or do as little damage as possible. Only twice had he been forced to wipe blood from his truncheon.

And after that second time came the promotion. Father must have waited for something to point to.

"Open the gate," Zenon repeated when Konrad had made no attempt. The private grimaced and coaxed the gate open.

They filed in, and Zenon pushed the gate back, making sure the latch didn't click closed. Not that the half-second taken to unlatch the gate would have made any difference, not rationally, but knowing he had saved that time, just in case—of what, he couldn't say—made him feel a tad less jumpy and more courageous.

The shed took a quarter of the small plot, and a rectangular area of mowed grass took another quarter; the rest was a garden. The plot belonged to a Mr. Zalewski. Ignacy Zalewski. The last name rang a bell. Whether Zalewski or someone else tended them, rows of tomatoes and cucumbers lined the soil with geometric precision, each plant perfect enough for a saccharine still life. Someone had given the garden water, fertilizer, and love.

The chimney sticking out of the shed made it clear that it was more than a storage space. The paint on the building wasn't fresh, but recent enough to adhere—no flakes, no mold. A curtain obscured the only window Zenon could see. A chrome handle stuck out of the door someone had painted green, in contrast with the shed's yellow.

"Knock," Zenon said.

Konrad shot him a look but took a couple of steps forward and rapped on the chipboard. "Open up! Milicja Obywatelska!"

"Move over!" Zenon whispered, using his throat.

Konrad did and glanced at Zenon again, now with uncertainty. "You think they have a gun?"

Zenon shrugged. "You do."

Konrad made no further comment as if that had answered his question. He slid a meter sideways, took his gun out of the holster, and held it like a hammer. A minute passed, then Konrad reached over and knocked again.

Zenon gave it a few more moments. "Check the door," he said, once the waiting had stretched.

Konrad pressed down on the handle, and it gave. Then he prodded the door with a little shove, and it swung in, roughly a quarter of the way, with a gentle whine of the hinges. Someone must have tended to them regularly, and probably planned to oil them again soon.

Zenon was about to tell the young man to check inside when Konrad stepped up, the pistol a shield, and sidled inside. Zenon lost him in the darker interior. He waited for something to happen. When nothing did, he called out, "Private, report!"

"You better come in here, lieutenant."

Zenon stepped inside, the hair on his neck erect, and he blinked to accustom his eyes to the shade.

Konrad stood to his left, the gun hanging by his side. A large shape lay on the floor in front of them. Flies buzzed around, taking a somewhat greater interest in the shape, the man on the floor, than in anything else. The flies seemed the most alive thing in the room.

"Is he breathing?" Zenon asked.

"Don't know. Haven't checked."

"Jesus! Check on him."

Konrad hunched his back and shuffled over to the body on the floor where he crouched and put two fingers to the man's neck. He tsked, then changed hands.

When he rose, Konrad turned to Zenon with a twist to his lips, wiping the fingers he'd used on his pants. "No pulse," he said. "Never seen a dead fellow before. Outside a funeral."

Zenon Drobina would have sworn, might have raved, but it felt useless. What's the point of planning? The relief he'd found in knowing his freedom was a day away turned into a bitter taste in his throat. Who else was going to take this case? Especially with the major nowhere to be found.

"Let's bring the regional folks in," Zenon said and stomped out. Before he got to the car and the radio, the stomp had turned into a shuffle. He fell into the driver's seat and pressed the button to call an ambulance and request a crime scene investigation team from Suwałki, forty kilometers away. Next, he'd fetch the gun from his room before going back to the HQ to fill out the paperwork. No dinner at *Albatros* tonight.

CHAPTER TWENTY-SEVEN

AMERICAN CASH

Monday, July 12, 1982. Zygmuntowo.

Roman Stelmach had marched down the street with the gravity of an iceberg when he sputtered to a stop, forced to make a decision. The road to the right, splitting off alongside the movie theater, led to the girl's apartment. The telephone station, if his memory of last December served him well, was in the opposite direction. Life liked to play tricks on a man. Roman had never had any interest in visiting Zygmuntowo, and now he found himself in this provincial shithole for the second time in a few short months. But this time he was here as his own man, a man about to reclaim his freedom. No orders from up above led him here this time but his own decisive action.

Left or right?

The apartment held a certain appeal. If the Sokołowskas were home, if either knew anything . . . bullseye. On the other hand, if his hunch—that the mother pretended loyalty while using her position to collaborate with Solidarity—was wrong, he'd probably have to kill both Sokołowskas and anyone else who might happen to be there to keep things quiet.

No. The telephone station might be a more conservative move, a brick toward building a case, but he was certain he'd get useful information. If he ended up having to kill the women—if he was right he would—it wouldn't be for the lack of trying to avoid it. Common decency demanded it.

Roman turned left and crossed the street.

In a few blocks, he approached the gray stucco building and stopped at the gate. Its vertical bars ended in spikes, and the same javelins fenced all around the visible perimeter. The building itself rose three stories, the staircase was placed in the leftmost corner, and Roman counted ten windows spaced evenly in each of the floors to the right of the entryway. This was no Gothic cathedral. Not even a proper brutalist piece. Just rows of prefab concrete upon rows of prefab concrete. The white "No Photographs" signs stood out against the station's ashen face.

"Who is it?" said the gate intercom's voice after Roman pushed the bell.

"Roman Stelmach. Major. Służba Bezpieczeństwa. Open up."

Roman found himself annoyed by the passive-aggressive buzzing that let him through. No human voice. No, "please citizen major, come in." Only a machine screech.

Once Roman climbed the stairs to the door, another buzzing announced that the station was ready to receive him. He pulled the door, stepped into a shady, cool hallway, and let the door close behind him with a slam. Some might have confused the sound for the clap of a Czak nine-millimeter pistol round. Roman wouldn't make that mistake. Besides, no casing fell on the floor.

He climbed another flight of stairs to a display case. Behind glass, a *Safety and Hygiene in the Workplace* sheet spelled out the dos and the don'ts of the Municipal Telephone Services Station. Roman didn't need the *Directoriat—3rd Floor* sign to know where to go.

Safety and hygiene. The key to any civilization. Roman took a moment to read through the sheet and felt his irritation subside.

By the time Roman Stelmach had climbed all the way upstairs, Czarniecki, the director, had thrown his office door open and stood in the threshold, stretching and flexing his fingers. It appeared that the intercom woman had alerted him.

Roman stopped for a second to stare into the man's eyes, then stepped inside, making Czarniecki shuffle sideways, rounded the desk, and took the director's chair with a sigh.

"Close the door and sit down," Roman said and rapped his fingers on the wooden armrest. If the chair wasn't real leather, it was close enough.

Far from standard issue for a replaceable asshole like Director Czarniecki. Roman had already decided on a line of inquiry, and now he felt even more certain about it.

The man's jaw made Roman think of a pot of milk coming to a boil, the meniscus of pale fat fighting against breaking, the points of muscle in the corners of Czarniecki's face popping up and disappearing. The director inhaled and, to his credit, took an inferior seat on the inferior side of the desk without protest. "What's this about?" he said and returned to grinding his teeth.

"Easy. We're colleagues, right?" Roman said. "We're both Interior Ministry people. Relax. I'm just working to get a few facts. I get what I need, you get me gone, and we're both happy."

Czarniecki blinked and said nothing.

"Fine," Stelmach said. "Emilia Sokołowska. She works here?"

Czarniecki nodded. "Major, you already know she does. She's on duty now."

"Notice anything unusual about the girl lately?"

"Unusual?"

In the next moment Czarniecki twitched in his chair after Roman had brought his palm clashing on top of the director's desk. Roman slapped the desk one more time, then again, and yet again. He left his hand on the surface and unclenched his teeth. "I know about your bribes," he said. "Been selling spots in line for new phone lines, haven't we?" When Czarniecki continued to breathe heavily but said nothing, Roman knew he'd struck the vein. All he needed to do now was draw blood and do it right, but that was far from simple.

"It's an awful thing," Roman said, once another minute of silence passed. He used a tone he might have with a friend if he'd had one left. "Hard. Living off that measly government salary. Believe me, I know." He let another minute go by. "Two to five years, if I were to guess. Not a terribly long time. You'll still be a young man—what, fifty?—when you come out. That's lucky. Because with a record, you'll have to use your hands and your back to make a living." Roman let the conversation hang again.

"What do you want?" Czarniecki said.

"Have someone bring the girl's call monitoring logs. The real ones."

The director reached out and pulled the telephone on his desk closer. He stuck his finger through the dial loop over the zero and ran it in an almost complete circle before letting the thing go. He dialed zero one more time, then finished the job with a short jerk of the finger. A moment later, Czarniecki made a calm, polite request of his subordinate on the other end, and Roman couldn't help but feel a measure of respect for the man.

Czarniecki hung up. Roman leaned back in the man's leather chair and closed his eyes. A man certainly could get used to plush foam and leather under his ass. He let his breathing slow down, and a casual bystander might have thought he'd fallen asleep. Roman knew that Czarniecki knew better. Though his eyelids were shut, he could as well as see the man stuck frozen in the chair across the desk. He wasn't going to get up and wasn't going to speak. If he'd put a leash on the fellow's neck the man wouldn't have been any more firmly under his control. In his mind, Roman smiled a grin that didn't reach his face.

When ten minutes later there came a knock on the door, Roman was ready for a change of posture. His left hip started to fall asleep. But Czarniecki hadn't risen or spoken until the knock repeated. The man got up, and Roman opened his eyes. Czarniecki dragged himself over to a spot next to his director's chair and told the person across the door to please come in.

When the woman entered, Roman struggled to place her face. It felt familiar but unremarkable.

"Thank you, that will be all," said the director and patted the woman on the forearm connected to the hand holding a thin, green folder. "You may go back to your work," the director repeated when the woman seemed to hesitate.

The woman nodded. She appeared ready to open her mouth, words seeming to force themselves to the surface, but must have thought better of it. She compressed her lips into a line, nodded again and slipped out, closing the door gently behind her.

"I find it's best to maintain boundaries," Roman said. "I never let things go beyond a solid working relationship."

Czarniecki turned and lay the folder in front of Roman. "Feel free to use my office as long as you need," he said. "I have business to attend to."

He had reached the door and begun to turn the handle when Roman said, "No, I don't think so. Sit down."

The man turned back around, said nothing but cocked his face to the left.

"Please sit," Roman said and pointed at the chair on the other side of the desk. "I may need you to clarify things for me." Roman kept his arm extended until Czarniecki sighed, and it seemed that more than mere air came out of the man. The director sat down and kept his eyes on the surface of his desk.

Roman pulled the three sheets of paper out of the folder and set the empty cover aside. The first sheet contained a formal report. A man alluding to listening to Radio Free Europe and Voice of America. Both parties in the conversation reported up to Central for investigation.

The report on the second sheet spelled out Emilia Sokołowska's suspicion that the man she heard on the line dealt in counterfeit ration cards. The man alluded to being able to get as much meat as his brother needed for his son's wedding, she had written. Roman pursed his lips in agreement. No one had enough meat for a wedding. A decent lead. But the director's evaluation at the bottom read: "negative."

Roman turned the sheet around, right side up for Czarniecki.

"What's the story here?" he asked.

Czarniecki focused his eyes on the paper, then reached out and held it up. "No story. She sometimes tries too hard. Her mother's a committeewoman. Must be in the blood."

"Seems suspicious to me."

When Czarniecki offered no further answer, Roman shuffled the sheet to the back and considered the third and last one. He skimmed it. Then went back up and read every syllable, voicing the words under his breath: eel, fresh, December. Coming here was the right call. Even if he might still have to kill both the mother and the girl. He extended the paper to the director.

"Have someone get me the names and the addresses for these two numbers. Why didn't you have this report sent up to Central?"

Czarniecki turned the sheet around. "Perhaps I erred in my judgment..."

"You did. Now, I'll need those names and addresses. I'll wait here." He watched the director rise, nod, and exit the room, his gait steady but his chest rising and falling rapidly.

That the man had not returned ten minutes later, came as no surprise. Roman didn't mind waiting alone. When another ten minutes went by and Czarniecki still hadn't come back, Roman picked up the director's phone.

"Major Stelmach here," he told the operator. "Find me Czarniecki."

There was no click indicating a transfer. Instead, a rustling told Roman that the operator took off her headset, and more of the same announced a new wearer.

"Still working on it," said Czarniecki's voice. "Both coming up as phone booths, but that can be faked if you know what you're doing and have the right tools."

"Phone booths where?"

"The number flagged as the male voice, the fellow in the market for smoked eel, was in Frombork. The other number is local. A Zygmuntowo booth. One of the two in the main square."

"This is all I will be needing," said Roman. "You can stop looking. Now give me the operator again. I need to make a call."

After a call to the local Milicja headquarters to order an investigation into Czarniecki's bribes, Roman strolled out of the building and through the gate. He looked around. A bench stood less than a block away. The code was child's play, and he had no doubt the supposed eel buyer was Piekarski. The money was here, waiting for Roman in this shitty little town. The sixth of July had already passed, but that was not what gave Roman the heartburn that made him sit down. Having lost Piekarski's trail, he had only one lead remaining. One thread to pull.

Lacking a better option, Roman Stelmach continued to sit in the shade of a maple, waiting for Emilia Sokołowska to start her walk home.

* * *

Two women came out of the phone station's gate at five minutes past three and turned down the street, away from Roman's bench. One was short enough to occasion comment. Her perm and high heels added a few centimeters, and she walked as if stabbing the sidewalk with each step. The other was taller, a brunette, and Roman appreciated how her skirt hugged her hips. He rose. He really would have preferred to follow just to watch Sokołowska walk, but there was work to do.

Someone else might have gone to wait for the girl at her apartment. Or might have knocked on her door later in the evening. Roman wasn't someone else; he liked to know his prey's habits, even those seemingly unconnected to the matter at hand. Sometimes one encountered surprises. Like the sanctimonious underground press operator in Sopot who was screwing his wife's sister. Alcoholic priests with stashes of kiddie porn; not one of those across the years, not two, but six. The doctor, high-up in Solidarity and a daily holy mass attendee, who charged beggaring rates for abortions in her patients' bathrooms. People were rarely reliable, but one could always depend on human nature, and Roman Stelmach had learned early how best to use it.

He hung about fifty meters back. Someone else might have grown uncomfortable with leaving such a long leash. But when Roman tailed a mark, most of the time, he felt as if he were the one leading. In the past he'd wondered if it was the artist in him—sensitive, empathetic—that had given him this gift. Now he simply put it to work but still sometimes wondered why so many confused empathy for conscience.

Work. Major Roman Stelmach, Security Services. That the idiot Zenon Drobina would use the term *ubek* to describe himself wasn't surprising. Many others embraced it, too, even if strictly speaking it referred to Bezpieka's predecessor agency. That was unfortunate. Roman never cared for it. People might fear an ubek, but few would respect him. And if a man couldn't have respect, what did he have? *Officer* was the least he was due. Roman had given up on correcting Drobina; one couldn't teach a fellow self-respect.

Roman Stelmach decided he would insist on being addressed as *General* once he got to Brazil with American cash in his pocket. He was done working for others.

The short woman—he'd seen her back in December, too, come to think of it—peeled off after patting Sokołowska on the arm. Emilia Sokołowska continued to sway her hips in the direction of her apartment building a couple of blocks away.

Roman Stelmach wasn't surprised by much, but when Sokołowska banked to the right as soon as the other woman was out of the line of sight, he stumbled ever so slightly. A secret. The girl had a secret. And a security services officer, even a shitty one, which he was not, knew precisely what to do with secrets. You tended them and grew them into cases and confessions, and sometimes, when the lousy government salary pinched, into power and small spurts of cash flow.

Roman, surefooted now, followed the girl up the street. One block grew to five, and she showed no sign of slowing down. She navigated past the cathedral's single rebuilt tower to her and Roman's left, then past the main square. She reached what looked and smelled sour—a creamery with puddles of spoiled milk by the loading dock—and kept on until four doors down. There, she stopped in front of an older, red-brick house and entered a moment later. Roman had had enough time to formulate a plan for just such an eventuality; he needed no time to think. Once at the building's door, he pushed the knob—unlocked—and walked in.

In the hallway's shade, he made out two further doors, each with a name plaque over the peephole. One was hard to read; someone had tagged it with "kurwa" in a black, permanent marker. The other said A. Burzym. And so A. Burzym it would be. Roman used a single knuckle of his right index finger to knock on the center of the door.

Rather than crack the door while holding it secure on a chain, like a normal person, the woman who answered unbolted it and threw it all the way open. "Yes? If it's a meter reading, they're out back."

Roman thanked the woman in his mind. He'd intended to use force from the start. Instead, he said, "Right. Just need to check the electric inside. The reading is a little high, and there might be a short."

The woman was short, too, though not quite as short as the one from the telephone station. When she nodded and stepped aside, her dark, brown bangs bobbed over matching brown eyes set symmetrically in an olive-toned face. Not a classic beauty, the arm holding the door looked thick enough to bench press as much as he could, but Roman suspected she didn't suffer a lack of admirers.

"Fuse box?" asked Roman, while he swept the living room, having closed the door behind him. Sokołowska sat on a sofa, legs crossed, seeming to focus her attention on the bottle of beer in her hand. She glanced at him, and he caught her eye, seemingly forcing her gaze to recoil. Then she looked again, her eyes widened, and then he knew she knew.

Major Roman Stelmach stepped away from the other woman, reached back, and pulled out his pistol. Back to plan A. The short girl froze. "Sit next to her," he told her. He didn't aim his gun. Instead, he made a friendly gesture with his other hand. The gun hung at the end of his right arm like a forgotten ornament. "Sit. Relax. And . . . I'll have that bottle." He stepped forward, the pistol still aiming down, took the beer out of Sokołowska's hand and put it on the floor. He rested his back against the wall and sunk to a crouch, the weapon suspended between his knees.

Roman breathed with intent, slowly, in and out, and waited.

After a minute, the short woman said, "I don't have much here worth stealing, but take whatever you want."

Roman gave her a smirk but remained silent. He watched.

Sokołowska's face trembled, and Roman thought she might start crying. Instead, her mouth twisted in slow motion into a caricature of a kiss and her eyes bulged out. The woman's chest pulsated behind the blouse. If she didn't get a grip, she'd probably pass out any moment now. That would be counterproductive.

"I'm not here to hurt you," Roman said. Well, he still might not. "My name is Roman Stelmach. I'm a Milicja officer, and I'm investigating a case. Just have a few questions."

The short woman shifted, and her eyes darted from side to side. Sokołowska's breathing might not have gotten better, but it stopped growing faster and shallower. Roman experienced a panic attack once, so he'd probably already lied; she would likely at the least end up with a monster headache. "What is your name?" he said, looking at Sokołowska's companion. The girl might be short and thick, but Roman liked the way she filled out her shirt.

"Agata."

"Are you a stripper?"

"What?" The confusion in her face got the better of the fear for a moment.

"They tend to forget their last names. Got one?"

"Burzym. Agata Burzym."

"Pleased to make your acquaintance, Pani Agato." Roman nodded at her from his crouch. "I suspect you know why I'm here?"

Burzym glanced sideways at Sokołowska. Neither answered. That didn't bother Roman. He was ready to get to work. He looked forward to the process of learning what he needed. He took in the details of the figures before him.

"Pani Emilio, whatever happened to your toe?" he asked. She'd taken her shoes off. The middle toe of her left foot ended abruptly. He tsked. "Whatever it was, it must have hurt. I'm sorry that happened to you."

Emilia Sokołowska took a deeper breath and held it for a few seconds before exhaling. "Infection."

So it probably didn't hurt all that much. People did nothing but complain and complain. Most didn't know how lucky they were. "Oh my," Roman said. "Thank goodness they caught it before more had to come off." Sokołowska's eyes darted to Burzym, but she nodded.

"Yes, lucky," she said.

"Is there anything specific you would like to know, Officer Stelmach?" Agata Burzym asked from her spot on the couch.

"Everything. Tell me everything. You know why I'm here and I'll know if you're telling the truth."

When no answer came, Roman rose to his full height and stepped closer. He considered Agata. She sat with both feet on the floor, knees together, like a schoolgirl. Respect. The woman's feet, huge, out of proportion to her body, ended in strangely delicate toes, their nails painted ruby red.

Roman Stelmach lifted his right foot and brought the heel of his shoe upon Agata's toes as hard as he could. He felt bone give and heard a crunch before the woman shrieked and tumbled from the couch. Before she could wrap around that pain, Roman kicked her in the kidneys, then he repeated. Agata Burzym began to struggle for breath. He stepped away, aimed the gun at Sokołowska, just in case, and took a couple of deeper breaths.

"If I kick again," he said, "I'll do it harder. The kidney will burst. Like a balloon. The bleeding will kill her. It's pretty slow. Lots of pain." He let the arm holding the gun fall again. "I'm thinking about doing it."

"Whatever he said, we didn't do anything wrong. You can't trust a drunk."

Stelmach froze in surprise for the second time today. He didn't like it.

He also didn't need to worry that he'd given something away in his face. Sokołowska kept her head down, staring at the weeping bundle on the floor.

"Keep talking," Roman said.

And the girl did. When, five minutes into it, it became clear that dollars wouldn't feature in the story, Roman raised his hand. "Stop."

"What?"

"I don't care about any of this. Look at me." Sokołowska met his eyes for a second before they slid sideways. "Look at me. Right at me." This time she followed his direction. "What I want to know is anything you can tell me about where your mother stashed the American money." When her eyes twitched, Roman found himself surprised for the third time. He'd stabbed with a vague idea of the target, but it seemed like he'd struck some soft flesh. He allowed silence to stretch.

"Please, may I check on her?" the girl said.

Roman now realized that the body on the floor had at some point stopped moving and whimpering.

"Stay where you are." He crouched and touched Agata Burzym's neck. Pushed harder. There, a pulse, but rapid, faint as a shimmer, and not likely to persist much longer. He was sure he'd struck just hard enough, not too much, not too little. Perhaps the girl had some cyst or a clot. Sloppy and unprofessional. Perhaps he'd lost a bit of control. If he wanted to make it all the way to Brazil, he couldn't allow himself to slip up again.

"How is she?"

"She's just out. Where is the money?"

"I hid it," Sokołowska said. "In my apartment."

Roman wanted to hoot but only allowed himself a grin. Though he would still have wagered on the mother, a likely turncoat, having done the hiding, it was enough the girl knew where it was. Well, perhaps there is balance in nature. His luck had started running shitty as soon as he'd left for this road trip. Perhaps it was time for it to turn.

"Anyone in this building have a phone?"

Sokołowska pointed toward the back of the room, and the door to Agata's kitchen.

"Here's what's going to happen. I'm going to call for a taxi. You and I will meet it at the curb and act like we're the best of friends. It will take us to your place. Once you show me where you've put the money . . . Do you have a phone line at home?"

Sokołowska nodded.

"Once I've recovered it for the Fatherland, you can call and ask for an ambulance for you friend. Agreed?"

She nodded again.

"I want to hear it. Agreed?"

"Yes."

"And if you misbehave, I will shoot you." Roman's grin returned. Surprises or not, this was turning into a good day.

CHAPTER TWENTY-EIGHT

BEARER OF NEWS

Monday, July 12, 1982. Zygmuntowo.

It was closing in on dinner time—three o'clock—when, with the crime scene secure, Zenon Drobina shut the car's door on his side while Konrad got behind the wheel. The dead man's identification rested in Zenon's pocket. He could swear it tugged with an unnatural weight. And the person to blame for that sat to his left.

"It's a matter of probability. No miracle," Konrad said, resuming his explanations, his voice thin with hurt pride. He had overreacted to Zenon's skepticism. All Zenon had said was *no way*. "There aren't that many Zalewski families in town. It may be a common name, but not here."

"Do you know where she lives?" By now, Zenon had come to believe that Konrad really had gone to high school with the dead fellow's daughter.

Konrad did not, but it would be easy to check once they returned to the Milicja station.

"She'd never have noticed a fellow like me," Konrad said. "She was the hottest girl in school. I don't know if anyone was up to her standards. Never heard of her really dating anyone. And now she rakes in the cash at *Albatros*."

Zenon blinked. "What's her name?" he asked to confirm what he already knew.

At the station, armed with Kalina Zalewska's address, Zenon told Konrad to stay put, changed out of his uniform, and washed up a little. Then he called *Albatros*. Kalina had a couple of days off. He checked a map. Then he drove to the place he thought the building ought to be. The concrete blocks with prefabricated walls sat crowded together but, thankfully, someone had the foresight to arrange them off perfect parallel lines. Somehow, Zenon knew, being among these would have been unbearable had they been lined up like ZOMO riot police.

He parked, then climbed to the third floor. After he'd knocked, Zenon waited a minute before switching over to ringing the bell. It didn't work so he knocked again, now using the full weight of his fist. He prepared to knock the third time when he heard the screech of a lock, and a door down the hallway squeaked.

"Who are you? What do you want?" The voice belonged to a woman. But not Kalina. Zenon shuffled over to it. Through a crack he could see a sliver of the face, a few strands of black hair and one tank-top strap. The woman had left the door chain secured.

"I'm a friend. Kalina's."

"Bullshit." The door closed, and Zenon heard the locks. He glanced down to confirm he'd changed back into civilian clothes. Did his face announce an ubek? Once he no longer did the job, perhaps with enough time the function and the guilt would wash off.

Zenon rang the bell. This one worked. He'd keep ringing it until something happened. But before he got to push the button again, the woman shouted from across the door, "Who are you?"

He sighed. Then Zenon pulled out his identification, stood back and presented it to the eye darkening the peephole.

"I'm Zenon Drobina. Milicja Obywatelska." That last wasn't strictly speaking a lie. He had the right to wear an MO lieutenant's uniform, even if his command structure stood apart. "I have news for her about her father."

After a minute of shuffling, the door cracked open again and a hand extended through the space. Two manicured fingers pincered a scrap of paper. Zenon took it.

"She's staying with a friend. A real one," the woman said. "Different building. It's number ten by eleven." Then the door shut.

Zenon glanced at the paper. He smiled for the first time all day. Whoever this woman was, her cursive was gorgeous, light, as if preparing to lift off the surface. Number ten, apartment eleven.

CHAPTER TWENTY-NINE

EEL FISHER

Monday, July 12, 1982. Zygmuntowo.

Antek sat in front of his tea, feeling rude. When he and Dorota had asked for Emilia Sokołowska, the middle-aged woman told them her daughter wasn't home yet, but would probably be coming any minute, and then invited them over for tea. The time of the day was right, and Dorota said yes, and he agreed. Declining would have been impolite, and it saved them from having to come back later, even if, depending on how involved the mother was, claiming the money itself might have to wait. Thinking of waiting now, when he was so close, made Antek's throat tighten and tingle. Sipping the tea—he detected a touch of honey—helped a little.

But now, as Pani Zofia Sokołowska—who, come to think of it, wasn't supposed to be home this early—began to peel potatoes for dinner, Antek, sitting at the kitchen table, felt like an intruder. He took another sip of his tea to wash down his reflux. Dorota, her hands hugging a teacup, smiled at the older woman. Antek's throat and neck relaxed. He began to count Dorota's freckles, as he'd often done, but now each of them appeared new, exotic. There was a time, back in Frombork, when he'd sit after work alone with his beer, that divorce appeared obvious and inevitable. He could even remember having convinced himself that he didn't mind it after a while. But that memory felt impossible, now, alien, implanted, as if coming from a different man. Antek watched his wife's face.

"How again do you know Emilia?" Zofia spoke over her shoulder while keeping her eyes on the paring knife.

"Oh, we haven't said." Dorota again beat him to it.

Antek cleared his throat. "We're friends of a friend," he said. He doubted it would satisfy the woman but hoped not to have to tell a lie. Suspicion mixed with relief when Zofia said nothing, only nodded, and moved on to dicing up a square of pork the size of a couple of matchboxes.

Zofia broke the silence once the pork had been cut up. "Potato babka with meat is Emilia's favorite."

She opened the cabinet under the sink, which revealed a thick, gray cannister with a valve and regulator on top. A propane tank. Antek's Frombork apartment also lacked central gas, and, without a true identity and ration cards, he'd had to buy it on the black market. Zofia unscrewed the tank's valve, closed the cabinet, then put the fatty pork in a frying pan over low heat. Not waiting for the bits of meat to begin to sizzle, she pulled out a small plastic tub and a grater and began to pulverize the potatoes.

"We should go," Dorota said. "We are in the way."

Zofia's hand stopped the stroking. "That is nonsense," she said. "I say, guest at home, God at home. If you leave, I'll take it personally. There will be enough babka for everyone. And if I know Kalina, she'll pick up a few beers on her way from windsurfing practice."

"We're very grateful," Dorota said and sipped again, but at the mention of the name, her ears seemed to stand to attention.

Antek found his tea had grown cooler now than he liked but continued sipping. Couldn't be, could it? Then he wished he could travel a moment in time and kick Dorota under the table after she added, "Is Kalina Emilia's sister?" She seemed to sense it because she tilted her head and gave him the eye.

"No," Zofia said. "Emilia's best friend. She's staying with us. Her father is impossible to live with. She's a good girl."

Once she'd grated all the potatoes, she mixed in the fried meat, spices, diced onion, and an egg and poured the batter into a couple of casserole dishes greased with lard. She put a couple of dollops of lard on top of each casserole. "I always add extra for flavor. My secret ingredient. Sometimes it bubbles over and stinks things up with smoke, but it's worth it.

Especially with the windows already open." Zofia put the dishes in the oven. "Need a warm-up?" she then said and pointed to her kettle. When Dorota and Antek declined, Zofia made her own tea and joined them at the table.

She met Antek's eyes for the first time since he'd entered her apartment. "I hope there is enough gas left in the bottle," she said. "I ordered a refill, but you know how it is. And I do not like asking to use other people's ovens." She grimaced, then let her lips relax. "You do know who I am, don't you?"

All Antek could do was blink.

"No, I'm afraid not," Dorota said instead.

"I'm on the district Party Committee. I'm a komucha, you know, a Ruski collaborator."

Now even Dorota didn't have an answer.

"Thought you should know." Zofia sighed. "Why are you here? Have you brought Kalina paper and ink for that little underground rag she's involved with? I know about that. I've kept the girl out of an internment camp. Don't put her there."

The apartment door opened before Antek could answer. A young blonde woman entered—Kalina—stepped aside, and behind her stepped in the fat ubek who had shot him. Now he regretted having compared this turncoat to a perfect ship. Was she informing last year, too?

Antek got up. His calm shocked him. His heart didn't race. The muscle in his temple refused to flicker. "When did you call the ubeks?" he asked Zofia. "I didn't think you ever left the room."

Zofia ignored him. She stepped over to the door. "You look familiar," she said.

"You might have met my father," the ubek answered.

Kalina raised her hand. "Excuse me. This is Zenon Drobina. He is a friend. Sure, he's a pig, but he's a recovering one."

Antek strode toward the large man and presented his arms. "I won't run anymore," he said. He meant it. Antoni Piekarski was suddenly exhausted.

But instead of putting handcuffs around his wrists, the ubek took Antek's hands in his. "I am sorry," said the man. "I can't ask for forgiveness. But I am sorry."

"What's going on?" Kalina asked. "We just ran into each other. On the staircase. Zenek here is saying he needs to tell me something but can't seem to get it out."

The big man let go of Antek's hands. "Kalina. This is private," he said, turning to the blonde.

Kalina shrugged. "I have nothing that's private anymore. An open book. That's me. No home. No dignity. What's privacy to me?"

The ubek Drobina swallowed. "Your father is dead," he said, his voice soft as if to blunt his meaning. "We found the body this morning in his garden shed. The ID isn't in doubt. I'm so sorry."

Kalina put a palm against her lips and turned away to face the wall. Something—a sob, a grunt?—escaped her chest, and she stepped away. Antek heard a door lock and guessed she'd shut herself off in the bathroom.

Zofia raised her arms. "Come to the living room everyone. Sit. I'll make more tea."

She followed this by herding Antek, Dorota, and the ubek to one of the apartment's two rooms and pointed to the sofa and the two chairs arranged around a coffee table.

Antek led Dorota by her hand to the sofa. The ubek took the chair to their right, his back to the open window and the balcony door. Antek avoided the man's eyes, and Drobina—a funny name for such a large man—seemed in no hurry to start a conversation, either. Kalina wasn't a traitor, after all? After ten minutes of silence, Zofia came back with a tray loaded with steaming glasses and a plate of what looked like butter cookies. "I see everyone's getting friendly," she said, her voice dry but high, as if short on oxygen. She put the tray on the table. "I'll be back after I check on the girl."

Antek kept staring at Zofia's wall of shelves, avoiding Zenon Drobina. He'd already noticed more books than one normally saw in private apartments. A small library. The usual pottery, picture frames, and a clock crowded the shelves and gave a resentful vibe. He focused on the spines now. Marx and Engels. Lenin. The Bible. Szymborska. Miłosz. Hłasko. Also, Irving, Tolkien, Dickinson, and many others in translation. A strange mix for a party aparatchik. He stole a sideways peep at Dorota to see she was also studying the tomes. Perhaps she sensed a kindred spirit.

Zofia returned and sat in the other chair. "She'll be a while longer," she said. "Citizen Drobina, tell us what you can while the poor child isn't here."

Antek allowed himself a glance at the man. The man's rosy cheeks paled, but he swallowed and said, "We found him in his garden shed. He was already cold when we got there. A bump on his head, but nothing broken. That didn't kill him. Heart attack maybe? He did some drinking last night, too, by the smell. We think . . . it's possible . . . that he killed someone, before. . . ." The ubek's voice died down to a whisper by the end.

Zofia bit her lip before taking a breath. "I'd believe it. And you just accidentally found the son of a bitch?"

The ubek swallowed. "Well, no. We got a call. Strange. Some woman reported a rape and a murder from a pay phone at night. He was long dead when we found him. Maybe the effort was too much."

Zofia grimaced. "Live by the sword, die by the sword," she said.

CHAPTER THIRTY

THE OPERATOR

Monday, July 12, 1982. Zygmuntowo.

Emilia rode planted in the back of the Łada. She clutched her purse on her lap. The man spread out to her left, behind the driver, and the gun shielded between his thighs, pointing at the floor, held her still. Usually, she would have gagged a little passing the creamery with its puddles of curdled sour milk; this time the sharp stench did little more than pierce her consciousness.

The cathedral flowed by. Emilia no longer went to church, even if Mother still made the point despite the looks and the whispered curses. Kalina went on an occasional Sunday and most other days of holy obligation. Agata . . . She had to be alright. She was Agata.

The man—Major Roman Stelmach. She now knew his name; he had not introduced himself back in December. The same bald Milicja man who led Marek and the other soldiers into the telephone station then. She recognized him as soon as she saw him.

Stelmach had now wrapped his left palm over the pistol grip and tapped his knee with the fingers of the right. The barrel seemed longer than before. It was longer. But the tightness in Emilia's chest had already peaked. It had begun to resolve into a bruise behind her ribs. The most recent glance to her left made her breath catch but thinking of who and what sat there no longer threatened to make her neck, shoulders, and stomach freeze solid again. Still, for now, she kept her eyes forward on the cobblestones and the lines of stucco and wooden houses on both sides.

Kalina had probably made it home by now. She may be drinking tea. Or sipping a Tyskie. With no idea that her father, if the Milicja did their job, would be going to prison for a few good years. With no idea that there was a man with a gun headed her way. Oh, God, Agata . . .

Tall and strong as she might be, there was no way Kalina would be stupid enough to challenge an armed brute. She wouldn't be reckless enough. The devil can take the money. Emilia will walk right in, pull the bag out and hand it over. No fuss. God willing Mother will stay quiet for once. If there is a piece of paper to sign, Emilia will sign it and assume all the guilt. Her fingers gripping her purse began to throb and had grown paper white, and she made them unclench enough to allow some pink to flow back over the skin. Nothing else in Emilia dared to relax.

The taxi groaned to a halt in front of her apartment block. Emilia could no longer sit upright. The weight in her stomach wrapped her around the purse until the front passenger seat stopped her forehead's forward momentum.

"Are you well, miss?" the driver asked.

"My daughter got herself pregnant. She'll be fine," answered the devil with the pistol. Then he handed the man in front a wad of bills, walked around the car and opened Emilia's door. "We all pay the consequences of our actions," he said. "It won't hurt forever. Take my hand."

Emilia didn't look and if a hand had been extended, she ignored it. Instead, she slid sideways and when she planted her feet on the ground, she gave the car's frame a straight-arm push. She found herself standing, hunched over but under her own power.

"After you, then," Major Stelmach said, having disappeared the gun somewhere, probably into a holster or his waistband. Emilia couldn't see it now but couldn't unsee it either. Charcoal. A metal gleam brought to mind a workshop. One of Kalina's old dumbbells. Emilia had learned to shoot a rifle in high school in Citizenship Preparation, but a handgun was new. More casual. Emilia shivered as she shuffled into the building's main entrance and toward the staircase. An engine's whine announced the taxi's departure.

In the concrete staircase, three floors below her apartment door, Emilia stopped.

She kept her eyes on the first step.

"Please don't hurt anyone," she murmured. "I don't care about any money. I beg you. By God, don't hurt anyone."

A hard point dug into the small of Emilia's back. She lifted her foot and levered her weight up. The other foot. Up. Up. She slid her left hand over the steel rail, now shod of the plastic sheath it had worn for the first few years. Once it had begun to peel, it took no more than a week for the full length, from the ground floor to the top, to come off like a mutant, hundred-meter-long snakeskin. Emilia wished she could leave her skin here, too, and fly somewhere else. To Japan. With Kalina.

Kalina will be reasonable. She will be. Mother will, too.

Step by step, turn by turn, Emilia ascended. On the third landing, she paused. She expected to feel the gun's barrel against her kidney, but it never came. She glanced back. Stelmach's blue eyes glistened. He blinked.

"When you're ready," Stelmach said.

"What do you want me to do?"

The man cleared his throat. "Nothing stupid. Just say I'm here to pick something up. Get the money, hand it over. Easy as that." He swallowed again. "This has been enough work as it is."

Emilia nodded. She shuffled to the apartment's door and put her palm on the handle. A taste of iron made her realize she'd bitten through the skin of her lower lip, and she forced her jaw to slacken. Emilia Sokołowska pushed the door open and stepped inside.

* * *

A moment after the door squeaked open, a voice from the living room called her name. Emilia flinched.

"Emilka? Emilka, is this you?" Her mother's voice sounded higher, more vulnerable than usual.

Emilia glanced at Major Stelmach who had leaned against the now closed door. The man waved her ahead but made no further move himself.

"Just me," Emilia said, her throat tight. "Just me," she repeated, louder now. But as soon as she stepped through the next doorway and into the living room, her feet shuffled to a halt.

A silent party had assembled around the coffee table to her right, halfway between the room's entryway and the apartment's balcony door. Emilia's mother sat in the chair closest to the entrance, the woman's neck twisted to let her eyes study her daughter. A large man, sweat glistening on his forehead, filled the opposite chair by the window in the far end of the room. On the sofa along the wall to Emilia's right sat a couple, the man dark-haired, moderately handsome, the woman petite and pretty. Like her mother, the other three watched Emilia, too, and said nothing.

When Mother broke the silence, it was to clear her throat and say, "Your friends have come to visit. Are you going to say hello?"

The man on the couch leaned forward. "Frania sent us. We're here to pick up . . . ," he paused, swallowed. "To get the eel."

Mother whipped her head back toward the man. Emilia rarely saw her mother surprised—the woman kept her expectations low—but there could be no doubt now. "What nonsense is this? Eel?"

The bathroom door unlocked behind Emilia.

"You?" Kalina's voice. A tremor in it.

Before Emilia could do more than glance back, Stelmach pushed past her, his gun on display but aimed at the floor. He stopped in the far-left corner, his back bumping into the wall separating the room from the kitchen. Emilia felt more afraid than she'd ever been but found herself wondering if he'd put a dent in the cardboard-strength floor-to-ceiling divider. Had something broken inside her? Her heartbeat suddenly even, Emilia waited for Stelmach to issue orders or start shooting. But the Milicja major appeared less alive all of the sudden than the browning rhododendron Mother insisted on keeping in the room's darkest corner. His pistol lifted a few centimeters, not enough to point the long barrel—a silencer?—at anyone in the room. His eyes had frozen, aimed at the fat man in the far chair.

Stelmach's right arm came to life and surprised Emilia by sweeping the gun toward her. "Both of you," the major said, his voice monotone, "get in here. Sit on the floor."

Emilia could now feel Kalina's breath on her neck but dared not look back. She stepped all the way into the room and lowered herself onto the rug next to the coffee table. Kalina followed and sat close enough for her hip to warm Emilia's, but little comfort came from it this time.

No one spoke.

CHAPTER THIRTY-ONE

THE RESISTOR

Monday, July 12, 1982. Zygmuntowo.

Nothing Antoni Piekarski considered felt like the right thing to say, but he was certain it was up to him to break the silence. His responsibility. A job to do. A heavy one; the bald man—Antek remembered him now from the staircase in Frombork—was still holding the gun. The man's face had scrunched up into a grimace. Antek would have preferred him confident. A nervous, uncertain gunman made his fear swell. He needed to find the right words before the Bezpieka man began to act.

"I won't resist arrest," he said. Were these the right words? Who knew? It was something. He leaned slightly forward, a centimeter, two; two fewer centimeters of Dorota for the man to shoot.

Instead of the bald man, Zenon Drobina spoke up from his seat by the window. "Glad you're here, Major. I have worked this cell out but now find myself in need of your superior professional judgment and expertise."

"What?" said the man, the Major. The grimace on his face slackened into confusion.

"You were sick, and I thought I'd give it a shot. I hung out with the locals until I heard the right thing, put two and two together. A small town, you know. Simple people. Wasn't so hard. Your experience would have been wasted on it, really."

"You son of a bitch!" yelled Kalina and would have scrabbled up to her feet if the other young woman, Emilia, hadn't put her in a bear hug and held on like a wrestler. After a moment Kalina's muscles appeared to slacken. "Hell is too good for you," she spat, then blinked, but Antek saw no new tears. Emilia continued to hold on.

Zenon looked away from them.

"What have you learned, Lieutenant?" the Bezpieka major asked.

Now it was Drobina's turn to give a twitch. "I tracked down this fugitive," he said, pointing at Antek. "What else is there? I was about to take him into custody." The younger ubek pulled out his gun and rested it on his knee as if to show how he would have gone on about things had his superior not shown up.

To Antek, the pistols looked identical, except for the silencer tipping the major's gun. Now, the silencer rose, and the barrel rang twice, the sound making his shoulders twitch. Something less material than air shredded the front of Drobina's shirt in a couple of spots.

Zofia Sokołowska pushed off with her feet. Her chair tilted back, and she fell into the shelves behind her.

Zenon Drobina's body spasmed, and the arm holding his gun rose until the big man clasped the gun in both hands in front of him.

The air in front of the major rang out with another metallic clap.

Drobina slid off the chair, to his knees, but his gun remained level, held in both hands like a candle at first communion. The man seemed to contract every muscle and the gun fired. The back of the bald head exploded in a spray, and the major's body fell, but Drobina kept pulling the trigger as if unaware of anything but the finger and the gun. These gunshots, without a silencer, made Antek's neck and shoulders contract, as if some atavistic instinct attempted to close his ears.

The bullets struck the interior wall and seemed to meet no resistance, and a moment later a roar loud enough to make Antek's eardrums pop removed both his hearing and his consciousness.

CHAPTER THIRTY-TWO

THE ESCAPE

Monday, July 12, 1982. Zygmuntowo.

As soon as Stelmach's gun had come up, Emilia scrabbled further over Kalina and flattened them both against the floor. When the louder shots rang out, she covered her ears and squeezed her eyes shut.

Emilia woke up with dust all around. Much of the interior wall was gone, and she could see right into the kitchen. The cinder blocks separating her apartment from the outside had held. No sink. No propane tank. Propane.

Instead, what was left of the wooden cabinets flickered with flames. They might have traveled along the wallpaper or maybe the initial heat had done it; in any case, her books were beginning to smolder.

A man with a hole in his head rested on the floor less than a meter away. Stelmach.

Why was it so quiet?

Emilia focused on the softness under her shoulder. Kalina's arm. The eyes Emilia loved blinked up at her. Kalina's lips moved, then again, but seemed to make no sound. Emilia struggled to push herself up to a crouch. Her legs and arms worked, even if they felt unsteady, woolen as if she'd been drinking all night with Agata.

Agata! Oh, God, Agata. The pressure in Emilia's head remained, but the memory of what had happened in Agata's apartment—the man, the kicks—cleared her thoughts enough that she gasped. The gasp should have been followed by rapid, shallow breathing, but Emilia made herself inhale the stinky air slowly. She offered her arm to Kalina, and they rose to their feet together, sharing balance and strength.

Emilia gripped Kalina's arm. "Agata," she said, or tried to, she wasn't sure a sound came out. "Agata!" she said again, anyway. Kalina shook her head, whether to clear it or in incomprehension, Emilia couldn't say.

The couple whose names Emilia didn't know had flown off the sofa and lay tangled up by the balcony door with its glass blown out. The man was on top, mostly, the woman somewhere under him, but the limbs began to move, and Emilia thought that enough of them did to account for both people.

Opposite the sofa and by the bookshelves, Mother was getting up, too, blinking and shaking her head. When she moved her lips, Emilia knew the woman said something—a garble reached her—but couldn't make out the meaning. Instead of attempting to respond, she stepped over the overturned chair and gave her mother a kiss on the forehead. Mother took the time to smile but then began to push Emilia toward the door.

Emilia planted her feet and pointed to Drobina's unmoving bulk.

"Fire," Mother said. Emilia heard clearly enough. She glanced back. The fire had traveled from the kitchen. The smoldering and smoke in the living room had turned in places to small tongues of flames. Before long, all the books, all the furniture, the clothes, everything they owned would begin to burn.

Six people couldn't carry Zenon Drobina. Emilia resisted the urge to check the man for a breath, a pulse. Best to assume he's already dead. She stepped sideways and instead of running for the door joined Kalina who had started to help the couple who had sat on the sofa to their feet. Mother lent an arm, too. The unnamed woman could walk, but Kalina and Emilia half-led, half-dragged the man out. Two unmoving bodies stayed behind.

On the staircase, they joined their neighbors rushing out of the building. None asked questions. Most hopped down several steps at a time. Two brothers from the fourth floor took over for Emilia and Kalina and began to carry the stunned man down. Most people skipped by like goats. But a few asked the three younger women if they needed help, and the red-haired woman whose name Emilia still didn't know accepted an arm. No one offered to help Zofia Sokołowska.

The apartment building's worth of humanity boiled out onto the square of grass between the surrounding buildings. When she judged that it was far enough, Emilia stopped and turned around. A crowd surrounded her, and yet her neighbors seemed removed. They might be speaking to their families, waving their arms, but their wide, near-unblinking eyes didn't allow the minds behind the eyes to range beyond a focus on their own concerns.

From here, Emilia could see her apartment's windows.

She swallowed. In the minute or less it had taken them to run out, the fire had already spread to the wooden window frames. They burned and the soot traveled up the outside wall, marring the gray concrete with black. It was unlikely the fire would spread to the neighbors, not with the cinder blocks making up everything but the division walls inside each apartment, but the thick block made each living quarter into an oven if a fire began. Books, photos, clothes. Everything gone. The two dead ubeks?

Mother stood next to Emilia, hunched over, with hands on her knees.

"Mama?" Emilia whispered.

Mother turned her head and squinted.

"Mama," Emilia repeated. "The men, those men . . . Zenon Drobina and the other."

Mother straightened and slid close enough to whisper in Emilia's ear. "They came for information. Started to argue and shot each other. All true. Understand?"

Emilia swallowed, then nodded. "Mama, we must get to a phone. The bald ubek hurt Agata. Bad."

Kalina had overheard. "I'll run over to my neighbors," she said and took off.

* * *

Zofia Sokołowska squinted after Kalina, then turned to face Emilia. "I'll file a report. You stay quiet. If anyone asks, you came back right before they started shooting." Mother took a breath and looked up at the apartment's blackened window. Emilia followed her mother's eyes and found that the flames had died down. Perhaps this made sense. They had little to burn. Mother grunted. "Good thing the propane bottle was almost empty. Come to think of it, if not for gas shortages, you and I might not be standing here."

Emilia's mind had cleared enough to find humor in her mother's quip, but she felt too tired and worried about Agata to smile. The idea of smiling lasted no more than a few seconds, anyway, and then she remembered where she stood and why. "Where do we go?" she asked.

"Right." Mother hesitated. "Do you think Kalina would take us in?"

"Her father would never agree."

"Oh, God, you don't know. Zalewski's dead. Drobina . . ." Mother looked back up and made a sign of the cross. "Milicja found him in the garden this morning. Cold and dead. The poor girl took it harder than I would have thought. All things considered."

Emilia closed her eyes as something grabbed her rib cage and squeezed, as if trying to bleed it dry. Each shallow breath pumped air out with nothing to replace it. It was her turn now to stoop over and rest her hands on her knees.

"Slow down. Breathe in." Mother grasped Emilia's shoulders from behind and gently forced her to unclench her chest.

Breathing as instructed, Emilia made herself ignore the pain. It would have been easier to faint and never wake up. Maybe she could close her eyes and refuse to speak for the rest of her life? Mother had never been a doting parent, but she would probably feed her.

Or she could run! Simply run away, without a destination.

It would start getting colder soon. She'd never be able to pay for a place to live somewhere else. Maybe she could get a room on a farm somewhere in exchange for mucking out and milking cows? It couldn't be that hard, right? Grab a teat and pull.

When Emilia's eyes focused again, she discovered that in addition to her mother, three other pairs of eyes were studying her. Kalina had returned and come up close enough for Emilia to see the tiny brown dots speckled against the green of her eyes. Kalina rested her temple on Emilia's shoulder, having to stoop a little, and let air escape between her lips to soothe her with a soft *shhh*.

The couple Emilia had met in the apartment stood a meter back. The woman, more than a head shorter than the man, blinked every so often, her hand closed around the man's wrist. The man, shuffling a bit in place as if struggling for balance, licked his lips.

"I'm Antek," the man said. "This is Dorota. My wife." His eyes flashed toward Kalina and he opened his mouth again, as if to say something more, but remained silent.

"You should leave," Mother hissed, after having glanced left, right and behind. "Leave. With . . . what happened, you may be able to get lost."

Antek looked up. "We can't," he said, keeping his eyes on the apartment's windows which were now only venting smoke.

Emilia pressed her neck against Kalina's head, then stepped over a few centimeters. She needed focus. "Eels?" she said. "About twenty thousand worth?"

Antek nodded.

"How would anything be left up there? Especially paper," she said. "It's gone."

The man grimaced, then nodded. His wife—Dorota?—switched her grip and hugged his arm to her chest. "It's gone," Dorota repeated. "We should go, too." Then she nodded at Emilia and Zofia and tried to pull Antek away. He had planted his feet, though, and recited a number at Emilia. "Please call if we can help in any way." Then he let himself be led.

Emilia watched the couple fade between the milling neighbors, caught another glimpse of Dorota's dress, and then the apartment buildings made Antek and Dorota disappear. She may not have cared about much more than her small life in her small town before this summer but now found herself hoping that losing the money wouldn't cause the couple much pain. She hoped there was more where it came from. Once she'd spoken with Kalina, if an unlikely forgiveness were offered, Emilia might ask about getting involved in her underground press, too. Might get back to poetry.

If.

"Kalina." Emilia turned to her lover. "Last night, Agata and I got your father drunk." She cleared her throat, then continued in a whisper. "Really drunk. And he tried to put his hands on me, so Agata hit him over the head. I swear he was fine when we left him. We had a plan to frame him for ... Such a stupid plan. We did it to put him in jail, so he'd leave you be. We didn't mean to hurt him. Forgive us."

Kalina's face didn't change, but from the corner of her eye, Emilia saw her mother blink. She must have heard. Kalina's body had stiffened, and she stared at something above Emilia's shoulder that only she seemed to be able to see. When she broke away from whatever vision had captured her, Kalina focused her eyes, glanced back at Mother, as if to include her, and said, "Both of you can stay at my place if you want." She drew back, however, when Emilia tried to touch her hand. "I'd better go call the hospital and check on Agata," Kalina said and shuffled away toward her apartment building, but not before giving Emilia an exhausted smile.

Mother then stepped up closer and looked her daughter up and down as if she were working to understand a sculpture in a museum. "Can you live with it?" Zofia Sokołowska finally asked. "With it on your conscience?"

Emilia took a deep breath, her chest open and loose. She nodded. "Yes," she said. "Maybe."

CHAPTER THIRTY-THREE

FIFTEEN AND FIVE

Sunday, August 1, 1982. Gdańsk.

Kalina and Emilia stood by a lowered window in the corridor of a train to Gdańsk. The further from Ełk—where they had gotten to by bus—the train carried them, the less apprehensive Emilia felt about standing with her shoulder touching Kalina's. By Olsztyn, she hoped they'd start holding hands. She planned to celebrate getting to Gdańsk, blessed by its size and metropolitan anonymity, by planting a big wet kiss on her . . . girlfriend's lips.

Gdańsk was no Japan, but maybe one day they could get there, too. Emilia put a hand on her side and felt the pouch hanging crosswise by a string around her neck and under her loose blouse. Her mind had felt both lighter and heavier ever since she and Kalina made the decision.

After Agata's surgery, after seeing her friend open her eyes a day later, once she could put her mind to it, Emilia returned to her apartment. As she had suspected, everything flammable had burned except for the twenty thousand dollars hidden under the thick, iron bathtub. Holding the money in her hands after she had made Antek and his wife believe it was gone should have felt like freedom. She was surprised to find little joy in it. And more than a little shame. She wished Frania had never thought to trust her with it.

Mother had already left for work that day. She didn't need the burden of knowing the money survived, anyway. Emilia had a late shift, and she and Kalina had been sitting most of the morning around Kalina's kitchen table with a surprisingly short stack of dollar bills between them.

"Still want to keep it?" Kalina had said.

"Still want to leave this damn place?"

"We don't need all of it."

Emilia could remember shaking her head. "We could use more. This isn't that much money in the West."

In response, Kalina placed her hands on Emilia's. "Yes, but what about you? The most valuable thing in the world is a peaceful mind."

Standing on the train with Kalina's warmth next to her, Emilia couldn't quite remember at what point she agreed that they should find Antek and Dorota and give them back fifteen thousand dollars. She could remember amusement at realizing that lying about the remaining five thousand didn't seem to bother her girlfriend, but now she'd come around to Kalina's way of thinking.

Her mind was lighter because this money had already brought enough pain; heavier because The Trinity was dead. Agata had left the hospital two weeks after the surgery, well after Emilia and Kalina had finalized their own plans—plans that didn't have room in them for Agata. The three of them would write and call, but Emilia knew that then the stream of letters and conversations would grow shallower until it dried out entirely, exposed to the elements of change, distance, and time. When she saw Agata again—if she saw her again—she would be meeting a friendly acquaintance.

***

Emilia kept her word to herself and kissed Kalina right outside the train station's arrival hall. Back home, it might have invited a stick or a rock, and definitely an enthusiastic wagging of tongues. In Gdańsk, two women kissing on the lips drew more stares than Emilia had expected, but no one glanced more than twice. No one made as if to comment. This was the right place for them.

They dragged their suitcases to the youth hostel a kilometer away. The room they'd rented at a rate that made her squirm wouldn't become available until Monday. They both would need to work multiple jobs and count on luck, besides, once the dollars ran out; only soccer players and whores could rent a place they didn't inherit with relative ease, and Emilia and Kalina had never been interested in either profession. Once freed from their luggage, they stopped by a phone booth to call Antek and make sure he still expected them. And that it was safe to meet.

A tram ride and a ten-minute walk later, Emilia was climbing the stairs to a second-floor apartment, watching Kalina's hips swing before her on the narrow staircase. Antek answered Kalina's knock immediately.

The man who opened the door had changed. This Antek seemed more rested, his skin less sallow. This time, a five-o'clock shadow made his face appear rugged rather than worn down. Handsome. He smiled.

"Come in."

Kalina and Emilia filed in then followed Antek to a small living room. They took his invitation to sit down and asked for a couple of beers instead of the offered vodka. A minute later, he returned with three bottles and a plate full of cold cuts and pickles.

"I had these ready," he said. "To go with the vodka. Would you like anything else? Something that goes better with beer?"

Emilia took a long pull. "No, this is exactly what I need."

They settled in and spent the required time observing that the weather had turned unseasonably cool for early August. They discussed the World Cup and toasted to Poland coming in third. They took turns asking about each other's health and the wellbeing of the families.

"We'd hoped to chat with Dorota, too. How is she?" said Emilia after Antek had offered a perfunctory *fine* in response to a question about his wife.

"Fine," he repeated. "She's spending most nights here but is still staying with her parents. We're working things out. Slowly. We want to get it right this time."

Emilia cocked her head but withheld further questions.

"We brought what we promised," Kalina said, face suddenly serious, lips pursed, and nodded to Emilia.

The small talk was apparently over. Emilia sighed and squeezed the pouch out through her blouse's neck. It was tight, but she sure wasn't going to unbutton the top for this man. Or for Kalina when she was acting this strange.

"Only about fifteen. The rest—"

"The rest is here," Kalina said. She pulled an envelope out of her purse and handed it over to Antek.

Emilia froze for a moment and glanced from Kalina to Antek and back. She considered the pouch. Lighter. Would she feel even lighter after this? She opened the pouch and handed the naked stack of bills to the man. "I'm keeping the pouch," she said. "It's real leather." She found Kalina's eyes. "I got it from a boyfriend," she added and immediately felt rotten about the lie.

What she got in response was a smile. "Maybe an ex-boyfriend."

"Fine," Emilia said. "We don't even have money for a train back. Let alone an apartment."

Antek cleared his throat. "We have two rooms here. You can have one now. And when Dorota moves back in, she says you can have the room at her parents' for next to nothing."

A suspicion wormed its way into Emilia's mind. "I see," she said. "Yes, we'd appreciate it." She paused. "When did you two arrange everything between yourselves?"

"Peace of mind," Kalina said and smiled small and thin. When she leaned in for a kiss, Emilia hesitated. Then she placed her lips on Kalina's, closed her eyes, and found that she didn't care if they made Antek Piekarski uncomfortable.

THE END

ACKNOWLEDGMENTS

First, I need to thank Meg. Without you, none of this, nor anything else, would have been possible. You are my best critic and the only one I care about. I write for you.

Ania and Rory, you've shown me how to be a better human, even though it should have been the other way around.

Thank you, Mama, for the inspiration, for your love, and for me being here.

To my sister, for keeping me grounded.

Dair and Elaine, thank you for reading the whole damned thing even though you didn't have to and for finding enough promise in it to encourage me to keep going.

Brandy Wilson, you helped guide this book into its final form and taught me much about perceiving the world through someone else's lens. Mary Miller, your mentorship made my writing so much better; I miss the workshop. Paulette Boudreaux, thank you for the lessons in listening.

Thank you, Jim and Peggy, for not running me out of town as soon as you saw me. In your place, I might have considered other options.

To Katie, Paul, Mark, and Mike, I'm grateful to be part of your family.

Steve Yarbrough, thank you for your advice and insight.

To all those in New York and Louisiana who helped me when I arrived in the US alone as a 20-year-old idiot, thank you for not letting me die.

I know I missed someone. I hope you can forgive me.

Places won't care, but I can't ignore the debt I owe Poland and my hometown, Augustów. You weren't always the kindest of friends, but you helped forge me into me.

Finally, I'd like to thank the forest. The one around Augustów and the one which surrounds me now. I couldn't write if not for the trees.

ABOUT THE AUTHOR

Karol Lagodzki, a native of Poland, is an exophonic author of English-language fiction. His stories have appeared in *Invisible City, Storm Cellar, NUNUM, Streetlight Magazine*, and elsewhere, and he has won *Panel Magazine*'s Ruritania Prize for Short Fiction. *Controlled Conversations* is his debut novel.

He holds an MFA in creative writing, buys more books than he can read or afford—usually novels and short story collections, though he's been known to pick up an odd book of poetry or accessible science—and gives back to the literary community by serving as a reader for literary journals. Karol's non-writing careers have ranged from fixing stucco while dangling from roofs in Paris to sorting through human cadaver heads in Florida to developing and marketing medical devices for critically ill people in the American Midwest, but his true ambition is to remain a student for as long as he possibly can and make sure more stories make it out of his head and onto the page.

Karol lives halfway down a Southern Indiana ravine with his wonderful, unconventional family, a scurry of squirrels, a passel of possums, a gaze of raccoons, a descent of woodpeckers, and a large dog.